STUCK UP
& Stupid

STUCK UP & Stupid

ANGOURIE RICE
&
KATE RICE

CANDLEWICK PRESS

First US edition 2025
First published by Walker Books Australia 2023

Library of Congress Catalog Card Number pending
ISBN 978-1-5362-3903-4

25 26 27 28 29 30 APS 10 9 8 7 6 5 4 3 2 1

Printed in Humen, Dongguan, China

This book was typeset in Adobe Garamond Pro.

Candlewick Press
99 Dover Street
Somerville, Massachusetts 02144

www.candlewick.com

EU Authorized Representative: HackettFlynn Ltd.,
36 Cloch Choirneal, Balrothery, Co. Dublin, K32 C942, Ireland.
EU@walkerpublishinggroup.com

To our mothers and sisters

1

Everyone knows that past performance is a good indicator of future behavior, so when four young people arrived at Pippi Beach's most expensive house by yacht, Lily wasn't surprised that her mother was the first to notice. Within minutes, Lydia was on the deck in her best bikini, eyes glued to the telescope.

"Mum!" admonished Lily. "They'll see you."

"I'm counting on it."

Two young men, who could safely be judged handsome even from this distance, were transferring luggage and supplies up to the house, assisted by someone clearly from the local marina and therefore unimportant. Two young women in sunglasses and flowing fabrics stalked the sand nearby, flicking their hair around.

"You looking?" Lydia asked.

"No," said Lily, her eyes fixed determinedly elsewhere.

"You will when I tell you who it is."

"I don't want to know who it is."

"Yes you do!"

"No I don't."

"Because it's Casey Brandon!" Lydia tore her eyes away momentarily from the telescope to gloat. "Casey! Brandon!"

"I don't think—"

"I know my rich and gorgeous megastars."

"Really?" An internationally famous visitor at their tiny beach settlement seemed unlikely to Lily, but she didn't like to confirm or disprove it by telescope. Not that she could have pried it from her mother anyway.

"Oh my goodness, there it is. He's taken off his shirt."

"Mum!"

"He clearly wants attention."

"Not from you!"

"How do you know? I'm not just your mum. I'm a hot mum."

"He's probably come here to get some privacy."

"He's American. They don't know what that is. It's our duty as Australians and neighbors to welcome him, show him around—"

"Please do not do that. Mum? Please?"

Lydia didn't reply. She was too busy monitoring the way shirtless Casey Brandon was carrying a box of groceries. All supplies to Pippi Beach had to be brought over by boat, and what people chose to bring offered quite a bit of insight into their lifestyles, tastes, intentions, incomes, and length of stay. This was all important information, especially to the few who lived in the pretty beach settlement all year round. Lydia had become a very experienced judge.

Six years ago, Lydia and her two girls had come to her older sister Jane's beach house at Pippi for a family Christmas and never left. Jane, who only came to Pippi for weekends and holidays, offered the house as a temporary solution until Lydia got back on her feet. Another apartment, another job, and another relationship had all fallen through, at least partly because of the girls' father, who had failed in pretty much every respect as a partner and as a reasonable person. Lydia felt it was only fair; Jane had practically sleepwalked into a high-income interior design career and then selfishly topped it off with a wealthy husband. And what were sisters for if not to share their good fortune?

At Pippi, Lydia found somewhere to bring up her girls. By overstating her ability to maintain the place, which comfortably slept six in the main house and six more in a separate pavilion out back, Lydia talked Jane out of requiring rent. She found work in a casual partnership with local entrepreneur Birdie-Round-the-Back, cleaning weekenders and holiday houses but not more than four hours a day and not at all during the summer holidays when the extended family gathered at Pippi. There were three other sisters between Jane and Lydia whose visits to Pippi with their partners and children provided Lydia with what she loved most: an audience.

Unfortunately, this summer would be relatively quiet. Jane and her family were there, and one of the other young cousins, but the rest of them had quite rudely decided to spend most of the holidays elsewhere. Lydia was determined to make this the best summer ever, to make it clear to her sisters that they had missed out—especially Elizabeth, who, as a successful children's author with a husband even wealthier than Jane's, was the richest.

"You watch," Lydia murmured to Lily as she observed the supplies being hauled up the steps and into the network of architectural decks at the cliff house. "I'll be best friends with them in no time."

"That is not a good idea."

"I'm thinking of you children."

"We're not children, we're teenagers, we're perfectly capable of amusing ourselves, and we don't need you spying on strangers."

"It's not spying if they're our friends," insisted Lydia, who, in her mind, was already up at the cliff house having a glorious time with attractive young people who never had to worry about boring things like money.

Lydia found a more appreciative audience for her news in her younger daughter, Rosie, and niece Kat, who were not at all averse to looking at movie stars in general and already followed Casey Brandon on social media. Aunt Jane agreed with Lily, who said that perhaps visiting celebrities ought to be left alone, rather like snakes in the sun. The younger teens took little notice of this opinion (even though Lily was the eldest of the cousins and recognized to be the smartest) and spent the entire afternoon lounging on the deck in their brightest bikinis, tense with anticipation, discussing how they would best engineer a casual conversation when Casey walked by. Which he was bound to do, sooner or later. The family house was right on the beachfront and very close to the jetty where Pippi time was marked by hourly loops of the ferry. All the theater of Pippi life played out before the front deck, or within sight of the many picture windows, so there was plenty of opportunity to both observe and show off. From inside, the family enjoyed beach, jetty, and water views. From outside, passersby and beachgoers could see straight into the high-ceilinged timber-furnished interiors and the lives that played out there. Lily had long ago stopped pulling the blinds down; Lydia always put them back up again. Sadly, there was no such exhibitionism on offer at the cliff house. No one emerged for the rest of the day and the girls had to content themselves with watching the lights go on in the evening and conjecturing which of the shadowy figures on the main deck was Casey.

It was actually Aunt Jane, who wasn't the least bit interested in meeting him, who was the first to encounter the one and only Casey Brandon while on her morning run along the beach. She returned full of smiles and rather happy to discuss the movie stars after all, which was lucky, as her sister Lydia and the younger girls could speak of nothing else.

"What was he like?"

"What was he wearing?"

"What brand?"

"Was he nice?"

"Was he as good-looking in real life?"

"Did you shake his hand?"

"Did he have an accent?"

"Why is he here?"

"Aren't you a lot of stickybeaks!" Jane declared. "You can find all this out for yourselves on Friday."

"He's coming to drinks," Lily pointed out. "It's not like he's doing anything important."

"He's meeting me!" yelled Lily's younger sister, Rosie. She was fifteen and for several summers now had been going through a loud phase. "What's more important than me?" she yodeled.

"My bikini!" brayed Lydia. Everyone laughed, and Lily seriously regretted weighing in.

As the conversation veered toward competitive wondering about what to wear and what to bring to make the best impression, Lily retreated to the back deck with Juliet, who was the cousin closest to her in age and temperament. Juliet was a pale city girl, the only child of glamorous Aunt Elizabeth. She and Lily had spent every holiday together since they were babies, and now that they had just finished school, they were closer than ever. The summer and their lives spread out before them, with all the delights of burgeoning adulthood. Together,

Lily and Juliet considered the celebrity issue in a way that was appropriate to their advanced maturity and coolness.

Lily did a quick internet search and found an impressive array of magazine covers and designer-sponsored content.

"How has such a star found Pippi?" Juliet wondered.

"And why?" asked Lily.

A few C-list celebrities had stayed at Pippi before—models-turned-TV hosts and former soap actors. They always treated Pippi like a quaint amusement park. They doted on the wallabies and gawked at the goannas, then left plastic champagne glasses on the beach and had bonfires during a fire ban. Lily often trawled the sand and the bush trails picking up after them and helped Lydia to clean their holiday rentals. She'd learned that people are a lot messier if they have the money to pay for incidentals.

"Perhaps he's only here for Friday-night drinks," Lily laughed.

"I mean, it must be very different from what he's used to," Juliet said.

"But he might love plastic bowls of dubiously flavored chips."

"Drunk dads."

"Ferocious little kids."

"Big dogs."

"Spilled wine turning the crackers soggy."

"I do hope we don't scare him off!"

"Ha! I kind of hope we do!"

For Lily, the only thing worse than cleaning up after careless celebrities was having to watch the locals—including her own family—try to impress them.

2

Lydia's community spirit, which tended to lag when it came to fundraising and volunteering, peaked around social events. Indeed, she rather felt that the collective success of the entire summer depended on the first Friday drinks: how long she stayed and how much fun she had. So she went early, decked out in a plunging bikini top and a sarong and carrying one of Jane's bottles of bubbly, secure in the knowledge that she did this every year, movie stars or no. Jane followed a little later with a cheese platter.

It had been years since Lily and the rest of the cousins had been young enough to really enjoy being anywhere near the adults when they got boozy. While little ones spent Friday-evening drinks capering on the green in view of their parents, teens tended to slink off for their own gatherings on deserted decks or among the rocks at the north end of the beach. But not this Friday. There was no way Rosie and her cousin Kat, age fifteen and thirteen, would miss this opportunity to meet Casey Brandon. They spent the afternoon showering, blow-drying, and curling, while Lily and Juliet didn't even get changed and insisted to themselves and each other that they were only going out of curiosity. The other cousin, Jane's fifteen-year-old son, Martin, forgot the drinks event was even on. His passions were video games and spreading awareness of the climate crisis, and as Casey Brandon was neither of those things, he went off with a local friend to find out whether the vines along the main hiking trail were strong enough to climb.

Word of the newcomers had spread well beyond the family circle. Pippi Beach was such a hidden pocket that overseas visitors were rare. It was a small beach settlement surrounded by dense bushland, only accessible by boat or a two-hour hike, with no shops, bars, restaurants, cars, or roads. Its pristine beauty attracted only those with the energy to seek it out. Locals and the wealthy businesspeople who spent their weeks in the city and their weekends in the top-tier waterfront properties liked to keep it that way, smug in the knowledge that they really did know Sydney's best-kept secret and only happy for publicity of the most exclusive kind, such as appearing on fashionable lists of Sydney's best-kept secrets. A small amount of social media was considered appropriate, preferably with ocean views and sunsets, good grooming, smiles, and expensive props, like boats. So a clutch of rich celebrities was most definitely on-brand for those at Pippi Beach who cared about branding, and was unlikely to disturb the peace and privacy of those who didn't. These were the long-term original residents, the nature-lovers, the boaties, and the retirees who lived in beach shacks or old cottages on the blocks back from the beach with no water views. Yet everyone, even Max, the local hoarder and plumber, seemed to have put a bit more effort into their beachwear and were more aggressively jovial than usual. Lily noticed that all eyes flicked regularly, apparently randomly, to the line of houses rising across the south headland, even though before yesterday, most of the over-forties, who made up most of Pippi's population, hadn't even known who Casey Brandon was. In just one day, all had become very familiar with his entire filmography and were able to conduct knowledgeable conversations about his upcoming releases.

The adults were on their second drink by the time Rosie spotted movement on the path from the cliff house.

"They're coming!" she shrieked. The adults paid no

attention to her but nevertheless proceeded to stand up straighter and laugh more loudly. The younger teens watched the approach from a safe distance, while the older ones steeled themselves for potential embarrassment by pretending not to care. They need not have worried. When the four newcomers—two young women and two young men—reached the group, any awkwardness was soon nullified by Casey Brandon's winning smile and genuine charm. He already appeared to know everyone. While his three well-groomed friends kept their distance, Casey fielded handshakes and backslaps and follow-up questions from previous chats. It appeared that Jane was not the only local he'd befriended, nor the only one who had invited him to the drinks. Lily watched with amusement as a handful of people jostled to introduce him to everyone else, only to find he knew them already.

Lily could see that, unlike his three friends, Casey Brandon had a knack for making everyone feel comfortable. He chatted with people as though there was nothing he would rather be doing right now. Lydia poured him a champagne and tried to fill her own glass at the same time, which caused her to spill half of it down her front. She shrieked with laughter and made a joke about a wet T-shirt competition. Casey's lofty friends visibly recoiled, but any embarrassment Lily felt was soon swept away by admiration for how quickly and easily Casey got his glass and moved on, somehow leaving Lydia with the impression that he found her delightful. Meanwhile, Fire-Chief-Steve thrust a beer at the other young man ("Here, have a real drink! It's local!"), who accepted it in a way that made it clear he would much rather not. In that moment, all the teenagers watching knew this wasn't just any young man. This was Dorian Khan.

Tall, dark hair, brown eyes, amazing posture, cheekbones and jawline that could cut glass, and a distant air of preoccupation with something important and devastating, like the environment. Lily marveled that he had remained at Pippi unrecognized for so long and mused that perhaps the weight of fame had kept him indoors. Casey Brandon was a relatively recent star; Dorian Khan had been in the public eye for over ten years. He first appeared at the age of fourteen in the lead role of a teen-spy franchise. Since then, he'd been in blockbusters, well-reviewed independent films, and further installments of the original franchise. He had an actual Oscar nomination and was currently appearing in moody black-and-white photos on magazines and bus stops advertising watches that no one his age could afford to buy. Lily noted he was wearing one now.

Rosie and Kat were beside themselves at the appearance of Dorian Khan. Lily and Juliet had to physically hold them to stop them from squealing and jumping up and down. Rosie wriggled away from her sister and squeezed in through the crowd on the pretext of retrieving a handful of chips. She came back bursting to report what she had overheard Casey say: nobody was anybody's girlfriend or boyfriend! Lily winced. Who would even ask that? But it was just Sheila, who was over sixty and beyond flirting, unlike Lydia, who had cleaved herself to Casey's side and was laughing way too loudly. Soon everyone knew that the exquisite tall girl with dark complexion was Casey's sister Cecilia, the delicate one who didn't speak was her friend Yumi, and Dorian was, of course, Dorian Khan. Mega movie star.

Kat wanted Rosie to go with her on another mission to get chips, but Lily talked them out of it by pointing out that if they went anywhere near Lydia, she would claim them as her young relations and neither of the girls wanted to make a first impression being labeled as mere children. Casey was surrounded by adults. Max was giving him advice on the best wind for sailing; Sue the artist was offering him her kayaks; and Fire-Chief-Steve was trying to tell him the history of the cliff house, Pippi Beach, and the greater Sydney area. The two girls who had arrived with him hovered nearby. Lily, Juliet, and local friend Nicola wanted to make a social approach. They were clearly quite close to the American girls in age, but somehow any attempts to make eye contact, or even get close enough to say hi, slid off and ended in distant smiles or turned shoulders. The American girls entertained some light chitchat when Casey drew them into broader conversations, but mostly they just took photos of each other and themselves and the sunset in a way that was appreciative of Pippi's glory. This was enough for word to spread among the adult locals that the girls were, indeed, very sweet. "Nice to see some smiles. You girls could learn a thing or two from them," Birdie-Round-the-Back told Lily and her friends.

Meanwhile, Dorian remained firmly on the outside of the group and refused to allow Casey or anyone else to draw him into it. Word spread just as quickly that he was arrogant, pretentious, and not at all nice. "Reminds me of your mum's ex," sniffed Birdie-Round-the-Back. Lily watched Dorian shut down an attempted approach by the president of the Pippi Beach Association. Yes, he might have been extremely old, but he had a sense of humor and a PhD in environmental law and it hardly seemed fair to give him the flick when poor Casey was stuck with Bob-with-Two-Dogs, one of the biggest bores at Pippi. Dorian hovered near the sand and looked at his phone, ignoring the crowd, the sunset, and the glowing water so comprehensively that many locals gave up on him and concentrated all their attention on Casey and the girls. But Lily kept an eye on him and concluded that a career playing sensitive, intelligent, and artistic young men in sensitive, intelligent, and artistic films didn't necessarily cultivate those qualities in a person. And in fact, might incline one more toward the exact opposite. She noticed Casey tactfully escape Bob-with-Two-Dogs, having just heard all about the distinguishing features of yachts, and seek out his friend.

"What are you doing, man? Lurking on your phone? You look like you're on the subway."

"I'm checking the weather." He spoke with a clipped British accent, so perfect it almost seemed like a cover-up.

"The weather's here," urged Casey as he spread his arms to the sky. He noted his friend's reticence and changed his tone. "It's cool. No one's asking for selfies."

"No need to ask when they're on offer."

"Don't make me babysit you."

"Go ahead and socialize. I'm not stopping you."

"You're ruining the vibe."

"Casey, these people are just kissing up to you. You know that bores me."

Casey tilted his head toward Lily, who stood nearby on the edge of a conversation with Juliet and Nicola. "What about her? She's not kissing up. She looks kinda fun."

"She looks suburban."

Lily's eyes flicked to Dorian's at this casual dismissal. She had heard every word, and as a look of recognition passed between them, he knew it and she knew he knew.

"Aw, she heard you, man!" complained Casey.

"I'm going back to the house." Dorian shoved his barely touched beer at Casey, turned, and strode off.

"Hey, wait for us," cooed Casey's sister, Cecilia.

Cecilia and her friend Yumi swayed after him, but Casey didn't follow. Instead, he turned to the three Pippi girls with a winning smile. "I'm so sorry, we haven't met. I'm Casey." And he shook hands with all of them, repeated their names, and asked questions with such unaffected charm that quite soon they were laughing along with him as though they'd known him all their lives.

Later at dinner, Lily told everyone of her encounter

with Dorian, which she thought was hilarious. Lydia, on the other hand, found it outrageous.

"Suburban!" she exploded. "We're not suburban, we're semirural! Anyway, who cares about Dorian bloody Khan."

"What?" Rosie frowned.

"You know he's originally from Geelong, right? Now, that's suburban."

"Mum, he's an Oscar nominee," said Rosie.

"So? Let me know when he wins."

3

Pippi Beach's unique qualities attracted an eclectic mix of people united by their insistence that they were all very different from everyone else. Of the hundred dwellings sprinkled across the beachfront, headland, and bush hinterland, only about twenty were permanently inhabited. The rest were weekenders and holiday houses. Everyone came here to escape, retreat, or regenerate. For the younger generation, weekends and holidays at Pippi meant freedom: from school, organized sports, uniforms, shoes, routine, rules, and expectations. As long as they appeared somewhere in view of their parents' deck before nightfall, they were free. Imaginations blossomed, anxieties dissipated. Things that normally dominated their lives, like timetables and the news and who liked whom at school, were nothing; the only thing that mattered was the height of the tide. The handful of young people who lived at Pippi went to school by ferry and appeared to lead a life free of care. When Lily and Rosie had come to live here, age just twelve and nine, they could hardly believe their luck. Lydia kept reminding them that someone still had to unpack the dishwasher and take the garbage out, but taking out the garbage was no hardship when it involved a walk along the waterfront to the public bins on the end of the jetty. Even something as tedious as garbage, collected twice a week by barge, seemed romantic.

The morning after Friday drinks, Lily and Juliet sat together on the deck, sipping tea in silence as Lily wondered how long it would take for Juliet to steer conversation toward the celebrity guests.

"He was surprisingly nice, wasn't he?" ventured Juliet.

"Yes, he was," conceded Lily. No need for clarification. Casey was gorgeous and Juliet was quite clearly smitten.

"And really funny."

"Mm."

"And good-looking. Objectively, I mean."

"Objectively, sure."

"You didn't like him?"

"Did you like him?"

Lily smiled as Juliet flushed.

"Oh, I mean—"

"I think he liked you."

"Really?" Juliet's face betrayed surprise and hope. "I mean, he was friendly with everyone."

"He chose to sit down with you. Not Bob-with-Two-Dogs."

Juliet smiled and shook her head.

"Shame about his friends," Lily said.

"What do you mean? You didn't like them? Why? They were so beautiful!"

"All the better to appreciate from a distance."

"I think they were just shy."

Lily laughed. "I don't think anyone who wears designer gear at Pippi can be shy. But I love that you think it's possible."

Juliet was kind and smart, but she could be a little naive. Casey Brandon was clearly special: generous, sincere, and unaffected. These were rare qualities anywhere, and possibly even rarer among the young and rich. Lily believed Cecilia and Yumi had been deliberately standoffish, and Dorian was just plain cold and unfriendly. The three of them had lived right down to Lily's expectations.

"I wonder what they thought of us?" mused Juliet.

"We know they didn't think much of me," laughed Lily. "But I think you made a good impression. Between you and the view, I think they can afford to overlook my shortcomings. And the catering."

Meanwhile, up at the cliff house, Casey, at least, had nothing but praise for Pippi, its views, and its residents. "I wanna move here," he announced as he looked out at the sparkling water.

"No, you don't," Dorian said with a shrug.

"This view, it's insane. Nature. It's everywhere. And the people, they're just . . . they're real, you know?"

"You're so American," said Dorian. "You're hyper-sensitive to any sliver of authenticity—which, by the way, is only a sliver here. They're just as obsessed with money and power as everyone else; they're just too embarrassed to admit it."

"Your cynicism is totally rotting your insides."

"I'm just saying, don't be fooled. Yes, they live in the middle of nowhere and talk with an accent—"

"You mean your accent."

"But people can be just as grasping and obsessive here as in LA."

"No one's obsessing over you here, man; literally no one cares!"

"That's not what I'm talking about."

"Then what are you talking about? No, don't answer that because I don't care. Look at that sun! The water, the sand, the wilderness! My God!"

"It is indeed beautiful."

"Then why don't you just enjoy it!"

"I am. I'm going kayaking," Dorian snapped. He proceeded to check coast maps and the weather report.

The tide was high.

For the kids at the beachfront house, high tide meant gathering at the end of the jetty to fling themselves up into the sky and down into crystal-clear water. They did this over and over and when they got tired, they lay in the sun, glistening with salt, sparkle, and happiness. This was their magic summer ritual and nothing could improve it. The international celebrities in the cliff house became irrelevant again, and even Rosie seemed to forget about them entirely.

In the heat of late morning, the younger ones retreated to trampolines and tire swings in the valley around the back of Pippi, while Lily, Juliet, and their friend Nicola lay on towels in the shade and reflected on the life ahead of them with all the gravity of young adults who had very little to worry about.

"I'm just so glad school's over," murmured Juliet.

"Oh my God, yes," exploded Nicola. "Finally. No more algebra, no more Shakespeare. And if anyone asks me for a piece of persuasive writing, I will say NO."

"Me too. And if they ask why, I'll tell them—with

a killer introductory paragraph, several awesome body paragraphs, and a devastating conclusion," laughed Lily.

"Can you stop being smart just for a second? Just to make me feel better?"

"She can't help it," said Juliet.

"Not smart," added Lily. "Indoctrinated. How wonderful to finally be in the real world—not be judged anymore."

"I'm still judging you," said Nicola.

"That's fair. But you're not judging me against some arbitrary set of learning criteria set by a disgruntled ex-teacher."

Nicola and Lily giggled. They had gone to the local high school, an establishment with a bit of a reputation for turning its teachers toward office jobs, stress leave, or out of the profession entirely. The school's biggest claim to fame was that its alumni included two world-class surfers. Juliet, however, had attended an exclusive city girls' school that had world-class everything. Nicola felt sorry for her—the school seemed to put so much pressure on study—but Lily rather envied Juliet's private-school education. Lily could hardly complain about disadvantage—her teachers had gone out of their way and had even run advanced classes just for her, which would have been socially ruinous if it weren't for Nicola. But at the end of her time in high school, Lily found herself adrift. She didn't know what to do next. She was interested in so many things—literature, art, science—and her teachers and aunts had all told her she could do anything she wanted. The problem was, she wasn't sure what that was.

"Poor Lily." Nicola pouted. "You know we're in the real world now, right? Thinking is optional."

"No thinking! How delicious," added Juliet.

"Definitely no thinking while we're away in America," warned Nicola. All three girls had planned a gap year, and Nicola and Lily were off to Los Angeles for four whole weeks in the middle of it.

"I won't know what to do with myself," Lily laughed. "Imagine going to a museum without a busload of kids and a notebook!"

"We are not going to museums."

"Not even to meet the love of your life while you're both sketching the same sculpture?" coaxed Lily.

"The love of my life doesn't sketch sculptures. And neither do I."

"Going to a museum gala event would be fun," put in Juliet. "Red carpet. Formal wear. Teeny tiny little canapés . . ."

"Champagne," added Nicola. "And lots and lots of guys who look like they put some effort into their outfits."

"There is nothing sexier than a man who cares about fashion," Juliet said with a sigh.

"So, was that an Italian designer Casey was wearing last night?" teased Lily.

"No, American. A new ethical brand, really interesting. Casey said the fabric is recycled—" She stopped at their laughter. "What? What's so funny?"

"There's nothing sexier . . ." Nicola echoed. Juliet loudly protested that they were just chatting, they had only just met, she was being polite, the designer came up in conversation and it didn't mean anything, and it certainly didn't mean she liked him. The truth was, since her conversation with Casey Brandon the night before, she had thought of little else.

"I'm not attracted to him or anything. He's good-looking, that's all," Juliet said with little conviction.

"He's gorgeous," agreed Lily. "A bit smiley for me, though. Too nice."

"Ha! Of course, you like a bad boy," said Nicola. "Someone with cheekbones and a moody glare."

Lily rolled her eyes.

"And a stick up his potato?"

"Right up there."

"I am so not interested in Dorian Khan."

"Not even a little bit?" asked Juliet, glad to have the spotlight thrown somewhere else. "I mean, he seems really smart."

"Acting superior does not mean you're smart. And I should know, it's my thing."

"And he is really good-looking," added Nicola, which sparked quite a discussion in which they agreed that Dorian was better-looking but Casey was more attractive and, in any case, in the greater scheme of things, what a person looked like was the least important thing about them.

"Anyway, the point is," Nicole went on, "if Dorian walked up to you right now and said, 'Lily, I love you, come away with me, my helicopter's waiting,' you'd be gone. In a second."

"I can assure you I would not," retorted Lily, laughing at the very idea. "I wouldn't walk with him to the end of the jetty."

"Liar!"

Of course, Dorian Khan didn't turn up with any offers at all and remained locked away inside the cliff house for the entire day. But Lily meant what she said and truly did not care.

4

Over the next few days, everyone remained on high alert for encounters with the celebrity visitors. Casey had been open enough with the locals for most of them, including Lydia, to consider him their particular friend, so he was often caught up in conversations while out and about. He was also clearly on trash duty because he walked past the beachfront house most evenings. He was always keen to have a chat, not at all conscious of the rubbish bags grazing the side of his brand-name board shorts. He stayed longer if Juliet was there, which she almost always was. She had abandoned even the most dramatic board game to run out and say hi to him. Lily began to suspect that the trash run was merely an excuse to talk to Juliet.

The fact that the two other glamorous girls kept to themselves, and Dorian Khan was rarely seen at all, confirmed the view, formed early by Lily and now shared by everyone else, that they were not that nice. So Lily was surprised when Juliet returned from a solitary walk down the south end of the beach chatting pleasantly—and even laughing—with Cecilia and Yumi. They turned their reflective sunglasses toward the deck as Juliet introduced them to Lily and Nicola. Then, with a great show of reluctance, they declined an invitation to stay.

"You're so sweet," Cecilia drawled. "We'd love to, really, later, tomorrow, for sure." She and Yumi ambled off. Lily knew they had no intention of ever setting foot on their deck.

"We too suburban for ya?" Nicola murmured after them.

"No!" Juliet defended her new friends. "They're lovely. Once you get to know them."

"And did you?" Lily asked.

"Of course!"

As the week went on, Cecilia and Yumi continued to extend smiles and occasional invitations to Juliet to walk and swim but displayed little interest in getting to know anyone else. The attention that Juliet took for sincere, Lily judged as exploitative. They probably just wanted a local who would take them to the best places and protect them from the many natural dangers. Most importantly,

Lily thought, they wanted someone to whom they could meaningfully show off. They told Juliet everything, and through her, Lydia and the younger ones extracted the most important details. Casey and Dorian were starring in movies in Australia that autumn. Dorian was doing some independent feature in Victoria and Casey was in a blockbuster on the Gold Coast. They chose Pippi for their holiday because one of Dorian's schoolteachers used to come here. Cecilia was an influencer ("Ha! She couldn't influence me to stand on one leg!" barked Lydia). Cecilia also did Casey's social media. Yumi was her plus-one and stylist to all four.

The younger teens hung on every word.

"You can do my social media, Lily," announced Rosie, "when I'm famous."

"Lucky me."

"I'll be your stylist," offered Nicola.

"Who can I be?" asked Juliet.

"Casey's plus-one," said Nicola.

Juliet blushed and protested loudly to cover how thrilled she was at the very idea.

"So, are they coming to Friday drinks again tomorrow?" asked Rosie.

"And more importantly," said Nicola, "are they bringing Juliet's dream man and Lily's nightmare?"

Yes, Cece (as Juliet was now allowed to call her) had said they'd be there.

Sure enough, as the sun was sinking the next day, the quartet arrived at the community drinks, dressed as though for a beach-inspired fashion shoot. Casey beamed and the two girls smiled from behind their hair and sunglasses. Dorian Khan followed with the air of one being held hostage. Casey and Juliet quickly found each other, while Cece and Yumi stuck close together. Dorian hung back, clearly uninterested in their conversation, in everyone, or in being there at all. Yet whenever his eyes flicked over the group, they always seemed to land on Lily.

"He's looking at you." Nicola poked Lily in the ribs.

"Who?"

"The man whose charms you are so resistant to."

"Ha! You are ridiculous."

"But he is!"

"You should be a chef, Nicola. Always stirring the pot."

"You should be a dad, Lily. Always making terrible jokes and avoiding talking about feelings."

"He's not even looking at me."

"Well, he was before."

"The python was back this morning."

"Stop trying to change the subject. But please tell me about the python."

As Lily proceeded to tell Nicola about the big black python that had taken to baking in the morning sun across the path outside their house, her eyes drifted toward Juliet, who was smiling shyly in conversation with Casey. Nicola followed her gaze. They both watched as Juliet talked and Casey listened and nodded as though his life depended on it.

"He looks like a bobblehead," remarked Nicola.

"Rude."

"Significant. Bobblehead nodding means he likes her."

Lily looked at Nicola skeptically. "Then he's head-over-heels for Bob-with-Two-Dogs."

"His ripped undershirt makes him irresistible."

Lily snorted into her drink.

"Anyway, she clearly likes him," Nicola continued.

"Who? Bob?"

"Casey, you idiot. She's doing that hair thing she always does when she likes someone."

Lily's stomach twisted in an urge to protect her cousin from whatever brand of trouble Casey might be.

"They're cute together," Nicola went on. "I reckon she should make a move. Tell her to make a move, Lily, she won't listen to me."

"That's because most of your suggestions are highly unreasonable. And anyway, what do you mean, 'make a move'? This isn't an '80s rom-com. They're both grown-ups. If they like each other, they can just say so."

Nicola rolled her eyes. "That is literally the very last thing grown-ups do when they like each other."

"Aren't we all a bit over playing games?"

"Games are fun!"

"Steeped in patriarchal norms? I mean, 'make a move,' what does that even—"

"Oh my God, oh my God, oh my God."

"Ow! Stop doing that." But when Lily turned around she was thankful for the sharp poke because Dorian Khan was navigating through the hubbub of muumuus and muscle tees right toward her.

Lily glared at Nicola, who just shrugged and smiled.

"Don't you leave me—" Lily began, but Nicola was already stepping backward.

"What was that? I can't hear you, my patriarchal norms are calling!"

"Nicola!"

"Byeeeeee!" and she was gone.

And Dorian Khan was standing right in front of her, a sweaty beer in his hand, complete with comedic souvenir can cooler, and a serious but not hostile look on his face.

"Hi," he said. "I'm Dorian."

"Hi. Lily."

"You're Juliet's sister."

"Cousin."

"And you live here."

"Yes."

Lily couldn't help smiling. Had he come over just to make pronouncements about her? And get half of them wrong? She wondered if he was working up to an apology for his remark last week, and if so, how would she respond? For him to apologize would be to acknowledge what he had said and that she had overheard. She should probably just jump off that bridge when she got to it.

"Are you hungry?"

That was not what she had expected. It was all Lily could do to stop herself from laughing. His serious expression, the red flush on his cheeks, the absurd question! She couldn't wait to tell Nicola about it later.

"Um, I guess so," she responded, wondering whether he expected her to ask him the same in return. That was how conversations worked, right? But never before had she had a conversation like this—if you could even call it that.

"There's chips and dips," Lily said. She gestured toward the sad plastic platter of supermarket nibbles and wondered if this guy ever laughed. "Flavor undetermined—I think that's French onion and I think that's just . . . yellow."

"Would you like to come to dinner?" he asked in a rush, almost aggressively.

If Lily had been shocked by his first question, it was nothing compared to the utter bafflement she felt now.

"You mean now?" Wasn't it only five thirty?

"Later."

"After drinks?"

"Sure."

What did that even mean? Was he inviting her or not?

"I can't," she said. "I have to make dinner for the family tonight. No one else knows how to work the oven."

She smiled lightly and his eyes went cold. It was true, as far as it went, that no one else had taken the trouble to learn the correct sequence of switches. But she and Dorian both knew that this was hardly an excuse. On a Friday night during the summer holidays on a virtual island, there was really nothing that would prevent her from going to dinner at the cliff house apart from her own disinclination. She didn't even say "maybe another time" to soften the blow and protect his feelings, if he had any. Why should she lie to protect him from a perfectly reasonable refusal of an invitation that was so clearly inappropriate? Or at the very least, too early? She hardly knew the guy, and what she did know was not inspiring. He appeared to struggle to find his words for a moment but managed a gruff "Right" before marching away.

Lily felt no remorse or regret for declining and guessed that Casey had put him up to it. God, she thought, Nicola is going to die.

On the other side of the throng, Dorian stood with his fists in his pockets, his half-empty beer discarded on someone's picnic blanket.

"Where've you been?" Cecilia sidled up to Dorian and draped an arm around his shoulder. He shrugged her off. Pretending not to care, Cecilia shifted her weight and followed Dorian's gaze into the crowd. "Talking to that girl? God, she's so boring." She yawned.

Dorian said nothing.

"Just being honest," she said, reading his silence as one of disapproval.

"You're being rude."

"I love it when you get all judgmental."

Dorian was silent again.

"Oh, I'm sorry, do you like her?" Cecilia teased in a singsong voice.

Dorian rolled his eyes and strode away, muttering something about dinner.

"Oh my God, you do!" Cecilia giggled loudly after him, her over-the-top hilarity hiding her disappointment that Dorian had a crush on someone and it was not her.

5

No one could quite believe Lily had turned down an offer of dinner at the cliff house. Lily, however, had no regrets and was somewhat annoyed that her friend, sister, and cousins were more outraged at her refusal than at the invitation itself, considering she'd barely exchanged two words with the guy. Even more regrettably, the noise Rosie and Kat made about it reached the ears of Lydia, who had just arrived home after a good couple of hours of drinking and flirting with Bob-with-One-Dog, only to discover his ex-girlfriend was arriving on the last ferry.

Lydia was declaring loudly that nobody ever got to know anybody properly by talking to them, when Casey jogged up from the beach and asked Juliet straight out, right there on the deck in front of everyone, if she'd like to join them up at the cliff house for dinner. Confusion immediately reigned. Juliet mumbled something about the lasagna being in the oven, and Lydia interrupted her, shrieking, "LORD, yes, of course she's free and don't you worry about US!"

Lily and Juliet made eye contact. Lily asked with her eyes, "Do you want to go? I'll save you if you don't!" Very few people could stop Lydia in full flight, and not even Lily could do it every time, but there was no way Lily would let her mother force her cousin to go on a date she didn't want. But Juliet's eyes responded, "Yes!" Within seconds, Jane was offering him a drink while Lydia shouted at various nearby daughters and nieces to "get him a chair, a glass, and for goodness' sake get Juliet fixed up, she looks an absolute fright, she can't go like that, he'll think we're BARBARIANS." She burst into braying laughter over the top of Casey's protests that Juliet was absolutely fine to come as she was. Jane rushed to find a suitably masculine beer while Lily whisked Juliet off to get her changed before Lydia said anything too obnoxious.

"Yes, that dress. No, you don't need to do anything to your hair. Yes, a bit of perfume. You look gorgeous. Now go before she starts talking about her acting career." They got back to the deck just as Lydia was mid-story about how one time she spent a whole afternoon kissing strangers at an audition for a toothpaste commercial.

"Didn't get the job, but I got a couple of drinks and a ride on the back of a motorbike! Ha ha ha ha ha!"

Juliet had never headed off so fast.

"Wait!" shouted Lydia. "You can't go barefoot! Here!"

Lydia hopped madly on one foot as she yanked off her own wedge heels and thrust them at Juliet.

"We're the same size," she huffed proudly. "Go on, take them!"

Lily tried to stop this horrifying exchange, but the wedge heels were off and dangling center stage. Lydia gushed, "Put them on, they do wonders for your legs, truly, put them on, PUT THEM ON!" So to shut her up, Juliet did as she was told and scurried away, practically pushing Casey before her down the path as he tried to shout back his thanks to Jane for the beer.

"Mum!" remonstrated Lily.

"What? She's got cankles just like ours; I was doing her a favor."

Lily retreated to the kitchen to take a breath. She felt a sense of regret that she wasn't going too, inspired mostly by the urge to protect her cousin. She judged Casey to be safe—genuine even—and it seemed he really liked Juliet. If Juliet liked him back, then Lily would be nothing but happy for her. But what about his friends? And his sister? She remembered Dorian's cold eyes when she told him no. She had to smile to herself as she flicked the oven off. She'd turned down a movie star for the sake of a dodgy switch.

Just as Lily brought the lasagna out to the front deck, Casey reappeared, out of breath and clearly shaken. "I'm so sorry, Juliet fell on the steps. She's twisted her ankle—badly—but she won't let me call an ambulance. She says there isn't one, but surely . . ."

A cacophony of loudly expressed concern and indecision erupted. Jane wondered aloud whether to call the water police, water taxi, Fire-Chief-Steve, or nobody at all, and Lydia insisted that if there was no blood or a snakebite, she'd be fine. Rosie and Kat clamored to go up to the cliff house to see, while Casey was still trying to get an answer to whether there was such a thing as a water ambulance or paramedic helicopter, like they have at the Grand Canyon.

"Stop it, Mum!" asserted Lily. "Aunty Jane, don't call anyone yet. I'll go up and see how she is and I'll let you know. Rosie and Kat, sit down and eat your dinner. Casey, please, just wait. I'll be right there."

Lily grabbed her socks and sneakers and cursed her mother for causing yet another vanity injury. Lily had dealt with a lot of them over the years—sunburned skin, infected ear piercings, blistered heels, and insect bites—sometimes Lydia's, sometimes Rosie's, sometimes her own. This time, poor Juliet was the victim. The steps to the cliff house were steep, uneven, and rocky, and now Lily would be ascending them that evening after all, cankles at their absolute worst, because Lydia thought that legs were not primarily for walking but for attracting boys.

Lily followed Casey down the path and up the steps at a brisk jog and tried to calm him along the way.

"Accidents happen at Pippi," she said. "This won't be the worst one, and even if it's bad, we can deal with it. The water police can get a boat here fast and an ambulance to meet it on the other side. But we won't call them unless we have to."

Casey breathlessly explained how he caught Juliet in his arms as she stumbled and fell, avoiding a greater tragedy, and luckily they were at the top of the steps so he was able to carry her into the house. The conversation was all a bit embarrassing as both knew the stupid wedge heels were to blame, though neither said so. Despite the clear emergency, Lily couldn't help admiring Casey's genuine concern. She imagined that the moment Juliet fell into his arms must have been just a touch romantic.

Lily found Juliet draped on an enormous designer

couch. Her ankle had swollen up like a balloon and was bright red from ice packs hastily cobbled together from tea towels and novelty cocktail ice cubes shaped like billiard balls. Cecilia hovered nearby making the right sorts of remarks and suggestions with little conviction, while Yumi stayed on the deck looking funereal and occasionally glancing at her phone. Dorian was attentive but quiet.

"We have to call an ambulance," he said in a tone that Lily found unnecessarily authoritative. "Don't worry, we'll pay for it."

"Money's not the problem," Lily shot back. "It's the boat, the resources. The paramedics have to come up by water police. They cover the entire peninsula and we shouldn't tie them up if it's not a genuine emergency."

"Truly, I'm fine," Juliet insisted as she gasped with pain.

"I don't like it," said Casey. "Not one bit."

A compromise was reached when Lily suggested they call the telephone nurse service, which they duly did, on speakerphone. Everyone added a bit to the story, including Yumi, who came in especially to say clearly that Juliet had been wearing three-inch platform wedges at the time. It was the first thing Lily had ever heard her say.

After some detailed description of the foot and the nature of the pain, the nurse concluded that it was probably a sprain, best to keep it elevated for twenty-four hours and see a doctor within forty-eight hours.

"I guess you're not going home tonight, then," said Casey in a way that suggested he wasn't altogether displeased.

"If that's okay," said Lily, at which Casey and Dorian both assured her quite firmly that any attempt to move the patient was entirely out of the question, while Cecilia murmured her agreement as she tossed a salad.

"I'm starving. Can we eat already?" Cecilia said.

Casey looked to Lily. "Please join us for dinner. I'll run back to get whatever Juliet needs from home."

Lily was about to protest, but Juliet stopped her with one look. Her red-rimmed eyes begged Lily not to leave her there alone in such a vulnerable state with people she didn't know well. Not yet. So Lily smiled, thanked Casey, and accepted the invitation gratefully, for Juliet's sake. She flicked a glance to Dorian and was relieved that he had the decency to smile briefly at her, in a way that was not triumphant or mean or at all like a potato on a stick. Just in a way that suggested he was glad that the crisis was over and he understood and respected Lily's decision to say no to dinner before and yes now.

"I'm so sorry," said Juliet. "I don't want to put you out."

Casey reassured her she was welcome to stay as long as she liked. The cliff house's rustic beach-shack aesthetic—raw wood, breezy louvered windows, and shabby chic furniture—was just set dressing for all the space and luxury of a five-star resort. With one suite farther up the cliff, another below, and three bedrooms on the main level, there was plenty of room for an extra guest.

"Oh! Yes, that's a bedroom, isn't it?" Cecilia said when Casey reminded her—upon his remarkably speedy return with a hastily packed bag for Juliet—that the smallest room was technically vacant, even though she and Yumi had festooned every available surface in it with clothes and accessories.

"The closet space here is so miserable," Cecilia explained to Lily as she moved armfuls of designer wear off one of the single beds. "Can you, like, not put that there?"

Lily obediently moved Juliet's small bag of belongings from the bedside table to her designated bed.

"I just don't want her to lose her stuff, you know, in this mess. I'm so messy. It's because I just don't care about material things," she explained as she fondled a watery-thin sweater. "See this, this is cashmere silk and

I've practically ruined it. It really should be in its own bag."

The beginning of dinner was awkward. Casey insisted on eating with Juliet on the couch to keep her company, and the two of them curled up in a private chat that no one else could hear. The dining table seemed rather too vast for four, and Lily felt like she'd never sat with people less able to conduct a sociable conversation. Yumi stared off into space, Dorian looked at his plate, and Cecilia checked her phone more than once.

"Oh look!" Cecilia squealed and thrust the screen at Dorian. "It's Sigrid! Oh my God, she's hilarious. Look, Yumi. That's so her." Her laughter subsided as she put the phone back down. "Dorian's sister," she explained to Lily. "We miss her so much."

"She's not joining you for Christmas?" Lily asked.

"No," said Dorian. "She's studying," he added shortly, as though there was nothing more that could possibly be said on the matter.

"She is supersmart," purred Cecilia. "Isn't she at, like, Oxford or somewhere?"

"Cambridge."

"It's like Harvard for England," she explained to Lily, who had to take a drink of water to keep from laughing. She didn't dare raise her eyes.

"I could never, like, study," Cecilia went on. "I was so glad just to graduate high school." Cecilia looked to Dorian for signs of approval and received none. "I mean, of course, I love learning. But I feel like you learn more from travel. Don't you think? Dorian?"

"I'm not in a position to say."

"I'm taking a gap year to work and travel before I go to university," Lily said. "My friend Nicola and I are actually going to the US."

Dorian looked up at this and Cecilia visibly bristled.

"That is so awesome! Where are you going? LA? Oh, that's so great, I know all the best places to go, you will absolutely love it." Cecilia smiled, showing her teeth. "I can't believe you've finished school. I thought you were, like, fifteen."

"It's because," declared Yumi, "she doesn't do her hair or wear makeup."

An hour later, Lily helped a drowsy Juliet into bed, handing over a small pack of painkillers she'd managed to source, said her goodbyes with much alacrity, descended the steps to the beach, and breathed a sigh of relief. What a debacle of a meal, just as she had foreseen. Yes, Casey was charming and fun, and Lily was confident he would take care of Juliet and shield her from any awkwardness. But the other three! Dorian, all guarded and taciturn, who took any kind of question as a personal slight. Cecilia, fluttering around in front of him, constantly seeking his attention. And Yumi, who was just rude. If that was what passed for fashion, success, and a movie star lifestyle, Lily wanted nothing to do with it.

Juliet, warm in the glow of Casey's charm and slightly high on painkillers, shared none of Lily's judgment. Despite her sprained ankle, she fell asleep thinking she'd never had a more delightful evening.

6

Thankfully, when Lily got home that night, everyone was too involved in a very exciting card game to notice her return. She crept off to bed, glad to avoid the inevitable interrogation.

The next morning, she woke up to a cheery text from Juliet assuring her that all was well. Cecilia and Yumi had been so nice to her, she felt they were quite good friends. It turned out they had spent a week in the very same village where Juliet's parents were right now, in the French Alps! Lily smiled to herself. Connections and shared privilege had, no doubt, brought out the haughty girls' best.

It wasn't until after breakfast, when Lydia was doing her habitual sweep of the water and the cliff house with her telescope, that she realized that with her own niece up there, she, Lydia, had a perfectly natural reason to supplement her long-distance stalking with a personal visit. Rosie and Kat whooped with excitement at the prospect. It was all Lily could do to dissuade them from trooping up the steps straightaway like some colorful parade of amateur cheerleaders.

"It's too early. I'll go later. You stay here," she begged. "There is absolutely nothing you can do for Juliet that I can't do better by myself."

Everyone agreed this was true, but it was no reason for them not to go because they had no intention of doing anything to help anyway. They wanted to check out the boys and the house, and Lydia declared that her status as a local resident more than entitled her to take a look at the recent renovation, injured niece or no. Lily was genuinely worried they would all barrel in and forget Juliet was even there. Lily persuaded them to go for a swim first (tide was high), then slipped off toward the cliff house while they were still in the water, hopeful to make it there and back without them noticing and to report no need for further visits.

To her relief, Lily found Juliet recovered enough to stop all talk of calling a doctor so close to Christmas. She could hobble with assistance, and Casey delighted in carrying her piggyback wherever she wanted to go. Unfortunately, the descent back down the steps was still impossible.

Lily refused Casey's offer of coffee, made a quick note

of what Juliet needed from home, and was just about to leave when Lydia's voice floated up from the beach steps below. "Yoo-hoo! It's only me!"

"No need to come, all good here," Lily yelled back—but Lydia was already there, red-faced, wearing silly shoes and a sparkling animal-print maxi dress and declaring how lovely the view was from this particular spot. Rosie and Kat crowded behind her, bursting with glee at their proximity to fame.

"Best view in Pippi," Lydia declared, "and I ought to know because I've been in every single house on the headland and, LORD, isn't this a nice reno?"

Before Lily could stop her, she was in the kitchen checking out the soft-closing drawers, commenting on the brand and model of the dishwasher, and talking prices.

"I mean, you can get a perfectly good kitchen for twenty grand if you're prepared to do your homework."

Casey asked if she knew the owners—a polite inquiry, designed to relieve the awkwardness—which Lydia took as an invitation for a long monologue about who owned the house now, who owned it before, the builders, the architect, and how much they spent on the renovation.

"You know how much those taps cost? Five hundred dollars. Each. And you can get the same thing at the hardware store at the Point for fifty. Have you been? You should go, it's Saturday. On Saturdays they have a sausage sizzle. You know, sausage in bread? Love me a sausage," Lydia laughed.

Dorian stood on the threshold to the deck, silent and serious, as Lily desperately tried to stop the unfolding disaster.

"Anyway, we'd better leave you all to it—" Lily began, signaling "no" with her eyes at Rosie, who had picked up an ornamental seashell. Lydia continued as though she hadn't heard Lily at all and segued into bragging about her own house.

"Mine and my sister's, but she's hardly ever here and I'm the one who cleans the toilets! Ha ha ha! Seriously, I mean, this view is great, but I nearly busted a lung getting up here. You need a bloody donkey. It's so much better on the beachfront than the cliffs; the houses up here are an absolute nightmare to keep clean."

Lily saw a look pass between Cecilia and Yumi that was as clear as if they'd said it out loud: cleaning and carrying things were not their concern.

"I know you're only here for three weeks," Lydia went on, "but you would have gotten the discount if—"

"Excuse me," interrupted Dorian. "How do you know how long we're staying?"

Lily and Juliet cringed as Lydia expanded, completely oblivious to Dorian's implication.

"Oh, my mate Michelle at the agency. No secrets here. So I know if you'd taken it for the full month, it's much better value, PLUS you get the cleaning included mid-stay, which you haven't, so—" She fished a gold-edged card from her cleavage. Lily wanted to die. "Ooh, it's all warm. Just popped it there for the climb." Lydia wiped it on her maxi dress and offered it to an astonished Casey. "Call me if you want a quick refresh. I don't do much myself over the summer, but my mate Birdie can get you her new girl, fresh off the boat. She can't speak English, but she does hotels and everything."

Lily went red, Yumi's face froze, Dorian went stony, Casey's mouth fell open, and Juliet bit her lip.

"Mum!" Lily said.

"What?"

"You can't say that."

"Say what? What are you, the PC police? We're among friends, aren't we?"

"I'm sure you didn't mean to offend," assured Casey to relieve Lily's (and Juliet's) obvious distress, to which Lydia remained oblivious.

"Now we really have to go," said Lily as she bodily

pushed her mother back out to the deck, wildly scanning the room to see where Rosie and Kat had gone.

"What's the rush?" protested Lydia.

"We haven't even seen the upstairs yet," added Rosie, wandering out from the bathroom holding a fancy bar of soap to her nose. "Here, smell this."

"We have to leave them to their holiday," Lily hissed as she snatched the soap and returned it, her face burning.

"It's so lovely," continued Lydia. "You must be loving it away from the big city."

"Very peaceful, yes," agreed Casey.

"SO peaceful!" screeched Lydia. "Get it while you can! Just you wait till New Year's, this place will go off. Boats everywhere!"

"We're not staying for New Year's," said Cecilia, as though this ought to be obvious.

"We're seeing the fireworks," explained Casey. "On Sydney Harbor, we have a friend with a—"

But he was drowned out by a chorus of dismay from Rosie and Kat.

"You have to be here on New Year's," whined Rosie.

"It's the best day of the whole year," Kat insisted. "Races, sand sculpture contest, there's a talent show—"

"A band!" added Lydia. "They play all the good

songs—everyone joins in—you'll absolutely love it," she shouted with the particular conviction that extroverts seem to have when it comes to the preferences of strangers.

"Sydney on New Year's is terrible," Rosie declared.

"You can see fireworks anywhere," said Kat. "Please stay!"

In the awkwardness of the moment, while Lily kept pushing them to leave and Dorian stood as silent as death and Cecilia looked inclined to laugh openly and Yumi ready to kill someone and Juliet about to cry, Casey promised that they would stay in Pippi Beach on New Year's Eve.

7

Lily slipped back up to the cliff house before dinner in the hope that Juliet would now be well enough to come home. She was indeed much better and thought she could probably get down the steps with help, but Casey insisted there was no need to be brave.

"We love having you here," said Casey, and Cecilia and Yumi backed him up so effusively that even Lily thought they meant it.

"You're definitely safer here," said Dorian with an air of authority that made Lily roll her eyes on the inside.

"He's done a lot of damage to his ankles, knees, whatever, on set," Casey explained. "We'll move you down in the morning after another twelve hours of keeping it elevated."

Juliet was easily convinced. Lily less so, but she was hardly in a position to object. When Casey asked her to stay for dinner again ("We're getting delivery! By boat!')

and Juliet assured her it would be fun, she gave in, accepted a cocktail, and shot a text back home to say not to wait for her for dinner. Two nights in a row at the cliff house. Yet this time the atmosphere was very different.

The previous evening had been overshadowed by Juliet's pain, the adrenaline spike, and the awkwardness of new acquaintance. The emergency was over now, and a whole night and a day later, Juliet felt accepted. She sat at the table next to Casey, perfectly relaxed and happy. Lily, however, was very aware she was on the other side of a growing gulf. While she was glad to be there for Juliet's sake, and enjoyed the lighthearted chat about previous emergencies, falls, and injuries, she was very conscious of the impression she—and her family—had made on Cecilia and Yumi. Last night, she felt they had judged her as smart and sly. Now, after properly meeting her mother, they knew she was most definitely the poor cousin.

But she cared too little about what they thought of her to be very uncomfortable. Casey was a charming host who kept the atmosphere buoyant. He entertained them all with anecdotes of on-set antics, pranks in five-star hotels, and encounters with outrageously famous celebrities. Lily enjoyed seeing him make Juliet laugh.

She found it even more amusing to watch the American girls' performance of being charmingly entertained, which she rightly guessed was very much for Dorian's benefit. Dorian himself, meanwhile, sat slightly apart, engaged little in the conversation, told no fun anecdotes of his own, and didn't even add to the ones in which he featured. Soon after dinner, he checked the time and stood up to leave.

"Excuse me, I have a meeting. I'll be back in twenty minutes."

"Nooooo!" whined Cecilia.

"Oh come on, we're on vacation!" complained Casey.

"I won't be long."

"Then why go?"

"Because it's a workday in London and my team is working for me."

"Ugh, that word," slurred Cecilia, who had already had a cocktail and two shots. "Work! How can you even say it? I won't let you go. No, I won't. You'll have to kill me first." She stuck a high-heeled leg across to the coffee table to prevent him from leaving.

"I'm going."

"You beast."

She ran her foot up his thigh. Dorian caught her ankle

and placed it on the floor casually but firmly. And while Cecilia visibly fluttered at his touch, he was unmoved, as though he'd just removed a slightly bothersome insect.

"If you're not back in twenty minutes, I'm coming out to get you!" she called after him. "In my underwear!" she added with a laugh. "I mean, no online meeting's complete without it, right?"

Lily suspected the scene of Cecilia interrupting a meeting in her underwear would have been a good one, but it didn't come to that. True to his word, Dorian reappeared within twenty minutes.

"Everyone! He's back!" Cecilia announced. "Working, on vacation, during a party. I mean, the rabble think that people like us don't work, but you know what, we work so hard. So hard." She mourned into her cocktail.

"You save the world out there?" asked Casey.

"I saved my schedule."

"Good for you, man, good for you. I would not sacrifice this moment—this view, this company—for anything." Casey spread his arms and looked straight at Juliet.

"Unless you had to," said Dorian. "And I reminded you."

"You would too! Meetings, schedules, budgets, scripts, endorsements. You're all—bam!" He punched a hand for emphasis. "And I'm all—what?" He fluttered his hands in circles. "Having a good time."

"Ha," said Dorian.

"What can I say. I'm embarrassed."

"No you're not; you're showing off."

"You're right!" crowed Casey, clearly enjoying himself. "You're always right!"

"I'm not always right and I'm not always working."

"Dude, you literally just came out of a meeting."

"It was important and now it's over."

"So what constitutes 'important'?" asked Lily.

All eyes turned to her. Should she go on? It was too late; she had waded in. She thought it was pretty rich for Dorian to call Casey out for showing off when he made such a performance out of a phone call.

"I mean, some things are more important than work," said Lily.

"That is true," conceded Dorian, with a sarcastic edge. "Perhaps I prioritized my meeting unfairly. Did I miss anything crucial?"

"Yes, actually," put in Cecilia. "My shoulder strap broke. See?" She pointed to where she'd fixed it with a safety pin.

Dorian remained unmoved and Lily remained determined to push him out of his smugness.

"I'm just pointing out that where we draw the line is up to us. Casey puts fun and friends before work. Is that such a bad thing?" Lily said.

"It depends on the work. What its needs are."

"What about your needs? Your family's needs, the community's needs. Your friends. The environment. There has to be a point where 'the work' comes second. Don't you think?"

"No offense," sniffed Cecilia, "but, honey, you don't work in the industry."

"The industry is irrelevant."

"No it's not," insisted Cecilia, who was pretty sure this Lily girl was making fun of her but was unsure exactly how. "He's Dorian Khan."

"My work is no more important than any other kind," interrupted Dorian. "I just have high standards."

"It's not like manual labor," Cecilia went on.

Lily smiled in the awkward pause that followed. "I'm sure whoever built this house with manual labor had standards too," she said.

"Do you think they compromised their work for their friends?" Dorian asked.

"The house would have been built faster if the builders never went surfing. It could have been bigger too, but the owners thought it was important to preserve the look of the headland."

"Come on, man, she's just messing with you," said Casey in a conciliatory tone.

Lily shrugged to make it clear that she was not at all invested. Why was he always so serious? "I'm just making conversation. Wondering aloud about how we decide our priorities."

"Well, there's nothing wrong with Dorian's priorities. He always shows up for the people who matter," Cecilia asserted, with a pointed look that suggested that Lily was not such a person.

"Now, that is true," agreed Casey.

Lily smiled at how quick Casey and Cecilia were to defend their friend—who also happened to be the most powerful person in the room. Perhaps the thought that he could ever be wrong about anything had never entered their heads. Or Dorian's.

Lily felt his eyes on her for the rest of the evening. She wondered why. She couldn't imagine Dorian was at all disturbed by what she had said, or was interested in her, except maybe as a curiosity. To him, she was probably a creature from another world or a deeply flawed individual who invited further study as some kind of example of how things could go wrong. Perhaps he was irritated by how little she cared about how she presented herself or what others thought of her. Surely he didn't get to his current position without caring deeply about both. He always seemed to be on guard, and that would take up a lot of energy. And his accent, part-London-part-posh, struck Lily as another aspect of his persona that just seemed careful and cultivated, especially considering he was born in Geelong. Perhaps behind it, he was an outsider too. She felt she disrupted his world somehow, but she wasn't sure whether it was her everydayness or her unique qualities as a Pippi Beach girl who lived among millionaires' mansions, whose mother's job was cleaning them. She couldn't help wondering if Dorian had ever encountered anyone who was not actively trying to impress him, working for him, or wanting something from him. Certainly, Cecilia and Yumi seemed to be all three.

While she couldn't work out what her effect on Dorian might be, she didn't spend too much time wondering. She had no doubts at all about what she thought of him, and he was quite clearly not worth her attention. Yes, he was obscenely good-looking; there were moments when Lily observed him thinking, or looking at the view, or bantering with Casey and it was like watching him in a movie. Lily half expected him to put in a call to spy headquarters on his watch. But she was quite satisfied that her first impressions of him had proven right. Whatever talent and intelligence this person may have was ruined by his arrogance, entitlement, and inflated sense of his own importance. And he was obviously paid too much.

When dessert was finished, Yumi called everyone out to the deck to admire the moon.

"Feel the vibrations," she demanded.

Casey and Juliet were far too comfortable on the couch, but Lily was drawn to the fresh salt air. Out on the deck, with the water beneath and the stars above, Lily caught Dorian looking at her again, and really, it was too much. Sure, the camera might love unreadable brooding glances, but in real life they were just strange. So she returned his stare.

"Do I have something on my face?"

"No, of course not."

He frowned slightly and looked away.

She laughed. "Sorry. I suppose I'm not as used to being looked at as you all are."

Which led to great protests from Cecilia, who insisted she was completely unaware of how she looked.

"I just never think about it," she opined as she lolled

on the railing in front of Dorian. "And so many of my friends are so obsessed with their appearance, they have, like, mental health issues. It's sad." She tilted her gaze downward. "Oh my GOD! Casey, why didn't you tell me your deck had a hot tub? I adore a hot tub. Yumi, come on!"

Cecilia and Yumi fled to Juliet's room to change into their bikinis.

"Did you want to join them?" Dorian asked Lily. At least he had the sensitivity to notice the slight.

Lily laughed. "Oh no. I wouldn't want to spoil the performance."

Dorian and Lily were now alone on the main deck with the moonlight, but it was Cecilia and Yumi on the deck below who commanded their attention as they splashed, giggled, and marveled at how peaceful it was and how little they cared if anyone watched.

8

Lily soon felt she had seen quite enough of Cecilia and Yumi in the tub, and as Juliet was deep in conversation with Casey on the couch, and Dorian had lapsed into silence, she decided it was time to go.

"I'll leave you to your evening. Thanks again. I'll just take these to the jetty with me," she announced, gathering up the food boxes and scraps. She was surprised when Dorian joined her.

"I'll come with you," he said.

"I'm going down anyway."

"So am I."

Lily suddenly remembered what she'd said to Nicola the previous week: "I wouldn't walk with him to the end of the jetty." But it wasn't as simple as that now. He had been oddly kind to her and Juliet, and though she knew she'd get an earful from Nicola later, walking down to the jetty laden with garbage was hardly a romantic stroll.

"All right. Thanks." And she offered him one of the bags.

"Taking out the trash, Lily?" Cecilia called from the hot tub as they passed the lower deck. "Oh, and you've got the garbage as well, how kind."

"Very funny, Cece," said Dorian without a glance in her direction.

"You know I love you. Wait there, we'll come."

Lily paused and shifted the weight of the recycling box onto her hip. Here we go, she thought. Mission accomplished. Dorian now had to stop and look as Cecilia stood up in the tub in her bikini, skin steaming as it hit the air, glistening in the light from the bedroom inside. Oh boy.

Lily observed Yumi struggle with the dilemma. Should she follow Cece as usual or stay in the warm water as the night air cooled?

"I'm never leaving this tub," Yumi said eventually.

Cecilia didn't seem to care. She dabbed herself with a towel and threw on a diaphanous robe. She didn't offer to carry any bags.

Cecilia led the way down to the beach, chatting airily, as Dorian and Lily followed in silence. All three of them kept to the shadows as they passed the beachfront house, though mercifully none of Lily's family was out on the deck. It wasn't until they had deposited the garbage and recycling in the public bins ("How adorably communist!" squealed Cecilia) that Lily realized she'd left her phone up at the cliff house.

"You can just get it in the morning," Cecilia offered. Was she eager to rid herself of Lily so she could enjoy a moonlit walk with Dorian? Lily would have been glad to leave them to it, but she didn't want Juliet up at the cliff house without direct contact with her only reasonable and tactful family member.

"I'd prefer to have it tonight," Lily said, and so they set off back toward the cliff house with a running commentary from Cecilia about how little she relied on her phone because social media could be so toxic if you didn't use it right.

Dorian silently ushered the party off the path and down the beach to walk back along the water's edge. Typical, Lily thought. Why should he lead the way? It was annoying how naturally he assumed control, even if this was the way she would have chosen herself. They all removed their shoes, and Cecilia's chatter subsided in the majesty of the night. Even after all her years of living at Pippi, Lily never got over its quiet beauty once the sun went down. Outside the pools of light from the houses, Pippi glowed with its own silvery energy. The dunes rustled with the breeze and animals, crabs scuttled across the sand, and cicadas buzzed.

"I feel so connected to nature right now," Cecilia mused as she picturesquely flicked long tendrils of damp hair and stretched her neck.

"You look it," Lily said with a smile.

"The water is so calm," Cecilia continued. "Oh my God. Let's swim!" She flung off her robe, stretched her arms to the stars, and lunged into the shallows with a delighted shriek. "What are you waiting for?"

Lily looked at Dorian.

"Too much nature?" Lily asked, amused.

Dorian didn't reply. She could barely make out his features to see what he was thinking, but she hardly cared. It was a beautiful night. Why shouldn't they swim? With as much businesslike speed as possible, she stripped down to the swimsuit she was wearing under her clothes and followed Cecilia in.

"Don't drown," Dorian called after them.

The water was lovely. The surface was as smooth as silk and still warm from the heat of the day. Lily dipped under and relished the feeling of salt water on her skin. When she resurfaced, Cecilia was standing closer to the beach, calling out to Dorian.

"Come on! It's beautiful!" She giggled and splashed toward him.

He didn't move. "I'm perfectly fine here. And I wouldn't want to deprive you of your chief pleasure."

"What do you mean?"

"Your audience."

Cecilia splashed him again in mock outrage. "Rude!"

"Honest."

Ha, thought Lily. Dorian saw right through Cecilia's display and refused to indulge it. Lily only hoped he didn't include her in his judgment. Not that she cared. Or did she? She knew she wasn't showing off for his benefit, but why did she have the urge to prove it? He could think whatever he liked.

"Not everything women do is for the benefit of men, you know," insisted Cecilia. "How should we punish him, Lily?"

Lily contemplated Dorian's shadowy figure cutting a casual pose against the glow of the sand and sky behind him.

"Easy," she said. "We laugh at him."

"I am! I do! Ha ha!" bubbled Cecilia as she twirled.

"Look at his serious face," Lily went on with a smile. "It's funny!" She started to laugh.

"There's nothing wrong with being serious," Dorian countered.

"Ah, but being serious and taking oneself seriously are two different things," she said. What the hell, let him squirm a little. She swam farther into the shallows. Cecilia followed her, striding out of the water, while Lily glided close to the sand.

"I laugh at you all the time," Cecilia claimed.

But Dorian kept his eyes on Lily.

"Is taking oneself seriously a flaw?"

"I didn't say that."

"My flaw is that I care too much," trilled Cecilia. "Come on, let's go. I'm freezing. Give me your shirt."

As Lily scrambled to dress herself, Dorian silently removed his sweatshirt and gave it to Cecilia.

"Oh my gosh, it's so warm! And so big! I'm swamped!" she declared with much laughter.

Dorian wrapped Cecilia's robe over his own shoulders and set off toward the cliff house. Lily couldn't help but wonder if that was a gesture for her benefit, to show her that he was indeed playful and spontaneous. Yet for some reason, even in an ankle-length sheer silk robe with frills, he still looked as serious as the grave.

9

Juliet's ankle was better enough the next morning for her to limp down the steps. Casey insisted on carrying her on his back across the sand and delivered her onto her own deck, where she collapsed into a chair with much laughter, thanks, and friendly touching of hands and arms as he knelt beside her and made sure she was okay. Aunts Lydia and Jane, cousins Lily, Rosie, and Kat, and even a reluctant cousin Martin clustered around the two of them in a cloud of thank-you-so-much and no-problem-at-all and really-I'm-fine.

Casey wasn't ten meters away down the path before Lydia, with eyebrows raised, exploded in a burst of whoops—more childish even than Rosie's and Kat's—and pretty much everyone said, "He is SO into you!" so loudly that Casey must have heard.

"Stop it! He's just a nice guy, that's all; he'd have done the same for anyone, even Martin."

"I wouldn't have twisted my ankle," grumbled Martin, but nobody heard.

Everyone was busy peppering Juliet with questions and supplying their own surmises and opinions. Had they kissed yet? What was it like? Does he always look that good? Are you in love?

Lily just shrugged her shoulders at the helpless Juliet and snuck off for a quick swim. She knew the truth and Juliet confirmed it herself later that day. Juliet was smitten—and they hadn't kissed. Yet. While their eyes had spoken volumes, nothing definite had been done or said. Juliet was worried that Casey was just being nice out of friendship, but Lily knew better. She could see that he was just as smitten as she was, and Lily was glad. Having spent more time with him, she was sure that his interest was genuine. With Juliet on the mend, and a new romance brewing, Lily needn't have much more to do with the rest of the cliff house occupants.

Christmas that year was wet, but nothing could dampen the family's holiday enthusiasm. Aunt Jane prepared an amazing meal; Lydia made cocktails and a pavlova. Everyone, even Martin and Aunt Jane, jumped off the end of the jetty in the rain. Most ran shrieking back to the house. Lydia floated back to shore in the inflatable flamingo, singing "Jingle bells, fat man smells" at the top of her lungs. Jane's husband, Charles, had turned up on Christmas Eve with a boatload of food, drink, and presents. He was the life of the party for ten hours straight, then promptly fell asleep on the deck, where he stayed for the rest of his holiday, only waking occasionally to jump enthusiastically into a kayak or a dinghy with whomever cared to join him. Jane found it delightful; Lydia was glad to have a man around to pull the boats up and down the sand for her.

Juliet spoke to her parents, who were enjoying their time skiing in the French Alps. Aunt Kitty called from Melbourne; she would be up to see them in January. Aunt Mary, who lived in India and worked for an international environmental organization, sent each niece and nephew notice of a donation she'd made in their name and a note asking them to match it instead of calling her to say thank you. She was uncontactable anyway. There were stockings filled with presents like nail polish, jigsaw puzzles, books, board games, new bikinis, bangles, and sketchbooks to divert them. The kids weren't really kids anymore, but Christmas at Pippi was no less magical.

The occupants of the cliff house were not to be seen, but everyone assured a slightly anxious Juliet that it was just the rain keeping them indoors. Then, when their yacht disappeared early on Boxing Day, everyone decided it was just respect for family time that had kept Casey from saying anything, and wasn't that sensitive of him, and good that the overseas visitors were taking the opportunity to explore the harbor even though the weather wasn't exactly perfect.

The household had something else to consume their attention: a visitor, whom everyone, especially Lily, was most curious to see again after many years. Wilson Collins was a few years older than Juliet and Lily. His mother, Charlotte, had been best friends with Aunt Jane and Juliet's mother, Lizzie, when they were young, and Juliet had vague memories of being forced to play with a pale boy who sulked when he lost at games and wouldn't share his building blocks. But that was a long time ago, and although Aunt Jane still kept in touch with Charlotte, she didn't really know much about Wilson. His social media was all pictures of Los Angeles vistas and expensive cars captioned with inspiring aphorisms.

Wilson, although Australian, now lived in the United States. His parents had separated about fifteen years ago and his mother promptly met and married an American property developer while on holiday in Bali. They moved to Beverly Hills, where Charlotte reinvented herself as a luxury real estate agent and socialite. She curated pictures of herself living a beautiful life wearing white linen in spacious living areas, with captions exhorting her Australian friends to visit. So when Lily expressed interest in traveling to the US, Aunt Lizzie got in touch with Charlotte, who was only too happy to offer Lily and her traveling partner, Nicola, use of her guesthouse whenever they liked.

"We'd love to have you both here," Charlotte had emailed. "Wilson will take good care of you! He misses Australia so much, you'll have so much in common and so much to talk about! He'll reach out to you next week!"

That was six months ago. Lily still didn't know how much in common she had with the mysterious Wilson, or how much they had to talk about, because he had never contacted her. But in early December, Charlotte had sent another email full of exclamation marks to say that Wilson himself would be in Sydney for Christmas visiting his father; maybe he and Lily could meet up then? So Aunt Jane invited him, through Charlotte, to Pippi for New Year's, and Wilson, through Charlotte, accepted. Lily was curious—and hopeful. She hadn't had time to think too much about her trip, but now with school over and Christmas done, the new adventure of traveling to the US was becoming real. She hoped she and Wilson would become friends.

Everyone trooped down to the jetty to meet Wilson's ferry, dressed in their array of swimwear and summer clothes, barefoot and tanned. There, in among the locals with carts of groceries, cases of beer, and parts of boats, was a young, trim man in a floral dress shirt, pants, shoes, socks, and a tie. Colorful resort wear, but still, a tie? It was probably the only tie worn at Pippi since Zen married Michelle at the north end, and even then, Zen had worn it with a T-shirt.

"Omigosh, look at you all, this is so magnificent, it's like Malibu, only Australian. Look, there's so many of you, I hardly know which is which! Wow. This jetty is adorable! A baby Santa Monica Pier! Oh no—don't take that one—DON'T touch it. Sorry to scare you, that's got my laptop so—" He snatched a leather briefcase from Rosie, who was trying to be helpful for the first time in her life and was only too happy to relinquish responsibility for carrying anything. Everyone else gathered up his enormous collection of matching designer luggage and dragged it up to the house, while Wilson kept up a constant commentary in a nasal, faux-LA accent that blared up and down the beach like a bugle call.

"Wow, I feel like I'm home. We talk about this place all the time, and you, you're my family. Now, which one

of you is Lily? Don't tell me, don't tell, I want to guess."
He ran his eye flirtatiously across the girls until he
settled on Lydia. "You! You don't look a day over seven-
teen! Ha ha, just kidding. You're gorgeous, by the way."
He switched his focus to Juliet. "Lily? Is that you?"

Juliet smiled, shook her head, and pointed toward
Lily, who was hanging back, already starting to wonder
if a month was too long to stay anywhere as a guest.

"Of course! Lily! I recognize you now. You and I," he
said, actually starting to laugh, "are going to have the
BEST time together, I know it, just you WAIT. I mean,
this is beautiful, but you wait till I show you Beverly
Hills."

Dinner that night was loud. Though their number
had only increased by one, Wilson's over-the-top manner
brought out the loud in everyone else as well. With
enough grasping energy to power a speedboat engine,
and an ear-splitting accent that dipped in and out, he
made the house that comfortably slept twelve feel like it
was bursting. The party had known nothing of Wilson
and his new life in America when he stepped off the
ferry, but after one hour over dinner, nothing about him
was a mystery.

"Yes, my boss is Stacy Black. Now, do NOT believe
what you have read about her; that lawsuit should never

have been brought—Oh, you don't know her? Yes you do. You know her work. Name any good movie from the last twenty years, she produced it. Or told someone else to produce it. Oscar-nominated period drama, check; gritty star vehicle, check; art-house thriller, check; war movie, check; blockbuster, check check check. You know the spy franchise Daniel Danger with Dorian Khan? Well, that is Stacy's. What? He's here? Dorian Khan? No, he's not, he's in London. Must be someone who looks like him. Casey Brandon too? Wait—let me see . . ." He bent over his smartphone for some minutes, then triumphantly rose to reveal what everyone at the table already knew, with many extra details (which invited no farther conversation beyond admiring remarks) about the two stars' past, present, and future schedules and their very close relationships with Stacy Black.

"She is so generous. I'm at her house in the Hills literally all the time."

Lily could still hear Wilson's voice ringing in her ears as she went to bed that night. She'd heard enough about Stacy Black and Wilson Collins for a lifetime. How could she survive a month of it?

The next morning, Lily and Juliet slipped out to prepare Nicola. She would be over later to meet him and they felt she needed some advance warning.

"He's very . . . consistent," Lily explained.

"What's that supposed to mean?"

"Come on, he's nice," insisted Juliet. "He just wants to make an impression."

"I know. I just feel like I don't need to be that impressed."

"I do. I love being impressed. Is he good-looking?" asked Nicola.

"Yes," admitted Juliet.

"I guess." Lily frowned. Wilson's looks weren't striking, but she had to admit he was very well put together. He'd said himself that everything about his appearance, from his tan to his teeth, had been very expensive.

"Good morning!" called out Wilson as he emerged from the beach, dripping wet, his chest bare, abs showing. He was flexing very, very hard. "You must be—"

"Nicola."

"So nice to meet you, I can't wait for you to visit LA. I'm so sorry." He paused and unexpectedly removed a phone from his board shorts. "Don't worry, it's waterproof. It's New York; I have to get this."

The girls tried not to laugh as he turned his dripping-wet back to them and ambled off shouting into the phone. But as they spent the day getting to know him while swimming, walking, and eating together, Lily had to admit that Juliet was right: Wilson's heart was in the right place and all he really wanted was to be liked. Lily just wished she could like him more.

"So when was the last time we saw each other?" said Wilson later, sidling up to Lily during a family walk along the beach.

"Long time ago now," Lily replied.

"I remember you. We used to play this HILARIOUS tickling game, do you remember?"

"No," said Lily.

She knew what he was doing. Wilson liked to collect and show off his luxuries, and a girlfriend was one he was missing. Unfortunately, it seemed as though Wilson had decided that Lily was his best chance.

"Well, it was a super fun game," Wilson said, undeterred. "Wouldn't it be funny if we, like, played it now? Ha ha! I'm kidding. Unless you want to?"

"Oh, I don't think it would be fair," she said. "I haven't been practicing! Better get some training in now and I'll let you know when I think I'm good enough."

She ran ahead to Nicola, bursting with laughter, and recounted the whole conversation to her.

"Ew!" Nicola screamed. Lily looked back, but Wilson had already attached himself to Martin. ("The beaches in California are just so much bigger. Overdeveloped?

I don't think so. A lot of people think that, but actually no, you're wrong.")

"He's such a squid," said Lily.

"Too slimy?"

"Too many tentacles and no backbone."

Her impression of him had proved correct, but Lily resolved the best way to deal with Wilson was just to tolerate quietly, and where possible, avoid.

10

The days between Christmas and New Year's at Pippi seemed infinite. Time, already warped by Pippi's isolation, became completely abstract. There was no sign of the celebrity visitors, which was disappointing to many, especially Juliet, but Lydia had already set her sights on new entertainment.

"Let's all get into our sexiest bikinis and meet the first ferry! No reason! It'll be fun!"

Ha, thought Lily. She wouldn't fall for that. She already knew that a gang of French backpackers was coming to work on the renovations of the gum-tree house, owned by Bob-with-One-Dog. Her mother must have discovered that today was the day. Lily shuffled down to the jetty in her pajamas with the others, but only to make sure that no one made too much of a fool of themselves.

"What? Backpackers? French? On this ferry? How

wonderful! Don't mind me, just lounging around in my red bikini my daughter disapproves of!" laughed Lydia.

Lydia, Rosie, Kat, and the French backpackers were all delighted to meet one another.

"Need help?" Lydia thrust herself forward to grab the handles of a shopping bag filled with six-packs of beer and was soon halfway down the jetty chatting away to two Frenchmen half her age, no doubt about to invite herself over for a drink. And Lily was suddenly face-to-face with a good-looking guy of about twenty-two, with curly sun-bleached hair, a tan, and a smile as warm as the sunrise. She couldn't help but notice his eyes were the exact green of the water currently being churned up by the departing ferry. Oh dear, she was turning into her mother.

"I'm Alex," he said, and Lily was surprised his accent was British. "This the welcoming party, is it?"

"You're from England?" chirped Rosie. "I thought you were all French, but that's okay, we'll allow it."

Alex smiled politely, with just the right amount of flirtatious twinkle.

"I'm Rosie," she continued. "And this is my sister, Lily, and cousin Kat and cousin Juliet."

"Nice to meet you, cousin Kat, cousin Juliet," he said with a half laugh. "And Lily."

Lily smiled and said hi and felt Juliet stifle a giggle next to her.

"That's our house," Rosie said, pointing to their front deck. "You're totally welcome to stop by whenever, everyone does that here. How long are you here? Oh my God, that's so awesome, you have to stay for New Year's! It'll be so great . . ."

As she chattered on, Lily noticed Alex's eyes drift and lock elsewhere. She followed his gaze over Rosie's shoulder and saw him focus on two kayaks paddling out in the morning sun. It was Dorian and Casey, passing close enough for her to see Dorian looking intently at the group at the end of the jetty, as though searching for the answer to a particularly important question, then turn away in what could really only be described as disgust. Lily was surprised at how mean he looked. She glanced back at Alex, whose face had clouded over with shock and possibly a little anger. Or was it fear? Rosie, too engrossed in detailing her party plans, noticed nothing. Lily watched as Alex blinked and returned his attention to her sister, though something in his face showed he was still thinking about what he had seen.

Lily exchanged a look with Juliet, who confirmed it. I saw that too, her face said, and it was weird. But they didn't have long to dwell on it.

"Juliet!" shouted Casey, waving madly. As the French backpackers and their enthusiastic bikini-wearing entourage made their way down the path, Juliet flew as fast as her injured ankle would carry her to the beach to meet Casey, where they had a long conversation in the shallows while Dorian idled out in the deep.

"Casey!" he called eventually. "The time."

Lily watched from the deck as Casey obeyed his friend and paddled back out to join him, while Juliet drifted back to the house, beaming happily.

"They're just anchored over at the Point," she said, and smiled. "He was so sweet, he couldn't stop apologizing. They left so early, he didn't want to wake us. Dorian wanted to explore. But they'll be back for New Year's."

It would be sooner than that, Lily guessed, if Casey had anything to do with it.

Bob-with-One-Dog's modular cottage was on the green stretch back from the beach, behind the waterfront. What he lacked in water views, he was making up for with grand vision—an extensive renovation that involved gutting the entire place and adding a second floor and a sweeping deck. To that end, he had turned the vacant lot next door, which he also owned, into a mini camping village for himself and his crew of cheap French labor. On the first night, he put on welcome drinks to show off his new battalion of muscle and introduce them to the Steves, Joels, and Sues who would help out with sourcing materials, boats, and any work that required signing off with a license (plumbing, electrical, or engineering). He invited everyone.

Usually, Lily would avoid a local booze-up at Bob-with-One-Dog's place. It wasn't fun to watch the adults getting loose and loud, and she wasn't really needed. Rosie and Kat would flirt outrageously, but they wouldn't get away with much drinking, and it was hours before her mother would have to be talked out of jumping off the jetty. But Lily had to acknowledge to herself that this evening was different. She actually wanted to go. She wanted to get to know Alex. Her main concern was that Wilson would get in the way. Wilson had been playing a new online video game about climate breakdown all afternoon with Martin, so Lily hoped it would keep his attention. No such luck. Wilson declared that there was nothing he would rather do than join a spontaneous event, and he was used to mingling because Stacy Black frequently hosted cocktail parties for visiting European filmmakers on her yacht.

They arrived to find music blaring. Lydia was already making good headway on a six-pack of cider and dancing with a muscly Frenchman. Rosie and Kat were giggling in their bikinis ("What do you mean, put something on? I have something on! Don't judge me!'), playing some sort of shrieking catch-and-freeze game with the two youngest French boys, who didn't speak any English but were very good at catching.

Wilson accepted a beer from Bob-with-One-Dog with much thanks and a smiling correction that no, really, he's not American at all.

"Born here, actually, but my accent is everywhere. Mid-Pacific, they call it in the film business."

When Bob-with-One-Dog started paying more attention to throwing the ball for his fox terrier, Grommet, Wilson attached himself to one of the Frenchmen.

"J'adore Paris. I'm more of a Rive Droite man; most people just don't get that there's so much more to it. Oh—Bordeaux? Yes, of course, never been myself, but Cannes—I'm in the film business, so—"

The Frenchman grabbed Rosie's waist, she slipped out of his grasp, and he took off after her.

"Good one!" Wilson shouted after him. "Ha, got you!" He grabbed at Kat, who brushed him off scornfully.

Lily slipped away to the steps up to the building site overlooking the green, where she could get a good view and easily fend off—or invite—anyone who came near.

She was pleased when Alex spotted her, waved, and pointed at a cider with a question on his face. She smiled, nodded, and tapped the empty space on the step beside her.

"Magical, no?" he said as he joined her. "I can't believe such beauty exists. I feel like I've stumbled on a lost civilization."

Lily laughed. "It will get less civilized as the night wears on."

"You speak from experience?"

"Years of it."

"You spend all your holidays here?"

"I live here."

Alex was impressed. "Really? Permanently?" and he demanded to know everything. The routine, the locals. He loved every detail and was especially delighted with the feud between architect Steve-with-the-White-Hair and Bob-with-Two-Dogs, which had started over who was supposed to mow the green and when.

"So how did you end up here?" asked Lily.

"Luck. I was just hanging out with Theo in this god-awful two-bedroom in Bondi—seven of us—and they asked me if I wanted to join them here for a building job. Why not? Strangely enough, I'd already heard of this place, though. One of my housemasters at school grew up over at the Point, used to tell us boys all about it. The fame of Pippi Beach extends farther than you might think."

"Yes," mused Lily. "When you arrived it actually looked to me like you saw someone you knew."

"Here?"

"Kayaking past."

"Oh. OH." He smiled. "You saw that. Well. Surely everyone knows the great Dorian Khan?"

"Not the way you know him, I suspect."

"Ah. No. Funny thing, we were at boarding school together for a while. Had that same housemaster, now that I think of it. Maybe that's how he ended up here too. Has he been here before? Do you know him?"

"Not really. I mean, we met—but only briefly."

She told the story of Juliet's accident, her evenings at the cliff house, and how she'd be quite happy to avoid everyone there in the future.

"Me too," confessed Alex.

"So you weren't friends at school, then?"

"On the contrary—we were best friends. Both very much into dramatics and that sort of thing. I got him into it, really, in a sense. He came back to England from Australia when his parents split up, and I'd been through something similar so we bonded, I suppose. Schoolboy productions. I believe I made a rather brilliant Titania to his Bottom."

They both laughed. Lily couldn't help noticing how natural and unforced his manner was, especially in contrast to the more self-conscious behavior she'd witnessed recently.

"It was one of those schools—boaters and blazers, etcetera. Anyway, long story short, someone saw us and signed us up. Started going for the same roles. Age fourteen. So cute we were. Two little Shakespeare aficionados, auditioning side by side for roles as street-wise hoodlums. Wot talked like 'at, guv."

"I'm sure you were gorgeous. So what went wrong?" What could have led friends to exchange the looks she'd observed on the jetty that day?

"I don't like to talk about it."

"Of course. Sorry, I don't mean to be nosy." Short silence. Lily quickly assured him he didn't have to talk about anything and changed the subject. "Did I mention my mother drinks a little?" Lydia, at that moment, was loudly trying to teach Theo how to say "Yeah, nah, yeah, nah." Alex laughed, a little sadly, but he steered her back. He wanted to tell, he said.

"Usually I don't, but there's something about you that makes me feel safe. Not that there's much to say, really.

We grew up. He and I both got a part in a movie—you wouldn't know it, some god-awful period drama—and embarrassingly enough, the producers thought I was all right and they expanded my part."

"Oh. Isn't that a good thing?"

"Well, yes. But by this time the Dan Danger thing had just started to take off for Dorian. God knows why he was threatened by little old me—maybe because I got him the part in the first place. Oops, did I say that out loud? Anyway. He wasn't happy about the attention I was receiving and got me fired."

"Fired?"

"Replaced. I know."

"Seriously?"

"Serious as cancer. So I was out on my ear, lost my agent, who of course sided with the money, and Dorian saw to it that I'd never work in the industry again. Which I haven't."

"That's terrible! But couldn't you—I don't know—tell people what really happened? I'm sure if people knew . . ."

"Oh no. Dorian Khan's connected. Honestly, the business at the top is worse than high school—everyone knows everyone—and he's a bankable name now. No one would dare provoke him. Call it luck, call it talent, call it a way of looking moodily up from behind a perfectly cascading fringe . . ."

Alex copied Dorian's signature look so perfectly that Lily had to laugh.

"Stacy Black, the producer." Wilson's voice drifted up from the green. "You know her? She has two Oscars. Two. I know."

"Your cousin?" asked Alex.

"Family friend," Lily corrected. "Also in showbiz. Apparently."

"Stacy Black IS showbiz. And so is Dorian, really. Which is why I don't want anything more to do with it. Don't tell them I told you. Let's just keep the past in the past."

"Of course."

Lily smiled at him. How wonderful to meet someone who so emphatically confirmed everything she already believed to be true: that the movie business was cruel; that Dorian Khan was an egotist; that success came most readily to those who were already privileged, lucky, and vindictive—not necessarily to those with talent. And how much more pleasant it was to sit here among building materials drinking warm cider with Alex than it was to be up in the cliff house watching the moon with anyone else.

11

Drinks at Bob-with-One-Dog's turned out to be quite revealing. Wilson took off his shirt, prompted by no one and awkward for all; Rosie revealed a little more than even she was comfortable with in an impromptu game of Twister; and Lily learned quite a lot about Alex King and Dorian Khan. She didn't tell anyone except Juliet, and even then, it was in confidence and only to get her opinion.

Juliet was in some ways the best audience, and in others, the worst. Her eyes widened and she gasped in horror at all the right places, but after Lily concluded her recount of what Alex said, Juliet refused to really believe it.

"Surely there was a misunderstanding," she pleaded on Dorian's behalf. "He's been so kind to me, I can't imagine him doing something like that."

"Can't you?" The portrait of Dorian that Alex had

painted matched perfectly with the Dorian that Lily had observed. It was not so great a step from taking Cecilia down a peg, even if she deserved it, to turning on a friend when he posed a threat to his success. Maybe that's why Dorian was friends with Casey—because he never challenged him.

"We don't really know this Alex person," Juliet argued. "I mean, he seems really nice, but we know Dorian."

"Hardly," Lily said, remembering Dorian's comment the first night she'd seen him. It didn't bother her, but it had been in bad taste and super arrogant. Her first impression of Alex had been nothing but delightful. "And why would Alex lie?"

"I'm not saying he's lying, I just—oh, I don't know." Juliet paused thoughtfully and reiterated, as if to close the case, "I just can't imagine Dorian doing something like that."

Lily didn't want to argue the point any further. She loved her cousin, but Juliet was a little too trusting and way too gullible. Dorian was a practiced actor, well experienced at manipulating people's opinions of him. What had Alex gained from revealing the truth about Dorian? Nothing. He didn't even want to tell her at first. And if she was being perfectly honest with herself, Lily recognized that she trusted Alex because she liked him.

He was witty and unselfconscious, unlike the reserved and mannered Dorian. Alex was an open book. Dorian always seemed like he had something to hide.

New Year's Eve drew closer. The Pippi Beach Progress and Advocacy Committee (known as the Pippi Committee) finalized plans for the races, talent show, and band. It was a tradition every year: races during the day for all ages (though the eight-to-ten and forty-to-fifty age brackets got the biggest turnout and were always the most competitive), and a talent show at night. The sign-up sheet was pinned up in the shed at the jetty and attracted all the usual acts, from a princess song written in little-girl-loopy script to a guitar standard scrawled by one of the Bobs or Steves. He would also take requests. Certificates for the races were printed, the plastic trophies delivered, and of course, out came the big talent show trophy that bore the names of all the winners since Lydia won in 1989 with a rather provocative song and dance that she continued to brag about. The usual buzz of excitement filled the air, only it had increased tenfold with the prospect that the French backpackers and the Hollywood movie stars would be there to see Pippi at its most quirky.

Lily didn't care whether Casey and friends came back for New Year's, except for Juliet's sake, but she did get a flutter of excitement when Alex mentioned he'd be there. Wilson, on the other hand, when Lily asked hopefully if he'd be going back to his father's place in Sydney to watch the fireworks, replied that he couldn't possibly abandon her on the most festive night of the year. Win some, lose some, she thought. And she definitely intended to lose Wilson before the countdown to midnight.

On December 31, as Casey had promised, the cliff house yacht motored back into Lydia's telescope sights. Immediately after anchoring, Casey ran down to the beachfront house to find Juliet and found himself swamped by the younger teens. Kat and Rosie, already excited about the festivities, bubbled at great length about the community games on the green. Casey was absolutely entranced and determined not to miss a single thing.

"I'll meet you there!" he promised, and gave Juliet a quick, apparently spontaneous and unthinking kiss before tearing back up to the cliff house to alert the rest of them that the races were starting SOON.

Lily strolled down to the green with the others, happy that Juliet's faith in Casey had not been misplaced, happier still at the prospect of seeing Alex. Since their chat, they had waved and called out pleasantries to each other, but this would be their first opportunity to spend more time together and Lily had been looking forward to it. Plus, she couldn't help imagining with amusement how Dorian's face would darken when he saw her chatting so easily with this particular person from his past.

They arrived on the green to find the French backpackers already practicing for the wheelbarrow races.

"Rosee! Kat! Come, we need yooo!" they called when they spied the girls.

Lily's heart rose in anticipation, hovered, and sank again as she scanned the whole area. Alex was nowhere to be seen. Dammit. Where could he be? Surely Dorian hadn't warned him off? She didn't put it past him. This was her turf and the thought of him policing it was intolerable.

"Lily!" exclaimed Theo. "Alex asked me specially to say sorry. He wanted to text you, but no number. You want me to give?"

"Oh. Okay." Lily quickly entered her number in Theo's phone and received Alex's in return.

"He had to go back to Sydney."

"Is everything okay?"

"I don't know?" Theo shrugged and skipped away.

Frustrated, Lily took a seat on the grass next to Juliet just as the entire cliff house entourage turned up with an extravagantly soft picnic blanket and a gourmet hamper. They arranged themselves in the shade as though for a scene in a high-budget melodrama. Casey whisked Juliet away to join them and Wilson quickly slid into Juliet's place beside Lily.

"I love this! Reminds me of summer camp. Oh, I keep forgetting, you wouldn't know what that is." (Lily knew what that was.) "It's like boarding school in nature with sports. Not to brag, but I am very good at three-legged races and I'm not leaving here without a trophy. Partner. High five!"

Lily miserably clapped hands with him, very aware that Dorian was watching.

Lily and Wilson did not win the three-legged race. Nor did they win the wheelbarrow race because Lily refused to enter it with him. She had no desire to see up Wilson's shorts or for him to see up hers. Luckily, she had a valid excuse as she'd promised to enter with her mother, which was just as humiliating, really, but also quite funny as Lydia was good at sabotaging everyone else and they ended up coming in second.

Casey won every single race he entered, including the men's open, although fourteen-year-old Hanson nearly caught him at the end. Dorian refused to participate, even with Casey's and Cecilia's coaxing. Wilson rolled his ankle halfway along, possibly on purpose, but it was clear to everyone that he had no hope anyway. During the trophy presentation he became very concerned about a phone call he hadn't received yet and returned to the house. Lily stayed on, happy to applaud and cheer her friends and neighbors—and unexpectedly found Dorian at her side, applauding each announcement with a degree of generosity that went beyond politeness.

"Is it always like this?" he asked.

"Sunny, loud, and oddly competitive? Absolutely. The winners change sometimes, but only if there's been a monumental event during the year. Like puberty. Or a death."

He seemed shocked, then smiled when he saw her laugh. They sat in silence as more winners were announced, and Lily had to wonder why he bothered coming down to watch this at all. And why, particularly, with her? Did he expect her to make conversation? If she hadn't felt so completely at home, she may have found it awkward. Instead, she was just mildly curious.

"So are you entering the talent show later?" she asked.

"Me? God, no." He caught her ironic eyebrow. "I wouldn't know what to do."

"It's been a while since anyone did Shakespeare," she hinted.

"Why would I do Shakespeare?"

"Someone told me you used to do it at school."

Lily enjoyed watching the cloud cross Dorian's face. For someone so reserved, his emotions were always unequivocal.

"I see. Would that someone be Alex King?"

"Bottom was your favorite role, I believe."

"That was a very long time ago."

"I imagine so. You don't seem to be into comedy these days."

"I love comedy. What I don't like is being made a fool of."

"And who could possibly do that to you? When you're so careful of your image you won't even take a risk at a community talent show?"

"Careful of my image?" he almost spat. "You don't know what you're talking about."

"That might be true," admitted Lily. "I don't know you well. I only go by what I see."

"And what other people tell you."

In one quick movement, he got up and walked off.

12

Lily was only slightly rattled by the exchange and didn't dwell on it for long. She was glad to have given Dorian a bit of a nudge on his untouchable high horse of fame and wealth. It was only a nudge and she doubted whether it had any effect on him at all. It wasn't as if he was enjoying himself anyway. He continued to show nothing but disdain for everything and everyone around him. Lily, on the other hand, was determined to have fun and refused to let Dorian affect her enjoyment of New Year's Eve, her favorite night of the year. She was particularly looking forward to the talent show as this year she was assisting the judges. Sheila, Sue, and Birdie-Round-the-Back routinely needed lots of help with keeping track of the acts, who was who, who performed what, and even which acts they liked. It was with some dismay that Lily discovered Sue had come down with a migraine that afternoon and, as chief judge, Sheila had co-opted one of the glamorous cliff house occupants to take her place. So in the many long minutes it took for Martin to set up the sound system, Lily distributed paper and pencils to Sheila, Birdie-Round-the-Back, and Judge Cecilia.

"Oh, thank you so much," purred Cecilia. "I'd rather just make notes on my phone but"—she made a face—"I forgot it up at the house."

Lily stretched a sigh into a smile. "Would you like me to go up and get it for you?"

"That's so nice, would you? You are such a darling. While you're there, can you grab another bottle of the sparkling water and also a champagne? This one. Not the other one, this one."

"No worries," Lily said as pleasantly as she could. "Anything else?"

"Get me a cushion," put in Birdie-Round-the-Back. "I told you before, these chairs are murder."

A Frisbee whizzed past, hit the tent post, and clattered to the ground at Lily's feet. Lily laughed and waved as she flung it back to Theo.

"Watch it," she warned him.

"Sorreee!" he yodeled back.

"New friends," observed Cecilia. "Cute."

"Yeah, they're nice."

"I hear you like a certain tall blond."

"Who told you that?"

"I know things, okay," Cecilia said. "Girlfriend to girlfriend, you know what I'm saying?" She leaned forward. "Alex King is as fake as these nails"—she brandished her manicured fingers—"and just as sharp. Don't go there."

Of course she was on Dorian's side.

"Do you know him personally?"

"Honey, I don't need to."

"Then thank you, I can judge Alex King for myself," Lily said.

Cecilia gave Lily the withering look of someone who wasn't expecting a challenge and, in the face of one, had no answer.

"Just trying to do you a favor," she muttered. "You'd better go, they're about to start."

Lily marched off to the cliff house, suppressing a smile at Cecilia's audacity. Fake and sharp? As far as Lily could see, Cecilia's nails fit right in with the rest of her personality.

Having watched almost every single Pippi Beach Talent Show in her lifetime and having entered a few herself, Lily knew from experience that the acts could be entertaining and excruciating in equal measure. There was something about the abundance of wine and a captive audience that made most performers feel hugely funny and uniquely talented and therefore deserving of at least six minutes stage time. Lily's family was no exception. Martin, usually sullen and quiet, took the opportunity to perform an original rap about the environment that managed to be both dull and terrifying. Rosie and Kat did what they did every year: chose an overplayed '80s love ballad and half sang, half giggled into the microphone, backed up by the original version of the song to keep them on key. Wilson, a last-minute entry, performed his stand-up "tight five" from notes on his phone, but most of his jokes appeared to be half-written and not many people laughed, which Wilson blamed on the audience's lack of sophistication and knowledge of pop culture. After four rosés, attention-shy Aunt Jane asked for the microphone, gave a rambling speech about staying safe tonight, then asked for a silent minute of gratitude, which lasted about four seconds. All in all, the Pippi residents and regulars agreed that any lapse in quality was more than compensated by the variety, length, and sheer number of acts and the visitors ought to be pretty impressed. It was a good year.

Lily, who had loved every minute, felt less confident that the overall impression on the visitors was positive. Dorian had watched the whole thing as though it were a murder trial. Yumi and Cecilia clearly got through the experience by exchanging snide texts. And Casey didn't pay attention at all because he spent the entire time gazing at Juliet. Then when the judges conferred, Cecilia had very little to offer outside of declarations that everyone and everything was adorable.

Finally, the winners were announced. Third place to an eleven-year-old princess with a truly beautiful voice who was visiting with her family for the summer. Second place to weekend residents, a father and son, who did a magic act. And first place to local boy Hanson and his older sister, who both did gymnastics and performed a dance-acrobatic hybrid routine. And with that, the real party could begin.

Fire-Chief-Steve and Bob-with-One-Dog set up the stage (portable) and cleared the dance floor (grass); the band hooked up their sound system and punched the opening notes of a '90s crowd-pleaser pop song. Two minutes in, Nicola was already kissing a French backpacker, Lydia was flirting with Sheila's husband, and Rosie was dancing with Kat. When one of the Bobs hijacked Casey into a conversation about surfing, Lily claimed Juliet to debrief.

"Where's Alex?" Juliet asked as they hung on the edge of the throng and sipped Aunt Jane's Moët. In her bubble of happiness, Juliet had barely noticed who was there apart from Casey.

Lily shrugged. "I think this lot scared him off."

"Dorian? No."

"He has deputies."

"Casey?"

"Cecilia. She actually told me to stay away from him!"

"That's not good," said Juliet. "She must know something."

"Did you ask Casey about him?"

"He said he didn't know the whole story—that Dorian wouldn't tell him—but he trusts Dorian."

Of course he does, thought Lily.

"But who does she think she is," Lily went on. "'Warning' me about a 'bad man'? This isn't 1813, I can judge for myself."

"You didn't really say that, Lily, did you?"

"Yup."

"What if he's dangerous, though?" Juliet's face was anxious. "Maybe she was telling you because . . . I don't know, girl code?"

Lily scoffed in derision. "Cecilia wouldn't know girl code if it did the chicken dance in her face. She doesn't even know Alex. She only knows what Dorian told her."

"I'm just saying," Juliet huffed, "Casey said it was pretty serious. You should look out for yourself."

"Don't you worry about me," Lily assured her. "I'm not the one running around kissing strangers," she added as Nicola joined them with a huge grin on her face and not a trace of lipstick left.

"Rosie and Kat are furious with me," she announced. "Where have you been all night?" she asked as she fished lipstick out of her pocket and reapplied.

"Hiding from Wilson," said Lily.

"Game over," said Nicola. The three girls watched in dreaded anticipation as Wilson edged through the crowd toward them.

"I'm going to find Casey," said Juliet, and she darted away.

"Nothing can save you now," Nicola said solemnly.

"It was good while it lasted."

Lily and Nicola steeled themselves for Wilson's approach, but as he advanced, he happened to notice Dorian nearby, possibly attempting to escape. Wilson stopped him in his tracks.

"Dorian!" he exclaimed.

Dorian turned on him with a stony expression that Wilson either didn't see or proceeded to ignore.

"It's me! Wilson Collins! From Stacy Black's LA office?"
Dorian was clearly unmoved.

"I've been trying to catch you since I got here!"
Wilson continued. "I've heard so much about you from
Stacy. How've you been, man? What are the chances
we're both here? Of all places!"

"This is a train wreck," Lily muttered.

"I can't look away," Nicola agreed.

"Thank you so much for coming up to say hello,"
Dorian said with the air of one who had no interest in
saying anything at all. "But I really must be going."

"Oh, okay," Wilson replied, slapping Dorian on the
back. "I'll tell Stacy you said hi."

"You do that."

Nicola choked on her drink and Lily suppressed her
laughter as Dorian disappeared into a clique with Cecilia
and Yumi. Wilson approached with a huge smile.

"Dorian Khan," he declared, "is such a nice guy. Do
you want to dance?"

And as it was going to be easier to avoid conversation
that way, Lily said yes.

The night was still young and there were more social
blunders to be made. Rosie flashed Theo (and everyone
else on the dance floor). Lydia twerked on both of the
Bobs (at the same time) and took every opportunity to

loudly point out Casey and Dorian, even once yelling, "Oh, yes, the good-looking one's seeing my niece Juliet. They haven't kissed yet." None of this was out of the ordinary—in fact, this New Year's was quite tame considering that last year Nicola rode her bike off the end of the jetty. It was just the right amount of crazy, barefoot fun.

But for some reason, Lily felt a little differently this year. There was something about seeing everything through strangers' eyes that made her self-conscious. New Year's Eve always got a bit loose, but it was still her favorite night of the year. Drunk dads saying "Hold my beer and watch this" while Lydia flirted outrageously with anyone who stood still long enough was all part of it. It was loud and messy, but these people were her family and friends. With Dorian's watchful eyes, Lily felt him judging the chaos. His strong glare made her feel like everything about this night and everything about Pippi wasn't good enough to be loved or enjoyed as wholeheartedly as she loved and enjoyed it, and she resented him for it.

The worst thing was that, at least in part, his judgment was justified. In every conversation, she overheard little hints and exclamations and reminders that Pippi felt itself touched with stardust tonight. Lily knew that

Dorian saw it too. The entire Pippi community, so proud of being so far removed from the world of Hollywood, was playing to the audience of real movie stars, relishing in its newfound status and hungry for more.

"Bet you've never been to a New Year's party like this!" declared Birdie-Round-the-Back.

Everywhere there was a lust for recognition. Nowhere more obvious than when Lydia squealed into the microphone after the midnight countdown: "Today Pippi, tomorrow Hollywood! We love you, Casey Brandon! They should have given you the Oscar!"— forgetting that he had never been nominated.

But despite all this, Lily was able to find a few hours of magic and commune with the real Pippi. She wandered along the sand in the dark, climbed the bush path to the headland lookout to watch distant fireworks, and danced into the New Year with a heart full of happiness. She unselfconsciously cheered Juliet and Casey as they kissed at midnight, and even managed to give Wilson a cheerful one-armed hug. She and Rosie did a crazy rendition of a dance they had choreographed when they were eleven and fourteen to a synth-pop, slightly creepy love song by a teen-boy heartthrob. Nicola held Bob-with-Two-Dogs' beer as he stripped down to his boxers and backflipped off the jetty and then Lily held the beer as Nicola jumped in after him.

At three thirty, Lily, Juliet, Casey, Rosie, Kat, and Lydia stumbled home. As Casey hugged Juliet and gave her a sloppy but sweet kiss on the cheek, Lydia insisted he join the family on their traditional hangover-curing New Year's Day kayak. He smiled, joked that he hadn't been kayaking since last year, and said he'd love to come. And with that, they tumbled into bed, just like the rest of Pippi, except for talent-show-winner Hanson and his mate, who danced wildly on the jetty until sunrise.

13

Lily woke to the movement of someone sitting on her bed. "Morning," she murmured, expecting to see Juliet.

"Morning, babe," trumpeted Wilson, right in her ear. Lily gasped in horror, suddenly wide awake. There he was, in an unbuttoned shirt, smiling in a very self-satisfied way, close enough for her to smell green juice on his breath. She recoiled, gathered the sheets to her chest, and sat up in a rush.

"You look so cute when you're asleep. Here. This is for you." He held up a cup of coffee.

"Wilson!" she protested, but he hardly heard her.

"I know how you like it. So."

He thrust the coffee at her and she took it reluctantly, automatically mumbling her thanks.

"But I'll have it on the deck. With everyone else."

Wilson smiled. "Your mom thought it would be nice, just the two of us."

"No," said Lily. "I'll meet you out there. After I'm dressed."

"I can wait."

"Get out, Wilson."

Wilson tilted his head and smiled as he stood up and headed for the door.

"Okay. I'll wait out there. But a guy can't wait forever. If you know what I mean."

"What?"

"You heard."

He saluted (what does that even mean? Lily wondered) and was gone.

Ew. That was gross. Worst of all, it didn't seem like just an ordinary case of an inflated ego operating in a culture of general male entitlement. Wilson had approached Lily many times before, but this time he'd had prior help. Lily flung on an outfit and took the offending coffee down to the kitchen, where she found her mother.

"Did you send Wilson to my room with this?" she demanded.

"You're welcome."

"No, I'm not welcome and he's not welcome."

"That's no way to talk about someone who's offering you free accommodation in America."

"He's not. His mother is."

"You should be nice to him."

"I am nice!" Lily barked.

Lydia sighed and looked at her daughter with nostalgic pity. It was a sore spot for her that Lily had never so much as been on a date, let alone had a boyfriend. She was eighteen. By that age, Lydia had engaged in all sorts of sexual activity and relationship dramas, most of which had caused nothing but grief, but she bore the scars with a sense of pride and felt that Lily was missing out.

"Honey, I'm just trying to help."

"I don't need that kind of help."

"The guy likes you! Now, I appreciate this hard-to-get thing you've got going on, but you're overdoing it, and then you rub his nose in it by flirting with Mr. Handsome British Backpacker."

"What?"

"That Alex boy is way out of your league, sweetie. And I mean that in the nicest possible way."

"I can't talk to you right now."

Lily stalked off, fuming. Her mother's insistence on seeing every interaction as some sort of hierarchical sexual energy exchange was nothing short of infuriating. Lily wasn't even thinking about Alex in that way! And even if she were, why should she pay any attention at all to Lydia's ancient codes of romance? Out of her league? This is not sports! And Alex hadn't come to New Year's Eve anyway.

"See, this is your trouble!" Lydia shouted after her. "Now you're being rude. You're not the only girl here, you know."

Lily stalked out onto the deck intending to let Wilson know nicely and clearly and firmly that they were just friends (not even that, if she was being honest), and furthermore, friends didn't go into other friends' bedrooms while they were sleeping. But the tide was up and he was already out on the jetty with the others. The deck was deserted apart from Aunt Jane and Uncle Charles, who were drowsing in deck chairs with hats over their faces, holding hands.

"What's up, love?" Jane asked.

"Oh. Nothing. Just Mum's being—"

"Mum's being helpful," Lydia shouted as she plonked herself in a deck chair. "You'll end up by yourself if you're not careful."

Lily appealed to Jane with a sigh.

"Mum is trying to get me together with Wilson."

"Oh. Don't do that, Lyddie," murmured Jane.

"I gave the guy a bit of encouragement," Lydia said defensively.

"And I was just on my way to tell him NO."

"Why, did he come on to you?" asked Jane.

"Kind of," said Lily.

"Not even," said Lydia.

"Well, you're both very naughty," Jane decided with a sigh. "You should leave the poor boy alone."

Lily harrumphed off toward the jetty, determined to put Wilson in his place, but her resolve waned the closer she got. Aunt Jane was right. Wilson annoyed everyone, not just her, and maybe she was reading too much into it. He would be gone in a few days anyway, and making a big deal out of a harmless coffee delivery could just make things worse. Best to let it slide and ignore him.

Lily refreshed her mind and body with a quick leap into the water with the others. If Wilson was at all disturbed by the whole coffee incident, he certainly didn't show it. Lily found it quite easy to brush it all off and see the humor in the entire episode, as long as she didn't have to talk to him or look at him at all. Wilson conveniently disappeared up the north end of the beach with Nicola and the younger ones and left Lily to talk it all over with Juliet in the kitchen as they prepared for the traditional New Year's Day kayak and picnic.

" 'Babe,' " she laughed. "He actually called me 'babe.' "

"Maybe that's normal in America."

"Ha! Bet he doesn't say it to his boss."

Juliet offered to keep him away from her for the rest of the day by taking him as her kayak partner. Lily laughed off the kind gesture.

"I'm pretty sure you're spoken for already. I'm not going to let Wilson come between you and Casey."

Lily was genuinely, unreservedly happy that Juliet had found someone, whatever that might mean and however it might play out. The distance between Juliet and Casey was vast—they truly were from different worlds— but Lily believed they could overcome it. They were both so nice and generous, and they had the money to turn their impulses into reality. If any couple could manage a long-distance relationship, it was them. And it was hardly an unusual thing. Every couple had to deal with some kind of separation these days. That's what the internet was for.

When the sandwiches were made, Lily wandered out onto the deck with her phone. She still hadn't heard anything from Alex. Her happiness for Juliet, the whole Wilson debacle, and her mother's insensitive reference somehow made it impossible to stop her thoughts from circling back to him. She was sure she didn't like him.

But she was interested in him. Her thumb hovered over the screen, hesitated, then quickly typed Happy New Year 🎉. That was genuine and not at all reproachful. She was surprised to receive a swift reply.

HNY to you too! Sorry missed the fun last night—would have loved to see the NY in with you but thought I should keep my distance—didn't want to ruin the atmos :). Still at the Point—back in a few days—we'll hang out then?

Clever boy. Such a perfect tone of unaffected charm—she could read into it just the right amount of frisson. She was in the middle of composing the exactly right reply (friendly without tipping over into creepiness or expectation) when Rosie interrupted her with an outraged shriek.

"O-M-freaking-G! They're leaving!" She was on the edge of the deck with the telescope trained on the cliff house.

"Who? What? Not Casey!" shouted Lydia from inside. She stormed out and grabbed the telescope. "He's coming kayaking. I didn't give up on my hangover to go on a picnic with just you lot!"

Juliet, following right behind, was certain that there must be some mistake.

But Lydia zoomed in on the activity at the south

end, and there was no doubt. Those were suitcases, the big suitcases, and the guy from the yacht hire place was back, helping them move luggage from the house to the boat. Cecilia and Yumi had switched bikinis and braids for full-flowing maxi dresses and carefully blown-out waves. Casey was hauling freight, head down, and Dorian, infuriatingly, was on his phone.

"Right. I'm going down there," announced Lydia.

Jane and a distressed Juliet tried to talk her out of it. In the end, it was only the sight of Casey tearing up the beach toward them that stopped Lydia from storming the house and/or the boat with a cricket bat. Luckily, at the same moment, there happened to be a kitchen emergency (Martin broke the toaster and set off the fire alarm again), so Lydia and Jane missed Casey's appearance on the deck completely. It was brief.

"I'm so sorry," he panted at Juliet, Lily, and a pouting Rosie. "We got a call—got to go now—so boring, just stuff. But Dorian says we have to, so . . ." He shot an almost furtive look over his shoulder at the yacht, as if he was worried he'd be in trouble if he were caught.

"Is everything okay?" asked Juliet.

"Yeah, it's just work. You know. God." He hugged Juliet close. "It's been awesome. Just . . . awesome," he said into her hair, with such intensity that everyone felt close to tears. And as speedily as he'd arrived, he was back on the path, running backward, making promises.

"I'll call you!"

"Wait! You don't have my number!"

"Soon!"

"My number, though!"

"I'll get it from Cece!" he yelled. "Love you guys!"

And then he was gone.

All Juliet and Lily could do was exchange a look of disbelief. The drama in the kitchen was over and the whole family gathered to watch the yacht reverse from the dock, turn, and glide away as though it were carrying strangers, all to a running commentary of Lydia's swear words. No one could quite believe it. What could possibly be so important that they should have to leave so quickly? On New Year's Day? When they had already made sandwiches? And Casey and Juliet had quite literally only just gotten together?

Nobody was in the mood for kayaking or picnicking anymore, except Wilson and Nicola, who went off together in a double kayak, found a deserted beach, hiked through pristine bushland, frolicked in a hidden waterfall, and later declared it was the best day of the whole summer. Wilson couldn't stop raving about it and said it was almost as good as a certain megastar's private beach hideaway in Malibu that he went to once with Stacy Black and, honestly, nobody should be at all surprised that the movie people left so suddenly, this is what the business is like. Unpredictable.

Juliet texted Cecilia but got no answer until late that night. "So sorry, we had so much fun hanging out."

And that was it.

14

The entire clan gathered on the end of the jetty to bid farewell to Wilson with promises that they would see one another again soon. Lily and Nicola would be in LA in just six months, and six months would fly by. At the first glimpse of the ferry chugging around the headland, Wilson began a solemn round of hugging each and every family member a little too warmly and too long, so that he hadn't even finished by the time the ferry was banging up against the steps. Lily, who just happened to be hauling luggage when it was her turn for a hug, fended him off with one of his own suitcases.

"I'll just take this down for you!" she chirped as she pushed past him. But he followed her, and as soon as she dropped the suitcase on the ferry deck, he clasped one of her hands in both of his and pulled her close with a meaningful stare.

"Bye!" she squeaked and kissed the air beside him.

He was so surprised that she was able to slip away and make good her escape.

"Bye, family!" he shouted from the open doorway as the ferry lurched off. "See you soon!" And he winked and pointed and touched a fist to his heart in a horrifying display that was very clearly aimed at Lily.

"Un-be-freaking-lievable," muttered Lydia. "You totally could have had that," she accused Lily. "Now what have you got? Nothing."

Lily and Juliet did their best not to laugh.

"Look at the two of you. Couldn't catch a guy in a brothel."

"Mum!"

"You're gorgeous, you're young, the pair of you should be getting it on every night of the week, but no. You had to scare them off, didn't you, with your stupid friend-zone attitude. And you"—she turned on Juliet—"there is such a thing as too nice."

"She didn't scare him off, Mum."

"And now you're miserable and alone, with nothing to look forward to but a bleak year of work and getting older."

The girls looked at each other and repressed bubbling laughter.

"Oh, Aunty Lydia," said Juliet. "We've only just finished school!"

"We're young, we're still excited by life's rich tapestry!" laughed Lily.

"She's not." Lydia tilted her head at Juliet.

"Of course I am!" Juliet protested smilingly. "I'm here at Pippi—my favorite place in the world!"

Lydia just grunted gloomily and stomped back to the house. She always had an attack of grumpiness after New Year's, but the stars' abrupt departure had hit her particularly hard.

For all Juliet's protestations, Lily could see that her mother was right. Juliet was really down about Casey. Her gap year, which she had been happy to keep flexible and free, now seemed empty and long. Juliet texted Cecilia several times, but the replies were vague and late. She was too polite to ask for Casey's number directly and Cecilia hadn't offered it. She followed him on social media but so did twenty-three million others and she doubted he even looked at it.

"Cecilia's in charge of it, remember," said Lily as she tried to comfort Juliet. "And I bet it's Dorian who tells her what to do. They're probably freezing you out deliberately and Casey has no idea."

"They wouldn't do that," protested Juliet. "He's

just busy, that's all. And you know what he's like—so spontaneous and haphazard—he'll call when he can."

Casey was easily distractible, it was true—and just as easily influenced, Lily thought.

"He would have called you already if Dorian and Cecilia weren't in the way."

"You are so funny. Like it's a fiendish plot."

"Nothing short of a fiendish plot could possibly keep you apart!"

Juliet laughed, but it was a small laugh that quickly subsided. "I don't like to think they could be that mean," she said.

But Lily had no doubts about how mean people could be or how easily they could walk over other people for their own advancement. She was sure that Cecilia and Dorian were behind Casey's silence. Juliet and the whole Pippi community were nothing to them. She trawled through their social media—always the brand names, the curated beauty, the calculated appearance of spontaneity. Of course, Dorian didn't post that much. He didn't have to; he was already at the peak of popularity. But it was clear that Cecilia was striving for more and more followers and attention. With Casey's best friend leading from above and his sister pushing from below, it was impossible for him to escape the constant pursuit of fame, money, and status. Because, Lily thought grimly, if you're not climbing, you're on your way down. Pippi was a diversion and a good photo op. Not much more.

Despite the shadow cast by Casey's departure, the summer was still summering on. And when Wilson departed and the French backpackers returned to work, there was plenty of fun to be had with lunchtime swimming off the jetty and knock-off drinks on the green or the deck.

Alex, Theo, and friends were now regular guests at the beachfront house and Lily was more than happy to join them, especially when Alex was around. Clever, fun, easy on the eye, he never failed to make her laugh. They became such particular friends that everyone assumed they would get together. But he didn't make any moves, and Lily, for her part, was grateful for it. She probably wouldn't have said no, but she didn't feel strongly enough about him to start anything herself. She was happy to enjoy his company with no expectation or pressure for more.

With Wilson and the cliff house people gone, they saw each other practically every day, and Alex was now free to let the gossip fly. He confirmed what everyone was already thinking about the movie business: Wilson was insignificant, his big movie-producer boss Stacy Black was an absolute nightmare, and Dorian Khan was a prime, stuck-up roast-on-a-spit. Alex told stories about Stacy's demands and Dorian's ego that had them all roaring with laughter. The stories even made Lily feel better by proving to her that she'd been right about Dorian Khan all along and people with money were, when it came down to it, more likely to be terrible than anyone else.

15

Lily loved all four of her aunts. Aunt Jane was like a second mother to her: always there, always ready to listen. Aunt Lizzie was a whirl of vibrant energy who inspired anyone who came into her orbit. Aunt Mary had only visited from India a handful of times, but she created a strong impression on Lily as a child with her scent of essential oil, her commitment to veganism, and her refusal to have anything to do with single-use plastics. But it was Aunt Kitty whom Lily had always thought was the coolest. She lived in Melbourne, where she had worked in theater (the experimental, fringe kind) for years before she became a teacher. After so many comings and goings of exhausting characters, Lily was glad to share what was left of the summer at Pippi with her favorite, least dramatic, and most reliable relation.

When they arrived on the three o'clock ferry, Aunt Kitty and her partner, Hanna, could not have looked more out of place: all pale skin and dressed in Melbourne-black from head to toe.

"It's like they're going to a funeral," muttered Lydia as they rushed down the jetty to meet them.

"Lyddie! Jane!" exclaimed Kitty as she buried herself in a hug with her sisters.

"You look like a vampire," said Lydia into her sister's hair.

"And you look like a cheap tropical cocktail."

The sisters reunited over gossip and early gin and tonics. Kitty and Hanna were most interested to hear about the famous cliff house visitors.

"Casey and Juliet are practically boyfriend-girlfriend!" spouted Kat.

Juliet's cheeks colored. "No we're not!"

"They kissed," insisted Rosie. "A lot."

"Shhh!" said Lily to her sister.

"You shhh!"

"When are you two coming down to visit?" Kitty asked Juliet and Lily, sensing their desire to change the subject. "Now that school's over you can come anytime. We can show you around—check out a museum or two, see some theater."

"Ugh," grunted Lydia.

Kat frowned. "Why would Juliet go to Melbourne when Casey's going to the Gold Coast?"

"All the more reason," declared Hanna.

Lily was committed to working and saving up for her trip to the US and couldn't visit until later in the year, but Juliet was easily convinced to go sooner. Lily was glad to see her cousin actually make a plan and smile. She had done neither since Casey's sudden departure.

Aunt Kitty and Hanna fit easily into the Pippi Beach lifestyle, despite their very Melbourne way of dressing. They jumped off the jetty with the young folks, shared gossip and jokes, and joined in socializing with the whole community, including the French backpackers—and Alex. Lily was quietly delighted to introduce him to Kitty and Hanna. He was as charming and smiling as ever, remembered their names after hearing them only once, and complimented Hanna on her vegan leather beach bag. Aunt Kitty's opinion of anyone and anything carried a lot of weight with Lily; Lydia's approval was too easily lost and Aunt Jane's was too easily won.

"He's very charming," Kitty said.

Lily waited, but she said no more.

"You don't like him?" Lily asked.

"I didn't say that. And my liking him shouldn't influence how you feel."

"But?"

"I've been around a while, Lily, and I've been stung by charming pretty boys and girls just like Alex."

Kitty paused, but Lily didn't say anything.

"You're a smart kid, Lily. I don't need to warn you or tell you what to do. I just know from experience—and your mum's—that a relationship takes more than a nice smile and sweet words."

"Nice line," said Lily. "Do you work in theater?"

"I don't want to see you get hurt."

"I know."

Lily thought of Cecilia's brief warning and what Juliet had relayed from her chat with Casey.

"You're not the only one who's wary of him," said Lily.

"He's got a reputation, then?"

"It appears so."

She turned her gaze back to the water to see Alex grab Rosie around the middle and tumble into the shallows with a splash and a squeal.

"I trust you to make good judgments, Lily."

"I will. I do. I have." Lily smiled back and wondered at herself for not feeling any sense of regret over Alex

King. In the end, she had been right to hold off, and she was glad she did.

The last weeks of January slid by in a wash of sparkle, swimming, kayaking, and jumping off the jetty. It was the perfect glorious summer of lazy hours with salt in your hair and nothing to do but enjoy yourself. Even Lydia relaxed for the last week. While she loudly lamented the end of the holidays, the start of work, and her sisters' departure, part of her looked forward to a return to life in which she was pretty much in charge.

On the last Sunday of the last weekend of the summer holidays, the locals gathered to say farewell to the last ferry of the day. Lydia had already shut up the back pavilion; Jane had taken Martin and Kat back to Sydney to prepare for the school year and go back to work. Juliet had gone straight to Melbourne with Kitty and Hanna.

Pippi returned to its natural state, where wildlife, locals, their boats, and their dogs dominated the social landscape. Even the building site slowed down. Half the backpackers split their time with another site over at the Point. The tents were taken down and the steady stream of passing backpackers and workers reduced to a trickle. Alex drifted out of Lily's life as easily as he had drifted in, and neither was more than superficially disappointed that the summer flirtation-that-never-really-was had come to its natural end.

"I think I did really like him," Lily explained to Juliet on the phone. "But only as long as he liked me more," she added with a laugh.

With Kat gone, Rosie started spending more time over on the other side of the bay at the backpackers' hostel, where she took up with a twenty-year-old surfer girl called Florence who wore a straw hat and sarongs. By the end of the first week of school, Rosie was in a straw hat and a sarong too, asking to be allowed to go and work on a farm picking fruit with all her new overseas traveler friends so she could save money to snorkel the Great Barrier Reef.

Lily felt the world shift beneath her feet. For the first time, the first school-run ferry of the year left the jetty without her. Nicola was on it, off to her new job at a shopping mall bakery. Both she and Lily had to save up for their trip to America, which was exciting, but it seemed a long way off and Lily felt the emptiness of the months ahead and beyond. She still hadn't made a decision about what to study or, in fact, what to do with her entire life. Over the holidays, she hadn't been so aware of the void in her future. Now it loomed large. While there was no immediate pressure to make a decision, she couldn't help feeling a little lost. She didn't want to repeat the mistakes her mother had made and drift along, letting accidental fortune or other people determine her life's shape. But she didn't know exactly how to take charge.

Lily watched the ferry chug across the bay just as she started her first big cleaning job of the year: the cliff house. The irony. She scrubbed out the tub that Cecilia had frolicked in, swept under the bed Dorian had slept in, removed cobwebs none of them had even seen, all the while listening to her mother's running commentary of judgments on rich people, architecture, cleaning methods and products, and how most people have more dollars than sense and if she, Lydia, had the chance, she'd show them all. At the end of the day, exhausted and grumpy, the family of three shared a plain little meal in the kitchen. Rosie complained about school the whole time.

"I guess this is adulthood," Lily laughed to Juliet on the phone later that night.

"It's not fair," cried Juliet. "Why don't you get a job in the city? You could stay with my mum. Or Aunt Jane."

"No, no, no," insisted Lily. "They've done more than enough for me already and they're paying for my flight to the US—the least I can do is earn my own spending money."

"I just don't think—"

"It's good work. It's just funny, that's all."

"As long as you're okay."

"I'm fine! It's mindless enough. While I clean I think about all my travel plans, where we'll go, what we'll do. Are you sure you don't want to come too?"

"To America? I don't think so. Melbourne suits me. It's pale and kind of thoughtful."

"You're not thinking too much about a certain someone?"

"Who? Oh no. I've practically forgotten about him. I know now it was just a summer fling."

She brushed away Lily's concern, but Lily could tell she was far from over Casey Brandon.

Lily stalked him on social media—and couldn't be angry with him. His open smile was just too guileless. It was Cecilia whom she blamed and, most of all, Dorian Khan, who glowered out from under his moody fringe on his social media, magazine ads, and billboards everywhere she went. How dare he be so good-looking— and so incredibly hurtful?

16

As the months passed by, Pippi got colder and wetter and quieter. Lily and Nicola worked hard all autumn. By the time June had settled in and the sky was permanently clouded, the daytrippers, weekenders, and holidaymakers who loved Pippi in all its summertime glory promptly forgot about it. The beach was deserted except for Lily and her family and a few other locals. It felt like a completely different place.

With the cleaning jobs drying up over the winter, Lily took a casual job tutoring history for a few kids at her old high school. Throwing herself back into the books was a comfort but also a reminder that her life was now untethered from school. Would it be like this forever now? Filling in time with unsatisfying work and a vague feeling that she should be doing something else? Nicola shared her frustration as she took double shifts at the bakery and came home with stories about her bitchy coworkers—and occasionally a few leftover iced buns, only slightly stale. As their travel departure date drew nearer, Lily grew all the more excited to leave behind the miserable mood at Pippi for sunny, shiny LA. Perhaps there she would find a key to her future, or at the very least be distracted from worrying about looking for it. Preparing for the trip soon consumed her life. Packing began and she and Nicola wrote lists of places to go and people to see.

"Theme parks, Hollywood tour buses, wax museums, give me it *all*, darling," said Nicola.

"And matching 'I Heart LA' T-shirts?"

"Worn totally unironically."

Lily was intent on seeing all of LA—not just hitting the famous hot spots—and she was glad she was going with someone like Nicola who could also enjoy LA's superficial side.

Lydia, Rosie, and Nicola's mum saw them off at the airport, and Lydia made a big show about her "baby" leaving her for a month.

"I'll be fine, Mum, you know I will."

"I know you'll be fine, but what about me? I'm going to be childless!"

"What am I, a potted plant?" said Rosie indignantly.

"You might as well be, you're never here," said Lydia, not paying much attention.

"Potted plants are literally always there," protested Rosie as Lydia talked over her.

"The most important thing, Lily," Lydia went on, looking quite serious, "is to HAVE FUN. Without getting arrested."

"And make sure you bring me back that eye shadow palette I asked you for," added Rosie. "And a key chain from every single theme park you go to. And a bikini from Venice Beach."

"Of course," assured Lily from deep within a very tight hug.

Fourteen and a half hours in economy later—not helped at all by the leopard-print neck pillows Lydia made them buy at the airport—Lily and Nicola stepped out of Tom Bradley International Terminal with big smiles on their faces and even bigger cricks in their necks. They jumped in a taxi and chatted excitedly about all that was ahead of them, jet lag completely forgotten.

"Omigosh, everything looks like a movie!" Nicola gushed as they exclaimed over everything from fast-food joints to street signs to enormous shiny black vehicles with tinted windows.

"We are totally in a reality TV show right now,"

agreed Lily. "About to meet the only-slightly-famous host!"

"Who is just a bit creepy."

"And way too effusive."

"Wilson," they said simultaneously and laughed.

"Do you think he'll take us to meet Stacy Black?" asked Nicola. "Or to hang out in a gorgeous mansion filled with movie stars?"

Lily laughed. "I kind of feel like I already did that. It wasn't that great."

"Well, maybe the problem was you," snorted Nicola.

"Probably. I'd better stay away from Stacy Black and her business."

"See, that is a definite problem. Stacy Black is Hollywood, Hollywood is money, money is life. I'm going to sip champagne at a gorgeous mansion with movie stars and dazzle them all."

"Good to set concrete goals."

"And I'm not leaving this town until someone declares their love for me at sunset."

The taxi pulled up in front of Wilson's mother's house in Beverly Hills.

"Oh. My. God," said Nicola. "Forget everything I've ever said about Wilson—he's my favorite person in the whole world."

The house was beyond the scale of anything Nicola had ever seen. Even Lily, whose aunts Jane and Elizabeth had comfortable homes in exclusive Sydney suburbs, was a little awestruck by the building's vastness. Everything was supersized, from the big trees to the big gate to the big front door, the portico, the terra-cotta roof, and the chimney three stories high and as wide as a car. Lily and Nicola piled their luggage out onto the curb and took a moment to take it all in.

"Show's starting," Lily whispered to Nicola as Wilson rushed out of the gate to greet them, followed by a middle-aged woman with sensible hair, and no makeup and wearing a bathrobe: Wilson's mother, Charlotte. From her social media photos, Lily had imagined Charlotte only ever existed in a neutral-toned linen tunic and draped scarf, leaning on or near expensive-looking furniture.

"Oh my, look at you two! You poor things! We would have met you at the airport! Grab their bags, Wilson, honey," she said as she enveloped Lily in a hug.

"Pilar!" Wilson bellowed back toward the house. "Can you get these bags?"

"You must be Lily," Charlotte said, smiling. "You look just like your mum. And you must be Nicola!" She hugged her too. "Aren't these neck pillows a scream? So comfy. I'd wear one everywhere if I could. Come on in. Don't worry, Pilar, Wilson's got them."

"I can carry this," asserted Lily to the obliging Pilar, who had materialized from a side door and looked somewhat confused about whose orders she should follow.

"Take the girls straight to the guesthouse, honey, I look a fright," said Charlotte. She disappeared back into the house, whereupon Wilson handed the biggest two bags back to Pilar, led the way up the driveway, and launched into a monologue.

"Right this way, mind your feet, Pablo's late with the leaf blower. How was your flight? Long way in coach. I just can't do it, I mean at my height, six foot one—" (Lily and Nicola exchanged a glance: five ten at the most.) "You're lucky you're both so small. There's the pool, no one uses it, we're all so busy, consider it yours. There's the hot tub, Pilar will show you how to turn it on, it's a little tricky, it's imported. And here's where you'll be staying . . ."

Wilson turned the lock on the door to the Spanish-style guesthouse. It was two stories, with an open-plan kitchen, living, and dining downstairs, and two bedrooms and a bathroom upstairs. The front windows in the living room faced the sparkling turquoise pool, which separated the guesthouse from the main house. The furnishings were simple yet elegant and, as Wilson constantly pointed out, expensive. He gave them a bragging tour of the whole place that would have been dull if it weren't so funny. And Nicola, who had never in her life considered the thread count of sheets or the provenance of floor tiles, made a good show of being both knowledgeable and impressed. At the end of the tour, with perfect timing, Wilson received a text and quickly ushered them all back to the driveway as a sleek black SUV stopped outside the gate.

"Cannot do without me for two seconds!" Wilson complained proudly. "I'm so sorry, you'll just have to get used to that."

"Is that her? Stacy Black?" asked Nicola.

"It's her driver. Come look at her car, it's amazing."

Lily assured him she'd make a much better impression on the car and whoever was in it after she'd showered. Nicola had no such reservation and with wide eyes scampered off down the drive after Wilson.

Lily laughed somewhat ruefully. Wilson's performance of superiority was so annoying and now Nicola was lapping it up. Lily had high hopes for her American holiday; the last thing she needed was for it to be tarnished by the hierarchical nonsense that had almost spoiled her summer. The very name Stacy Black reminded her of Dorian Khan, and he was the last person she wanted to be thinking about.

Before Lily had time to even unpack anything, Nicola came charging back into the guesthouse at a run.

"How amazing was the car?" Lily asked in an exaggerated American accent.

"So amazing!" said Nicola.

"Really?"

"What? Yes. It's electric. BUT. That's not it: Stacy Black has invited us to dinner at the Sunset Room!" Nicola squealed.

"Sunset Room?"

"Oh my God, Lily, this is why you need me here. It's a super fancy restaurant."

"And you're going?"

"Yes and so are you."

"What if I said no?"

"Wilson already said yes, so you'd better just change your mind."

"I hate doing that."

"Oh, come on," wheedled Nicola. "You didn't come halfway around the world to say no to things!"

"I didn't come here to be pushed around! By Wilson!"

"Yes you did!" Nicola gave her a friendly shove. "We're his guests!"

Lily shoved her right back and laughed.

Nicola was right after all. Lily was here to experience something new—and she would take every opportunity that came her way, however strange or uncomfortable, and at the very least, she would always find something to laugh about.

Wilson disappeared back to work in the amazing car, leaving Charlotte, now showered and dressed in immaculate athleisure, to look after the guests. Charlotte turned out to be the best kind of hostess. Practical, friendly, generous, and the kind of person who would happily invite you in to sit and chat if you encountered her in the kitchen but sensitive enough to know that you might not want to.

"You just treat our place as you would your own," she assured Lily and Nicola in her strange hybrid American-Australian accent. "And let me know if you need anything; I'll be around." As she rambled with them through a tour of the three living areas and the cavernous kitchen and the den and the vast array of bedrooms upstairs, Lily felt that it would be entirely possible to stow away somewhere in this house and never encounter another living soul.

"Wilson's so excited about your visit, bless his heart, and he will do anything for you. Anything," she emphasized with a significant look. "But he works so hard, he's hardly ever home. Have you got his cell? You just text him any little thing and he'll make it happen for you. That's my husband, Javier." She indicated a framed wedding photograph that was mostly of sand and ocean. "You probably won't see him. I never do."

Lily and Nicola recovered from the flight by the pool.

"Sun is the best thing for jet lag," Nicola, sprawled on a deck chair, murmured from beneath her hat while Lily frolicked in the water and enjoyed the clear Californian light.

"Nicola, look! Squirrels!" she chirped.

"Where?" Nicola angled her hat to peek at the lawn without actually sitting up. "Oh, cute."

And they had to agree that although the squirrels were physically less impressive than the wallabies that roamed around Pippi, they were much more romantic.

Just at the point when they were wondering if they were hungry or not, Charlotte called out that she had "thrown a platter together" and they were free to eat whenever they liked as she was headed out and Wilson should be home any minute. Lily and Nicola showered and changed and ventured into the main house, where they found the biggest grazing plate ever seen in the history of the world, which they devoured despite their weird light-headedness. They became rather giggly and silly, to the point that when Wilson finally appeared, they found him delightfully funny and took note of every suggestion he made for the following day. He expanded under the light of their attention, like a flower unfurling in the sun, and Lily wondered if he was close to six feet after all. Perhaps he was only so unpleasantly intense all the time because he was afraid of being minimized. But she was too tired for serious reflection. The thrilling rush of having arrived on the other side of the world caught up with the travelers and hit them in the face before it was dark outside, and that night they slept the deepest, heaviest, most dreamless sleep they had ever thought possible.

17

Lily woke up to a surge of excitement about finally being overseas and a text from Wilson reminding them about their date at the Sunset Room that evening with Stacy Black. Nicola was already up and surveying the exploded contents of her suitcase.

"This?" Nicola asked as she held up an item of clothing that was mostly sequins. "With these?" She held up a platform heel.

"Maybe not to breakfast."

"Breakfast? I've sorted breakfast," said Nicola scornfully, indicating an ensemble arranged on the floor, complete with bag and hat. "I'm talking about dinner."

"You know it's twelve hours away, right?"

"You don't seem to appreciate the gravity of the situation, Lily. Even I was too stupid to fully grasp it yesterday but I've done my research and now I know.

The Sunset Room is THE restaurant. Nobody gets in there without celebrity status or booking a year ahead."

"So turning up with clothes on should be the easy part."

"It's a big deal!"

"It's dinner."

"I might see a superhero."

"Well, if you do, and they happen to notice you, I'm sure they'll appreciate you wearing something tight. With a cape. Now come on, let's get out there and see some sights!"

They spent the day exploring as much of Beverly Hills as they could comfortably reach on foot. They wandered up and down beautiful curved suburban streets, took photos of themselves on impossibly green lawns in parks, and exclaimed over every little thing. Look! A convertible! A silver fire hydrant! A dog in a bag wearing a collar of diamonds! They giggled their way through boutiques selling clothes and accessories and jewelry that they couldn't possibly afford. "They don't know that," Nicola pointed out, and Lily quite agreed that they were as entitled to look at expensive things as anyone else. They made it back home with an hour to get themselves ready for dinner, only to find Wilson already home from work, dressed, and in a bit of a state.

"Where have you been? Quick, you'll never be ready!"

"Has the time changed?" wondered Lily.

"One of you will have to use a different bathroom, oh my God. Mom?"

Charlotte materialized out of nowhere and made soothing noises while Nicola berated Lily for not listening to her.

"Honestly, I told her we had to come home," she insisted. "But we'll be fast, promise!" She scooted off to the guesthouse.

"Don't worry, I can shower after her, we'll be fine," assured Lily as Wilson demanded to know which bathroom she could use and Charlotte tried to calm him down.

"I haven't even seen what they're wearing!" he complained to his mother.

"I'm sure Stacy will understand they're from out of town," Charlotte reassured him.

Lily laughed as she slipped out to the guesthouse. She was not at all nervous about attending a fancy restaurant or meeting Wilson's famously powerful movie-producer boss. What did either of them really mean to her? She was independent and glad of it. Wilson's extreme investment in the markers of status was just sad . . . when it wasn't incredibly amusing. Her unique experience of living close to wealth but not with it had taught her that most rich and powerful people got that way through luck rather than merit, and self-interest rather than beneficence. Her experience with Dorian had confirmed as much. Yes, Stacy Black had made a lot of great movies. But Lily would wait to see what she was like in person before making any judgment about Stacy Black herself.

Exactly forty-five minutes later, she and Nicola presented themselves for Wilson's approval. He sighed deeply and declared it would just have to do.

"Oh, honey, don't! They look perfect!" declared Charlotte.

Wilson looked despairingly at Lily's feet. "You don't think a heel?"

"I don't have a heel."

"Really? Oh. Maybe . . . what size are your feet? Mom, have you got—"

"No, really," Lily protested. "I'm perfectly comfortable in these."

"Oh my GOD, the car's here. Mom, go get her some pumps."

"Don't be silly, honey, my feet are enormous and those sandals are lovely. No one will see them sitting down anyway," soothed Charlotte.

But Wilson's focus was on the street outside. "Is that

our car? Did he just drive away?" he said, and charged out, waving furiously.

Nicola took the opportunity to quickly get a bit more reassurance from Charlotte that their outfits weren't totally embarrassing.

"Are you sure we're okay?"

"You both look divine," she reassured them. "There's no dress code. It's only underlings who dress up for the Sunset Room." She gave them a conspiratorial wink as Wilson started shouting from the driveway that the car was here and they had to go now. "The truly rich and famous go casual."

They were met at the restaurant door by a smiling greeter with impossibly long nails and lashes, who ushered them to a booth with a view of sprawling magnificence that took in all of Hollywood, Beverly Hills, Century City, and Santa Monica, all the way down to the distant ocean. Nicola breathed a sigh of awe and reached for her phone, only to score a brisk slap on the hand from Wilson.

"Ixnay on photos!" he hissed.

As they slid into their seats, Wilson leaned in for a breathless military-operation-style scope of the celebrities currently there, from the A-list Oscar winner in the corner to the brand influencer at the bar. Lily was fascinated, not so much by the celebrities themselves, most of whom she didn't really know, but by Wilson's deadly serious cloak-and-dagger identification of them. She had to work hard not to laugh, but luckily Nicola had the presence of mind to remain super impressed.

They were ten minutes early. Exactly ten minutes late, the greeter ushered a person to their table who was barely visible behind enormous sunglasses, a floppy hat, and a blow-dry. Wilson sprang from his seat and gestured frantically for everyone else to do the same.

"Oh, don't get up," drawled the figure as she slipped into the best seat at the table, where Wilson had been, and directed the nondescript teenager trailing behind her into the seat next to her, which had been Nicola's. Everyone moved down and sat, with much fussing and moving of water glasses, as a waiter appeared from nowhere and set a shallow glass in front of Stacy Black.

"Skinny martini," she said to everyone and no one. "They always make them too cold here."

She took a sip, removed her sunglasses and hat, shook out her orange locks, and turned pale eyes on Lily, who smiled pleasantly in return, and Nicola, who trembled.

"So the Aussies have invaded. I didn't think you'd look so tired."

Part of Lily had really hoped that as Stacy Black had produced so many sensitive, profound, and elegant films, there would be some evidence of those qualities somewhere in her personality. She wasn't an actor like Dorian, a gun-for-hire who made a living out of pretending. She was actually in charge of making those films. But on reflection, Lily realized that to recognize the commercial potential in someone else's creative work, then facilitate that work with money, required its own set of skills. Throughout the meal, Stacy Black snapped at her daughter ("Sit up straight, for God's sake, Inez, you look like a goddamn prison inmate"), alternately commanded and ignored Wilson ("Order the fish. Pass me that. What is this? Look it up."), and interrogated Lily and Nicola.

"So you live at this island place?"

"Yes," said Lily. (Nicola couldn't speak.) "But it's not an island."

Stacy turned her pale eyes back to Lily with faint surprise.

"Wilson said it was an island."

"It's actually on the foreshore of a huge national park. It's surrounded by thick bushland and steep cliffs, so the only way you can get there is by boat."

"It feels like an island," mumbled Wilson.

"If you need a boat, that's an island," Stacy Black continued over the top of Wilson. "I hear there are no shops, no restaurants, no cars, quite idyllic."

She looked at Lily as though she shouldn't really come from anywhere idyllic.

"It is." Lily smiled back without flinching.

"And private." She contemplated Lily thoughtfully. "How many people actually live there?"

"It varies because a lot of places are just weekenders. In winter, during schooltime, there's often only about thirty people there. But during summer holidays, there's three to four hundred."

"And how do you shop? You get things delivered?"

Lily laughed. "Nothing is delivered."

At this, Stacy Black's teenage daughter looked up from her phone, which she was holding beneath the table, with a look that was half-disbelieving and half-scornful. Her mother noticed.

"See. That got her attention. A life without unboxing."

"I don't unbox," muttered Inez.

"She lives to shop," Stacy Black explained, talking over her daughter.

"No I don't, you do."

"I would adore to live on an island with no shops."

"Wilson told me it doesn't have flushing toilets."

Inez flung the remark at Stacy Black like a grenade. Her mother just tilted her head in a way Lily knew from experience was infuriating to a daughter looking for a reaction.

"Disappointing. If true."

"It's not," Lily laughed, interrupting Wilson's immediate attempt to both apologize and explain. "We have plumbing; we just have to save water sometimes. When we're in a drought. The water supply is all rainwater."

Lily thought Californians might understand the sacrifices one had to make in a drought.

"Can't you buy water in Australia? That's what we do."

Maybe droughts didn't exist when it came to Stacy Black's lawns.

"Yes you can," put in Nicola, a little too enthusiastically. "We have friends, they've got a farm and they had to buy tanks—for their farm. They have a weekender. At Pippi." Nicola flagged a little under Stacy's gaze, but she rallied. "You can definitely buy water in Australia."

"Good to know."

"But at Pippi you'd have to drop it in by helicopter," added Lily.

"I love helicopters," Stacy murmured. "You take one to school?"

"I took the ferry."

"Huh. I suppose your mother works remotely?"

"No. She's a cleaner."

"A what?"

Wilson intervened. "I believe she runs some kind of—"

"Hush," said Stacy Black, and Wilson hushed.

"She's a cleaner. Cleans houses. And I help her."

Stacy looked like she'd never heard of anything so delightful. Inez smirked, while Wilson and Nicola looked dreadfully unhappy. Lily just smiled. She'd long ago learned to enjoy the challenge of revealing her modest means.

"And how," Stacy Black went on, "does a cleaner's daughter—who also cleans—get a vacation in LA?"

"I'm very lucky," admitted Lily. "I saved up and I'm only staying a few weeks. My aunts helped me with the airfare."

"Aunts, you say."

Wilson could restrain himself no longer. "My mother is best friends with Lily's aunt Elizabeth—the children's author who won—" but Stacy Black silenced him with a flick of her pale eyes.

"Well," she said to Lily, "so this might be your only trip here for some time. We'd better make the most of it. You just go ahead and order whatever you want."

"Thank you," Lily said, and couldn't help but wonder if the others also needed express permission.

18

Lily and Nicola packed their days in LA with tourist attractions. No shop, theme park, or photo op was left untouched, which allowed little time for lounging at the Beverly Hills home and none at all for Wilson, who was in any case extremely busy working on various important projects—as he frequently reminded them via text. But at the end of the week, amid apologies for not having done it sooner, he cornered them into accompanying him to work to see the "real" Hollywood. He'd been planning it for weeks, Charlotte whispered. There was no getting out of it. It was an errand-running day for him, and so Wilson, Nicola, and Lily piled into his car and launched into the sunny, traffic-jammed streets. As they were bumper-to-bumper on the highway, Wilson ran them through the agenda for the day.

"Contract delivery, personal, discreet, you won't be allowed in, I can't even tell you who it is. Then we've got wardrobe pickup, production-wrap gift selection, and restaurant reservation."

"That's a lot of nouns," Lily remarked.

"Yes, it is. I know it's a lot, but really it's all about one thing and that's what most people don't realize."

Lily wondered how long before they would be allowed to realize.

"What is the—" Lily began.

"Relationships. That's it. That's everything. That's what this town runs on. I was away for a month in December; I'm still undoing my replacement's mistakes."

"This traffic, though!" exploded Nicola. "Couldn't you do most of these things on the phone? Get things delivered?"

Wilson laughed patronizingly.

"Oh, Nicola! No, no, no. You don't understand. This is Stacy Black. Any loser can get on the phone, get a delivery from some delivery guy. Winners need other winners to work for them. And winners go the extra mile, they go in person."

"Even to book a restaurant?"

"Especially to book a restaurant. This place is booked out months in advance and Stacy wants it this weekend. A winner goes in person, and if they get told no, they beg."

He said it as if it was the most natural thing in the world. And Lily thought that perhaps Wilson was really well suited to this job.

The traffic was terrible, but they made it to the mysterious house in Beverly Hills, a big-gated thing completely obscured by trees, to deliver the contract. Lily and Nicola stayed in the car and watched Wilson buzz the intercom, go through the gate, and return a minute later without the folder.

"Oh, she's always so lovely," he said as he got back in the car, though no one asked. "She always asks me to come in for a coffee, if you know what I mean. So awkward! I'm half her age! I always just smile and say another time. Thank God you're here, I've got a proper excuse!"

Lily just looked at Nicola and shook her head in disbelief.

Next was the dry cleaner, which was sized and staffed like a high-end medical facility, to pick up Stacy's designer dress. Most people wouldn't even know that such a dress required specialist attention, Wilson explained. Lily had to admit she thought it just looked like a large black sack, then had to bite her lip as Wilson continued to explain in how many ways she was wrong.

The production-wrap gift turned out to be a large blue-and-gold vase, selected under Stacy's watchful eye via text and video call.

Finally, after much more time in traffic, they pulled up among the topiary out front of a restaurant in Santa Monica, where a valet in uniform stood ready to park the car while Wilson did his official groveling.

"Come on! It'll be fun to watch!" Nicola urged, but Lily had seen enough for one day.

She wandered down to the waterfront, stood on the sidewalk with a long line of buildings to her right and left, gazed across the vast expanse of sand and water before her, and felt revived. How marvelous that this sun-blasted ocean, right on the edge of a city of millions of people, was directly connected to the delicious wild green water at Pippi.

In less than ten minutes, she got a text from Nicola: DONE!!!

Back at the car, Nicola was beaming.

"Lily, you will NEVER guess what just happened!"

"You finally saw a superhero?"

"I AM a superhero!" Nicola squealed as they hopped in the car to drive to their next location, Wilson staying curiously silent. "I convinced them to make room for a booking for Stacy Black! It was all me, me, me!"

"After I played it into your hands," corrected Wilson.

"Oh, come on. I was brilliant!"

"I was brilliant. You were lucky."

"I groveled like no groveler has groveled before, even squeezed out a tear or two! They were totally convinced I was Stacy's new hopeless assistant and that my job was on the line! It was HILARIOUS! I am so good at improv."

Of course, Nicola did stuff like this all the time when they were in school: convincing kids to swap assigned groups so she could be with Lily (or whomever Nicola happened to be crushing on that week), or bargaining for better seats at the movies, persuading the ticketing assistant to shift another group so they could sit front and center. Lily never really participated in her antics, but she felt it was kind of okay considering Nicola hadn't been dealt the best hand in life and so she sometimes had to trick her way through it. And now that they'd come to a place where immature cheating could be seen as a smart business move, that inspired some respect.

"She's really a natural," observed Wilson with genuine approval and only a little resentment.

After another hour in rush-hour traffic, Wilson, Nicola, and Lily arrived at Stacy's production office in a chic Beverly Hills high-rise that was all sparkling glass doors, white tiled floors, and uniformed security.

"Thanks, Pam," said Wilson cheerily to the unsmiling receptionist who signed them in. "That's Pam," he explained as they stepped into the elevator. "She's so funny."

Stacy's production office was bright and open, with one wall of beautiful big windows looking out over the Hollywood Hills, and three walls of framed film posters—including, Lily couldn't help but notice, all three Daniel Danger films, featuring Dorian's face age fourteen through to twenty years old. The assault of handsomeness had a confusing effect, and Lily was quite glad that Wilson directed them to Stacy Black's private lounge to wait for him.

"Emails, couple of calls," he explained. "It's okay, Stacy's gone home and you'll be out of the way. The green chaise lounge." He thrust the vase and the dress at them.

Lily and Nicola raised their eyebrows at each other and ventured down the hall.

"Should we be getting paid for this?" asked Lily.

"I think I've already earned at least seventy-five percent of Wilson's salary for my excellent reservation swindling."

"What did he—" and Lily stopped short. For there

in the waiting room, sitting on the green chaise lounge, was Dorian Khan. And right next to him, Lily noticed, another handsome man in his late twenties. How was it that everyone in this town was so good-looking?

"Hi," said Dorian.

"Hi," said Lily and Nicola at the same time, both too baffled to say much else.

"I had a meeting with Stacy this afternoon," Dorian said. "She told me you'd be coming back so we waited. Just to say hi."

Lily looked at him and wondered why in the world he took the trouble. Did he imagine they'd be thrilled? He certainly seemed as unmoved as ever.

"This is my friend and assistant, Franklin."

"Pleased to meet you," said the other man in an American accent and with a flash of ice-white teeth. He extended his hand, which was a little awkward as Lily had to put down the vase and Nicola had to drape Stacy's not-sack dress on the chaise lounge to avoid creasing.

"He pays me to be his assistant," Franklin joked. "But not to be his friend. I do that for free."

Dorian smiled faintly.

"Aw, he's embarrassed." Franklin gave him a shove. "So Lily, I've heard so much about you."

Lily glanced at Dorian in surprise but he appeared not to notice.

"How do you like LA?"

Franklin made conversation easy, with a relaxed charm that reminded Lily of Casey. Dorian sometimes added small remarks, asked where they were staying, and politely asked after their families. In turn, she asked him if he'd heard from Casey recently.

"We've been in touch."

"Oh really? We haven't heard from him at all," Lily said as lightly as she could. The ghosting of Juliet still rankled her, but if Dorian was at all provoked, he didn't show it.

"Do you have plans for tomorrow?"

"No," said Nicola immediately.

"Stacy's hosting lunch at her house and she asked me to invite you. Wilson has the details."

"Omigosh, thank you!" bubbled Nicola. "That's so nice! Isn't that nice, Lily?"

And Lily had to admit that it was nice—and also surprising and unnecessary. She didn't want Dorian or Stacy to go to any trouble on their account.

"No trouble at all," clipped Dorian.

Dorian and Franklin left, neatly avoiding any conversation with Wilson, who came running in minutes later to tell them, at great length and with much side detail, what they already knew: they were invited to lunch and it was special. Nicola was thrilled at the honor. Lily, however, once again felt ambushed. Instead of steering clear of the world of Stacy Black as she had intended to do, she was getting deeper into it.

"I can't believe Dorian waited around to see you," Wilson said, clearly impressed. "You know who does that in LA?"

"No, who?" asked Nicola eagerly.

"No one."

19

The next morning, Lily and Nicola found an envelope slipped under their door. Inside was Wilson's credit card and a neat list of fashion boutiques at the Beverly Mall, each one with a name next to it.

I've reached out to them all and these are stylists I trust, he underlined. *They'll know what you need for a pool party at Stacy Black's. I'm at work all morning, I'll pick you up at 3:00 SHARP,* underline, underline, underline. *Kiss, kiss, Wilson.*

"Is he serious?" Lily couldn't believe it. "What am I saying, he's always serious."

"How much do you think we can spend?" wondered Nicola.

"Nothing! We can't accept this. We're not charity cases!"

"Yes we are!" pleaded Nicola. "We're going to a pool

party at a Hollywood producer's mansion, Lily! I don't want to look like I work at Bready-Set-Go Bakery!"

"But you do."

"But I don't want to look like it. And seriously, Lily, what are you going to wear? It's casual classy. We don't have that."

Lily had to admit that in that particular style category, their travel wardrobes were a little limited. She remained reluctant, but Nicola persisted and enlisted Charlotte's help.

"Of course you should get something! That's the family credit card; Javier pays that and, honestly, he won't even notice. You don't have to get anything over the top. Just something nice that you can take home and remember us by. Please. For me."

Charlotte made a convincing case, and as long as they only bought what they really needed—ethically made and sustainably sourced—Lily was almost as happy as Nicola to oblige.

"But we're not doing it for Stacy Black's benefit—or Wilson's or Dorian's," she asserted.

"Of course not," agreed Nicola. "It's for us."

"The only person I wouldn't mind impressing is Franklin," Lily mused.

Wilson arrived just before three to pick them up.

He was suitably satisfied with the girls' new outfits and felt personally responsible for their choices as he had directed them to the right stores.

"You look amazing," he gushed at Lily.

"And me?" asked Nicola.

"Oh yes, amazing. Now get IN, gosh. NO, Mom, we don't have time! We'll take photos when we get there!"

The car snaked along the curved streets, past lush lawns and palm trees, and up into the crazy curly corners of the Hills. The mansions became more and more opulent and less and less visible from the street. Lily caught glimpses of sun-drenched terraces and sparkling pools beyond hedges and gates and on the distant slopes of narrow canyons. Finally, as they reached a peak and a dead end, Wilson delivered them to the most majestic gate yet. He entered the code, the gate swung open, and in they slipped. The car crunched to a halt in a circle of gravel. Before them, a white concrete edifice of angles and curves sprawled across and down an expanse of terraced landscaping cut into the hillside.

"I know. It takes your breath away," said Wilson. "Don't worry," he assured Lily, who was not in the least bit worried. "She likes you."

He led them in the front door, which was wide enough to admit all three of them side by side, to an interior of sweeping surfaces and views from rooms so minimally furnished that some were completely empty. Then down an oval-shaped staircase that seemed to have no visible means of support, and out to a pool deck where clusters of people in beige, black, and white were arranged, with LA quite literally at their feet.

Lily was more struck by the ordinariness of it all than its opulence. The sun hits all houses the same way, she reflected. Without a frame around it, even the most dramatically social-media-worthy setting is still just another moment in your life, connected to all the other ordinary moments, with all the attendant ordinary feelings. She felt a twinge of sympathy for Stacy Black, locked up here behind a high fence and a huge gate, filling the space around her with people closer in age to her teenage daughter.

The daughter herself, Inez, sat on an oddly shaped bench with her face in her phone. As the afternoon progressed, she occasionally changed location when the party moved from pool deck to dining area to kitchen, without even looking up. She was like some walking black hole. Luckily, there was plenty of personality bouncing around to fill the void. In addition to Dorian and Franklin, there was a handful of young industry types who all seemed to know each other. Introductions confirmed Lily's suspicion that, directly or indirectly, they all worked for Stacy. This was not really a social occasion. Everyone was on show and on the clock. Stacy Black drifted around in a caftan and a floppy hat, telling everyone about the various and many things she had done or had other people do to her house, garden, belongings, or body and advising everyone what they ought to do as well. Wilson followed her around, lapping it all up, assiduously taking notes on his phone when necessary. ("The pink place on Sunset—ask for Letitia and tell her I sent you.")

Dorian let her talk and managed to remain coolly polite without attracting her disapproval. Indeed, Lily thought she detected a slight—just a slight—air of neediness from Stacy Black toward Dorian Khan. He was certainly the only person there whose opinions she solicited or whose replies she listened to. Luckily, with Stacy Black dominating the conversation, it wasn't too difficult for Lily to just enjoy the food (no one else was eating it), the view, and the swimming pool, and take what opportunities she could to engage with others one-on-one, away from the monologues about travel, design, shopping, movies, body maintenance, and other people. She found a willing conversationalist in Franklin, who turned out to know quite a lot about Pippi Beach.

"I'm so sorry I wasn't there with you on New Year's Eve," he said.

"I'm sure you were somewhere more glamorous," laughed Lily. "Like this." She gestured to the infinity pool and the city glittering beyond it in the afternoon sun.

"Do you really think this is better?"

"No!"

They both laughed.

"But Pippi is special to me," said Lily. "I know it's beautiful in a conventional way—you know, sand, water, sun, nature—but it's not just that."

"The people, maybe? I always think people make a place."

"Yes, partly, but that doesn't quite explain it either. Some of the people there drive me crazy. Like my mother."

Franklin laughed good-naturedly. "So Pippi has something else?"

"What? What does Pippi have?" shouted Nicola as she drifted into the conversation. One week into her Hollywood experience and one drink into the party, Nicola had become rather expansive.

"It's got you," Lily said with a smile. "And plenty of other contradictions." She was aware that Dorian was hovering nearby and wondered what he had told Franklin about her home. "It's wild but also comforting. It's a world you can see the end of, with everything you need inside it, but then somehow the water and the bush around it extend forever."

"No shops," put in Nicola. "No theater."

"Apart from the New Year's Eve talent show," said Dorian, who had edged closer.

"Talent show—what?" Now Stacy Black had overheard. "This place has a talent show?"

"We have one every year," said Lily.

"It's just for kids, really," Wilson explained quickly. "I did a tight five, but—"

"And did you perform?" Stacy ignored Wilson and kept her eyes on Lily. "What is your talent?"

Lily laughed. "I haven't performed in a while."

"She won too many times, they wouldn't let her enter anymore!" crowed Nicola.

"You didn't tell me she was a performer too, Wilson," accused Stacy Black. "So what are you? Dancer, singer, actor?"

"I'm none of those things."

"Then what is it that you are?"

Lily felt the color rising in her cheeks. What indeed was she? In this place where everyone was pursuing a goal or ensuring the security of one they'd already attained, her lack of direction felt like failure. But how did someone like Stacy Black measure success? Was this it?

"I don't know what I am," Lily had to admit. "But I can play the ukulele."

"Then we must hear you. Wilson, get a ukulele."

Wilson, not knowing where he could find such a thing, rushed off to ask the housekeeper.

"I'd rather not," Lily protested.

"Nonsense. This is a party."

"No, really, I wouldn't like to."

"Of course you would," purred Stacy Black. "You're among friends. No judgment. It's not like the movies when the pool boy sings or the waitress gets caught rehearsing and then suddenly I notice them and they become a big star." (Nicola was hanging on every word.) "That literally never happens. I can tell if someone has what it takes the moment I see them, and you and I both know you don't."

"Oh. Well, thank you, I suppose," said Lily as Wilson thrust a ukulele at her.

"But you do have something, I'll give you that," went on Stacy Black. "So go ahead and show it off."

Lily could only laugh at the absurdity of the situation.

There was desperation in Wilson's face and some creeping embarrassment among the others. It was quite clear that Lily could not get out of this without a confrontation. Everyone, including Dorian Khan, appeared to know that Stacy was being impossibly rude and a bully, but nobody was going to say so. Out of everyone there, Lily was the one who cared the least about pleasing Stacy Black, with the exception of perhaps her own daughter. Stacy was just like a cat choosing to sit on an unreceptive lap, and Lily knew her only defense was to choose not to fight.

So she went ahead and sang her 1920s novelty song in a light but pleasantly charming voice, in a way that was so unaffected that Stacy Black appeared quite confused.

"Well, you certainly don't have a voice," Stacy said at the end as the applause died down. "But you've got guts."

Lily just laughed. She may have performed for Stacy, but she hadn't submitted to her judgment and that is what raised her in the eyes of everyone else there. As Franklin told her later, it wasn't putting on a show that intrigued this audience of performers—it was that she seemed to enjoy it without caring much whether anyone liked it.

Lily took care to keep her distance from Dorian and

was somewhat surprised and a little annoyed that he always seemed close by.

"Are you trying to scare me?" she asked Dorian jokingly as she chatted with Franklin on the pool deck, well away from the others.

"Not at all," Dorian replied.

"He wouldn't scare anyone," laughed Franklin. "He's too sweet."

"You'd be surprised," Lily shot back. "He was not known for his sweetness at Pippi Beach."

"Really? All dark and mysterious, were you?"

"Positively threatening," assured Lily. "The very first day—a fabulously casual gathering—Dorian Khan did not speak to a single person."

Franklin gasped in mock horror as Lily dropped her voice so Inez wouldn't hear. "And spent the entire time looking at his phone."

Franklin laughed. "Ah yes—the ultimate sign of disdain."

"Or the last refuge of the socially challenged," Lily said.

Dorian seemed annoyed. "I didn't know anyone. I'm not like some people who can just throw themselves into a situation with strangers and make friends. I'm not good at it."

Lily raised her eyebrows and looked over at Nicola, who was nodding as Stacy Black told her which kind of eyelash extensions to get. "Hm. Well, that's a funny thing, isn't it? I'm not that good at the ukulele, but I've always thought that's my own fault for not practicing."

Franklin laughed loudly and easily. "Ha! She got you there!"

Dorian's lips twisted a little. "You sell yourself short. Everyone here thought your performance was just perfect."

"But apparently not my voice."

Dorian winced at this reminder of Stacy Black's rudeness. "But you don't perform for just anyone. And neither do I."

"Dorian! Hey, Dorian," called Stacy. "Get over here. Did we make Dan Danger two in the Czech Republic?"

"Yes."

Somehow, Stacy annexed Dorian, Franklin, and Lily into a conversation about the suitability of landscapes for various kinds of filming ("Europe has versatile geography but not architecture"). Lily attempted to drift off but was instantly roped back in with more questions from Stacy about Pippi Beach.

"So is there a mayor, or something? Who runs the show?"

"No one, really, although I'm sure Bob-with-One-Dog would like to think he does," laughed Lily. "There's also a Bob with two dogs. But Bob-with-One-Dog has the most property there so he usually gets his way."

"Interesting," mused Stacy. "So Bob-with-One-Dog is really Bob-with-All-the-Say? What does Bob-with-Three-Dogs think?"

Lily had to laugh. Discussing the power machinations of Pippi Beach in such a setting was nothing if not amusing. But if Stacy insisted on engaging Lily in conversation, then she was glad it was at least about a topic she knew.

20

The next day, Lily's thoughts kept returning to the mansion. She was more troubled by Stacy Black than she felt she ought to be and she struggled to get to the bottom of it. Was it that Stacy was a creature of the movie business, somehow magically skilled at capturing attention, holding it, and subverting a person's sense of the way of things? Lily knew she wasn't dazzled by wealth and power. Was she just seduced by the superficial glitter of this desert town, as Nicola was? Had she fallen victim to it herself? She winced as she thought of herself playing the ukulele, laughing and talking about Pippi Beach with people who would never understand what it meant to her.

Nicola was not bothered by any such reflections. The only impressions she took from the pool party, Stacy Black, and LA life in general were favorable ones. Nicola adored the way everything looked and felt and refused to be bothered by troublesome details like where all the water came from.

"I think Stacy Black is magnificent," Nicola declared. "Don't you? You know she went to a state school, just like me. Grew up without a dad. Just like me. And she's a Scorpio."

"Fierce work ethic, steely ambition," teased Lily. "You're practically twins."

"Oh, ha ha. Omigosh, that reminds me, I have to get to the mall."

"Why?"

"Manicure."

"You got one yesterday!"

"Yes, but Stacy says with my skin tone, this is all wrong."

"But you love that color."

"Stacy says no."

"Stacy's not wearing it."

"But I said I'd change it and I booked it right in front of her yesterday! With her favorite technician!"

"You could cancel."

"Are you insane? She'd find out! Wow, Lily. Rude. I'm wearing your hat. Thanks. Bye." And she was gone.

Lily was happy enough to have a morning to herself. She made a cup of coffee and wandered out to the pool deck, where she spied Wilson through the kitchen window and made an abrupt about-face. It was too late. He had seen her.

"Hey! What a beautiful morning! I'll be right there!" he called. And while Lily would have much preferred him not to join her, the sun was too nice to retreat, and after all, it was his pool deck, not hers.

Wilson emerged from the house in a colorful floral print shirt buttoned way too low, bearing a large oblong box, which he placed in front of her with a flourish.

"My lady."

"What's this?"

"A present."

"Wilson, really—"

"I know, I know, you have some weird aversion to gifts, but honestly, I can afford it. So. Go ahead."

Lily steeled herself and opened the box. Inside, nestled among clouds of orange tissue paper, she found a very pretty ukulele and a pair of satin high-heeled pumps.

"Wilson!"

"Try them on! They fit. I know they do, I got your size."

Lily slipped them on and had to admit that they were supercool and made her legs look fabulous. Then she stood up and remembered why fabulous-looking legs were not worth the price.

"I can't wear these!"

"Yes you can. It's practice, that's all it is."

"But I don't need them!"

"This is LA. You need heels."

"I've already been to the Sunset Room."

"Are you kidding? Nobody goes just once. And there are so many cool places—"

"I don't go to those places."

"I'm gonna take you."

"And I already have a ukulele at home. It's really sweet of you, Wilson, I'm touched. But it's too much. I couldn't fit them in my luggage anyway." She started to pack the gifts away. "You should return them. Or save them, give them to someone who can use them."

"You can use them while you're here."

Lily laughed. "I'm not here for that much longer."

"But I want you to stay."

Lily paused and checked Wilson's face. Yes. This was it, for real this time. She knew what he wanted of her, he was making it clear, and she needed to make it equally clear that it wasn't going to happen. But before she could draw breath on a firm but kind speech—he had, after all, put some thought into these very nice gifts—Wilson leaned forward and pressed his open mouth onto hers, tongue first. Lily backed away with such urgency that the lovely box on her lap slid to the deck and one heel bounced off into the pool, causing her to reflexively lunge after it as Wilson called her name and lunged after her. Somehow they both ended up at the edge of the pool, Lily with her hands on a dripping shoe and Wilson with his hands clasped dramatically around Lily's face.

"I love you," he declared solemnly. "I always have and I always will. Lily. We are going to be magnificent together!" And he leaned in for another kiss.

But Lily was ready this time and jumped to her feet.

"No. Wilson, stop!" She fended him off with the heel. "I said no."

At which, horrifyingly, he smiled. "You don't mean that."

"Yes I do."

Tense pause. Then he turned and sat down on a deck chair with the air of a professor patiently waiting for a student to grasp the obvious.

"So it's like this, is it? After all we've been through?"

"I don't know what you're talking about."

"You want to keep on playing some weird friend-zone-type game?"

"It's not a game."

"Everyone knows. And everyone's happy for us."

"Us?"

"You and me. Our relationship."

"What do you mean, everyone?"

"Stacy. Mom. Nicola." He smiled indulgently at her frown. "We can stop playing. Finally. And be together." The emotion moved him to approach again. He took her hand and Lily was too confused to stop him.

"Stacy?" was all she managed to say, but Wilson barely heard her. He was already waxing lyrical about their future together as boyfriend and girlfriend. Everything was all planned. Nicola was happy to fly home alone, Lily could stay for several months more on a tourist visa, which would give them plenty of time to apply for another one, and in any case, Stacy and the entire production office were moving to Sydney later in the year to make a couple of movies in Australia, wasn't that great? Not that it mattered that much; it wasn't as if Lily was committed to going to college there or anywhere else. If she continued to build on the good impression she had already made, Stacy might just straight-out give her a job.

"I know you might want to stay on in the guesthouse at first," he went on. "I can see you want slow, I can go slow. You know that about me, I'm sensitive. But with the housing market the way it is, and the money we could both be earning, we can look at getting our own place within a few years." She stared at him with incomprehension. "I know, it's a lot to take in. But imagine it. Our own place in West Hollywood."

"West Hollywood?"

"Only for the first couple of years, babe; we would be back in Beverly Hills so quick and if Mom lends us—"

"No!"

"Okay, we can make it on our own if—"

"NO!" Lily screamed. "You're not listening to me!"

"You don't need to say anything. I understand."

"No you don't!" She snatched her hand out of his grasp. "I'm not into you, Wilson. I have never been into you."

"Ah—well, that's a lie."

"It's the truth."

"The way you look at me—"

"I've been polite!"

"And smile at me, it's pretty clear."

"Polite! Nothing more! And if you've misunderstood that, I'm really sorry, but I want to make it perfectly clear, right here and now. I don't want to be with you, Wilson. Not now. And not ever."

Wilson finally seemed to hear her. He paused to think, which was a little frightening, and then he started to smile, which was much worse.

"I don't think you can say that."

"I am saying it."

"You're forgetting one thing."

"No, I think I've covered it."

"You're forgetting the power of love, Lily. Love does not give up on people. Love does not die. And I love you, enough to look past whatever game this is, whatever feminist statement you feel you need to make by denying what is obvious. To everyone. And when you fully understand that, I will be here. Waiting for you."

Lily gave up. She returned to the unlucky box of gifts, shoved the sodden shoe back in among the tissue paper, well away from the ukulele, jammed the lid back on, and dumped it in Wilson's hands.

"Thank you, but no."

"These will be here for you," he replied. "Whenever you're ready."

But Lily had already disappeared back into the guesthouse, cursing herself for letting this whole situation slide for so long, and cursing Wilson more for creating it in the first place.

The next week was tense. Lily avoided Wilson as

much as she could, which was relatively easy when he was working, but he kept up a steady stream of texts that walked the line between apologetic and creepy. Nicola found the whole thing hilarious and reassured Lily that Wilson would get over her soon enough, but when they opened their door to a massive delivery of flowers on Friday morning and a card featuring nothing but a question mark, Lily declared that something definitive must be done. She marched the elaborate floral arrangement and its card straight back into the main house and placed them in front of Wilson's mother.

"Wow! Someone has an admirer."

"Yes," said Lily. "I think you know who it is."

"Oh, honey, Wilson is such a romantic boy, always was, and if it's too much, you just tell him."

"Actually, I did tell him, but he doesn't seem to be listening."

"You want him to slow down?"

"I want him to stop."

Charlotte's face fell. Lily felt sorry to disappoint her, but she had to stand her ground. "I'm not his girlfriend. And I don't want to be."

"I know he can be a bit intense, but he worships you. Honestly. He will move mountains for you. If there's anything he can do—or I can do . . ."

"No."

"You just want to be friends," Charlotte confirmed, a little sadly.

"Yes."

Charlotte sighed. She turned to the flowers and adjusted some of the orchids, which were colored like candy and bigger than her head. "I told him he should have gotten something more delicate. Roses. Pilar?"

Pilar appeared from nowhere.

"You want these? They just don't go in here. Take them with you when you leave. Actually, pop them in your car now."

Within seconds the offending flowers were gone and Lily had Charlotte's word that Wilson would not bother her again.

"But you might want to keep your distance from him this weekend. I can get him to leave you alone. But I can't get him to like it."

21

"Hi, Lily, this is Dorian. I hope you don't mind, I asked Stacy for your number. I know Wilson has a busy week of work ahead and I wondered if you and Nicola would like to see Griffith Observatory."

Lily finished reading the text aloud to Nicola, who immediately snatched the phone from her.

"No. Way."

"I know. How does Stacy Black have my phone number? I don't have hers."

"She would have gotten Wilson to give it to her, you jellyfish. The important thing here is that YOU have DORIAN KHAN's number in YOUR PHONE! Do you know what that's worth?"

"Yes, it's worth a trip to the Griffith Observatory, which I'm actually desperate to see but you have refused because it's up a hill. Now we can go in style!"

"With him?" Nicola made a face.

Lily shrugged. Sure, she and Dorian had clashed a little at Stacy's party, but the experience was more amusing than actively annoying.

"It could be fun."

The two of them spent five minutes composing a text with no emojis and a restrained use of exclamation marks. ("Just one smiley sunglasses face?" pleaded Nicola. "No!" insisted Lily.) Just as everything was settled, Lily all the while wondering why on earth an internationally famous person would voluntarily leave his luxury hotel to go to a tourist hot spot just to show two Aussies around, Nicola's face fell.

"Oh no!"

"What?"

"The launch!"

Wilson had gotten them tickets to the launch of Vegan Eggs' new album at a cool record store in West Hollywood, back before what Nicola was calling the Great Rejection.

"I know you love cultural landmarks and astronomy and whatever, but I love this band much, much more—"

"It's fine," said Lily.

"I'm sorry."

"Why? Go to the album launch. Take Wilson. If I'm not going, I'm sure he'd be delighted."

"And you'll go to the observatory?"

"Why not?"

"Alone?"

"I'll be with Dorian."

"Exactly! Alone with Dorian! It'll be like every single romantic Hollywood movie ever."

Lily laughed. "Yes. A bit superficial and unconvincing, terrible dialogue, with very pretty scenery. I'm looking forward to it. And this time, no one is telling me what to wear."

The next day, at one o'clock sharp, Lily opened the door to Dorian looking surprisingly ordinary in jeans. They exchanged casual greetings and Lily noticed how much more comfortable she felt without the pressure of a dress code. It was much easier to own being an outsider than to pretend not to be one.

Dorian led her to his top-of-the-line (compact size) electric vehicle and she climbed into the front seat, suddenly very aware of how close they were. They'd been this close before, even closer, but there was something about being confined to a car, where every outside sound was muffled and every internal sound amplified, that felt very intimate.

"Thanks for taking me," Lily said.

"No, of course," Dorian said. "I'm glad you could still make it."

He didn't smile. He was so awkwardly aloof, Lily wondered if Franklin had put him up to it. He seemed a little put out.

"Do you want music?" Dorian asked.

"Sure."

He turned on the audio player in the car, which immediately began playing a 1950s-era crooning love song from a playlist named "D-Dawgz Sik Beatz." Lily stifled a chuckle and Dorian looked alarmed.

"Casey named it." He frowned. "Nobody calls me that." But Lily thought she may have caught the tiniest self-deprecating smile.

As they drove up the winding road, the hill became steeper and the sky bigger. The shaded houses and swaying palm trees fell away and glimpses of the city beneath them expanded into commanding views. They parked in a small parking lot at the base of the mountain.

"I remember you like hiking," he announced.

"I do," replied Lily with a smile, wondering if there was anything that Dorian liked.

A black SUV pulled up right next to their car, and as she got out Lily found herself practically face-to-face—or rather face-to-chest—with a big, burly man. As she slipped around the car to join Dorian, the man followed close behind her. Oh dear. Lily had thought this might happen. Dorian was the face of one of the biggest movie franchises and he wouldn't have the same anonymity that Lily enjoyed while traveling. Although she'd expected Dorian to be hounded by teenage girls Rosie's age, not six-foot-two men with thick eyebrows and biceps. But to her surprise, Dorian shook the man's hand.

"Good to see you, David," Dorian said. "Lily, this is David. He's, uh . . . well, he's my security. Sometimes. When I need it."

"Nice to meet you," said David in a surprisingly light voice as he took Lily's tiny hand in his massive one. "Don't worry, you won't even know I'm here."

He said this more to Dorian than Lily and winked, at which Dorian turned red and just nodded, then led Lily away toward the hiking path to the observatory.

"How long have you known David?" Lily asked as they started walking. She checked behind her to see David's tall form following, just behind an older couple walking their dog.

"About five years," said Dorian, clearly not wanting to talk about it.

Lily felt sorry for him, that going outside was such an

194

ordeal. It was a bit surreal, being tailed all the way up the hiking trail. She kept wanting to turn around to see if David was still there. She thought maybe she should just ask him to join them so she wouldn't feel so weird. It was strange to her that this man's job was to watch Dorian and ensure his safety but still be separate from him.

As they reached the top of the hiking trail, the observatory came into view: a cream stone building with beautiful domes like a castle, overlooking the Los Angeles haze. To her right was the sign that spelled out HOLLYWOOD. Nicola was right, it did feel like a movie. Except it was swarming with tourists, the harsh midday sunlight made everything too bright, and the leading man was as silent and stony as the observatory building itself.

Lily and Dorian made their way up the steps, where they were welcomed by a uniformed attendant who ushered them onto the highest balcony, which had been roped off, apparently especially for them. The attendant magically disappeared and David stood sentinel at the ropes. It was a strange maneuver of privilege that left Lily astounded at its speed and at how naturally Dorian accepted it all without comment. She decided it was best not to mention it either.

Observing the view gave both of them an excuse not

to say anything. As she watched all the tiny cars glittering like beetles down below, she wondered why Dorian had invited her when he appeared not to enjoy her company. Aside from their little joke in the car, he had been sullen this whole time, and Lily thought it might be easier if she just turned and said to him, "Don't worry about me, you can go home now." It'd put him out of his apparent discomfort and leave her to enjoy the view, and the play of shadows on the building's angles and curves. It was all so beautiful and Dorian didn't even seem to see any of it.

Her thoughts were interrupted when a loud American woman directly below them blurted out to her friends, "That's my apartment! Look, you can see my TV! I'm so glad I got sixty-five inch."

Dorian and Lily exchanged a private smile, an acknowledgment that they both heard the remark and found it amusing.

"Do many locals come here?" asked Lily, taking this opportunity to try to start a conversation. "I thought this place was just for tourists."

"Pretty much everyone who lives in LA started out as a tourist here," he said. "It sounds romantic but it's true—it's full of runaways. People running from family, small-town life, expectations."

"What are you running from?"

She was half joking, but Dorian didn't see the comedy.

"I've never lived here," he replied.

"Well, it's very different from home," Lily said. Then she wondered if it was tactless of her to use that word. Though they were both technically from Australia, he certainly didn't live there anymore. Where was home for Dorian Khan?

"It's so magnificent here—truly spectacular," she went on, drinking in the view of mountains and sprawling city below.

"It is extraordinary," he mused. "But this has nothing on the natural beauty of Pippi Beach."

Lily smiled at his honest praise of the place she loved. "I didn't know you liked it that much."

"How could I not?"

"Not everyone does."

"I expect you'll move away to study next year."

"Not necessarily. I don't know what I'm doing next year."

"Of course, the biggest challenge about it is the community," he went on. "Those people. No privacy. Even worse for you, living on top of your family. Your mother. You must love being away."

Lily whipped her head to look at him. Was he making a deliberate dig? Or just being carelessly rude, dismissive, and judgmental of her, her family, and her entire community? He kept his gaze on the distant horizon and betrayed nothing.

"I miss them all very much, actually," she said coldly.

He said nothing in reply.

They walked around the building a few times, neither of them taking any photos or engaging in anything more than necessary small talk. A frostiness grew and they descended the hill not long after. Lily made no further attempt at conversation and became angrier as the silence between them lengthened and he didn't even seem to notice or care.

When his car pulled up in front of Wilson's house, Lily felt she couldn't thank him and get out of the car fast enough.

"I—" Dorian began, then stopped himself.

Was she finally going to hear an apology from him, she wondered, for being so distant, for hardly opening his mouth except to insult her family? Was he finally going to say something real? But whatever he was originally going to say, Dorian seemed to change his mind.

"I'll see you later," he said. And that was that.

Lily got out of the car, more certain than ever that

whatever strange friendship might have begun to form was definitely gone now.

Nicola, however, did not see it that way.

"Lily, I'm telling you, he likes you," she said the next day as they sat by the pool, both in big hats and sunglasses, though Nicola's were more to dampen her hangover than to protect her from the sun. The Vegan Eggs album launch had raged until two in the morning, and Nicola had even kissed the drummer, so she said. After hearing all about Nicola's brilliant night, it was Lily's turn to divulge her awkward outing with Dorian. She included every stony silence, every insult, and she was shocked that Nicola had come to this conclusion.

"Did you listen to anything I just said?" said Lily. "He assumed I was happy to be away from my family and my entire community because he thinks they're unbearable, which they can be, but only I'm allowed to talk about my family that way behind their backs."

"That was off," Nicola conceded. "But he's totally got the hots for you."

"I can assure you he does not. He was friendlier to his bodyguard."

"But he's so dreamy," she said, as if that was at all relevant.

"My opinion of him hasn't changed since that first

day at Pippi. He's stuck-up and he thinks my family and I are stupid."

Lily said this with such power in her voice and fire in her eyes that Nicola dropped the subject and offered her a sparkling water to cool down.

22

Lily didn't waste too much time worrying about what Dorian Khan was thinking. The following week, she and Nicola were off on the next part of their adventure: a weekend in Las Vegas, a day at the Grand Canyon, three nights in Palm Springs. Their break was not quite as wild as Nicola wanted it to be, but they still managed to spend a lot of money, laugh a lot, eat a lot, drink a lot, and take way too many photos.

Their return to the guesthouse in Beverly Hills felt like a new beginning. Having been away and come back again, they were filled with comfort and confidence at the sight of their very own curved, palm-lined street. They were no longer tourists. They belonged here. There was no more exclaiming over squirrels or the pool deck or Pablo mowing the lawn or the strange ongoing absence of Charlotte's husband, Javier. This was just their life now. As promised by Charlotte, Wilson continued to keep his distance. Any invitations were texted directly to Nicola with an aggrieved air of cool formality, which she found hilarious. Would they like to attend a screening of a new movie at the end of the week? And a press junket for the opening of a different movie tomorrow? Nicola was thrilled at the idea of lurking near real celebrities giving real interviews to real journalists in a fancy hotel. Lily politely declined and sought out an art museum instead.

Lily was happy to discover that on a weekday afternoon the sprawling maze of galleries was practically deserted. So she was a little surprised when someone came and stood right next to her to admire an intricate eighteenth-century oil painting and quite shocked when she turned to discover that that person was Dorian Khan. David the bodyguard was lurking behind a sculpture of Cupid.

"What are you doing here?" asked Lily.

"I always come here."

"Always?"

"Often."

"So I could have come anytime and I still would have run into you?"

"Quite possibly."

"Aha. You were at the junket today," she guessed.

"No, at the office actually. I saw Nicola without you and wondered if you'd gotten lost."

"I'm not lost. The Impressionists, however . . ." Lily had no trouble finding the museum but once inside had been unable to find anything.

"I know, this place is a labyrinth."

"Did you seriously come all the way here to be my guide? I could just ask her." She pointed at an octogenarian gallery attendant.

"I think she's asleep."

Lily had to smile and felt the coolness between them fade. But all the same, it was a bit weird for Dorian to turn up like this, with his security detail in tow.

"I was planning to come this week anyway," he assured her. "And I always go to the Monet first," he added.

"This is not a Monet. So who's lost now?"

She accepted his help on the condition that he didn't try to explain history or art to her, to which he agreed as long as she didn't either. They each solemnly accepted that they were equally knowledgeable.

"Is that what you're going to study? Art?" Dorian asked.

"No. Maybe. I don't know. I love art, but I love science too. And history and literature. I guess I haven't found what I want to do with my life yet."

"Or it hasn't found you."

They wandered to the Impressionists, then onward through the Cubists and Modernists. Conversation remained superficial and fairly easy as long as they talked about the paintings. If Lily asked or volunteered anything too personal, he would freeze up suddenly and change the subject. Not that Lily cared too much either way. She was merely being polite; she didn't really know what he was doing. Showing off, presumably, in some rather twisted reverse psychology way that maybe was common among celebrities. Maybe he just wanted to come across as cultured as well as rich.

"There's a bookstore downtown you might like," he suggested casually. "It's all secondhand books, great range, very quirky design."

"I'll have to check it out."

"Franklin's picking something up for me there tomorrow; he could take you if you like."

"Sure." Lily wondered at the ease with which he made an offer on Franklin's behalf. "If he's okay with that."

"Of course he is," Dorian returned, as though Lily

had somehow questioned something as basic as the color of the sky.

Aha, Lily realized. Franklin is staff first, friend second, and his preferences are no more relevant than those of bodyguard David.

They had wound up in a courtyard next to a charming water feature surrounded by café tables. The scent of freshly baked bread and coffee filled the air. Lily was thirsty and hungry and her legs were tired. Would it be rude to say goodbye and then stay? Considering Dorian had just very pointedly not asked her on a date? And if he had, she would have refused. Would it seem like she was asking him on a date if she suggested lunch? And where would David sit? Lily was just at the point of announcing she was going to sit down, to hell with the consequences, when Dorian abruptly announced his departure, thanked her for her time, and left.

Nicola agreed the whole interaction was rather odd but was in no mood to go over it in detail. The junket had been extraordinary, she said, and as Lily was still a little unclear on what a junket actually was, Nicola felt the need to explain its intricacies in great detail. Lily eventually came to understand it as a kind of party for journalists at which producers trick them into being nice to their actors. Nicola bubbled with importance as she explained it all. The cherry-on-top of her revelations was that she had actually been chosen to welcome members of the press in the lobby because she was hanging around being so friendly and everyone loved her accent. She had to go back tomorrow and she urged Lily to please come.

"Thank you, it sounds amazing and I'm sure you're doing a fabulous job, but I would only be in your way. Anyway, I'm going to a bookstore downtown."

"Dorian asked you on a date?"

"Most definitely not. I'm going with Franklin."

"Aha! He's road testing you on his assistant!"

"Not so much. He's taking credit for showing me a cool spot without actually taking me there."

Franklin picked Lily up in a sexy convertible.

"This old thing? She's a hot mess and I love her," he said. "Probably won't even get us there, but trust me, if she breaks down, everyone stops to help push."

Lily felt unselfconsciously happy as they cruised the streets from Beverly Hills to downtown Los Angeles. Franklin laughed easily, like Casey, and Lily wondered at Dorian's apparent preference for people with a sense of humor when he so clearly didn't have one himself.

The bookstore was every bit as quirky as Dorian had promised. Laid out across the ground floor and mezzanine of an old department store, the space was a maze of staircases, shapes, sculptures, and shelves, all made from or jam-packed with books. Wandering through its galleries and corners afforded an ever-changing vista of literature that filled Lily with joy, while everywhere around them young tourists busily snapped and posted selfies. Lily found herself constantly dodging other people's photo ops.

"Ah," she said. "Is that why Dorian didn't come? Too many cameras?"

"Yes," admitted Franklin. "He only ever comes here when the place is closed. He doesn't like being recognized in public. It can get very ugly very quickly."

"It's hard to imagine."

"He manages it well. But it's hard work and he's lucky he's had the time and the intelligence to work through it. Can you imagine how exhausting it is to feel watched and judged all the time? By people who think they know you?"

Lily remembered how at the observatory and the art museum Dorian had steered away from people and was always looking over his shoulder. She thought of all the moments she'd been part of a crowd at a museum or landmark or show and she felt sorry for Dorian that he couldn't experience that.

"That kind of fame is dangerous," Franklin added.

"What do you mean? Are the fans really a threat?"

"They can be. But it's not just that. Imagine a world where no one ever says no to you. Where you can have whatever you want, do whatever you want. Pretty soon the normal limits you put on yourself start to disappear. When you're constantly surrounded by people who adore you, who want to impress you, who will quite literally do anything for you, it's easy to believe that you are more important than everyone else."

"Yes, I can see how that could happen." Lily thought of Stacy Black and her empty rooms and Dorian's standoffishness and the offhand way he'd delegated Franklin to take Lily out. She was a little surprised that Franklin thought him so very down-to-earth.

"But Casey Brandon seems to have escaped that trap," she commented.

"Ah yes—Casey Brandon. Perfect example. If it weren't for Dorian helping him out, he would have been cheated out of most of his money and spent the rest on parties and cars."

"So Dorian taught him to save?"

"There's nothing sexy about good financial management but you've got to think about it in this town. But it's not just that. Casey's so naive, he doesn't know when people just latch onto him for fame and prestige. Dorian's been part of that world a lot longer, he can recognize it sooner. He's always rescuing Casey from entanglements."

"Really?"

"Just recently, in Australia—some local fangirl at Pippi got a bit infatuated. Dorian had to step in. You were there; you probably know who it was."

Lily felt her cheeks flame.

"I have some idea," she said, trying to keep the emotion out of her voice. "And what did Dorian save Casey from exactly?"

"Heartbreak. At best."

"And at worst?"

"Stalking. Blackmail, exposure, slander, extortion. Not to say it definitely would have happened in this case."

"No."

"But it might have."

"And Dorian picks it beforehand, huh?"

"He's a really good judge of character."

Lily fumed inside but said nothing. She was convinced Dorian had been talking about Juliet. Her cousin. The sweetest, nicest girl on earth—not to mention someone with a very comfortable background, thank you very much. For Dorian to think her capable of using Casey for her own advantage was so outrageous, it would have been funny if it weren't so hurtful. And wrong.

"Casey needs someone like Dorian. The whole journey into sudden fame and wealth—it does something to you," Franklin went on.

Lily couldn't help but agree. She reached out for the nearest available book, which happened to be an atlas.

"Interesting. You go on ahead," she said to Franklin. "I'm going to take a closer look at this one. Meet you back downstairs?"

She collapsed into a convenient armchair and stared unseeingly at the atlas, aghast at Dorian's cruelty. This wasn't unthinking, casual disregard for Casey and Juliet's relationship. Dorian had intervened in a way that was deliberate and calculated. He said he rescued Casey and then bragged about it to Franklin. How could Dorian be so horribly judgmental? Of poor Juliet? When she was injured? He probably thought she hurt her ankle on purpose. Impossible.

But the more Lily dwelled on it, the less surprised she was. She was angry with herself for not seeing it before. As Franklin had said, fame does something to people. It cuts them off from the rest of the world, inflates their sense of importance, and makes them suspicious and cruel. She thought back to what Alex King had told her, about the terrible way Dorian had treated him. The whole world of privilege and excess made Dorian think more of himself and less of everyone else. It was abominable. She felt it in his coldness toward her. And now here was Franklin praising him as a great friend because he was able to convince Casey of something that wasn't even true. He had projected his own fears onto Juliet. She wasn't grasping for fame or approval, but Dorian couldn't understand that because in his world, that's how everyone was and he was never wrong. Ha. Lily knew better. How she wished she could fling her contempt for him right in his face.

23

Lily was so disturbed by what she had found out that she wanted nothing more to do with Dorian or anyone connected with him, even if it meant forgoing Franklin's sexy convertible. She thanked him for bringing her to the bookstore and insisted she would find her own way home.

"Everything okay?"

"Absolutely. Thanks." She felt sorry that someone as nice as Franklin had somehow been sucked into Dorian's evil empire.

It's all about money, she thought ruefully as she climbed into the back of her reasonably priced and decidedly unsexy rideshare.

She was cheered by the sight of her own cozy guesthouse. She hoped that Nicola would be home by now so she could unburden herself of this awful new knowledge about Dorian's underhandedness.

"Nicola?" she called out as she opened the door.

She was answered by silence, followed by a thump, a strange rustling, and a giggle coming from upstairs. "Are you home?"

"Yes!" Nicola called back thinly, then dissolved into giggles. "No!"

"There's nobody here!" called out . . . Wilson. From Nicola's bedroom. At four o'clock in the afternoon.

Please no! Lily gritted her teeth. But yes, this was really happening. Within seconds, Nicola was on her way down the stairs, tying on a robe, smoothing back extreme bed hair, and assuring Lily that it wasn't what it looked like. And then Wilson descended soon after, with his shirt completely undone, and suggested they all have a drink and talk about this like adults.

"There is nothing to discuss," protested Lily, but there was no escape.

Wilson and Nicola insisted on discussing at great length (while fondling each other's hair, arms, and faces) how very attracted to each other they were and this didn't mean they loved Lily any less. In the end, Lily found the only way to get through this horrid conversation was to stand on the stairs, poised for flight, and keep saying "Okay." When Wilson was sufficiently satisfied that no, she wasn't hurt, and yes, she was happy for them both, he finally left the guesthouse on the condition that Nicola join him the second she was ready because they were going out to celebrate their one-day anniversary.

Lily turned to her friend with her eyes blazing. Now it was Nicola's turn to try to escape. But Lily chased her down.

"Wilson? You have scorned him this whole time!" she accused.

"I have not," Nicola protested. "You have."

"How could you?"

"He likes me."

"That's news; last week he was in love with me."

"He wasn't serious about you."

"He gave a pretty good impression of it!"

"But he is about me and you'd better start being happy about it because this is long-term."

"We're going home next week."

"I'm not." Nicola stuck her chin out. "He loves me and I love him and he's offered me a job. Work experience. It's called interning, look it up. Wilson's going to look after me, then when the production moves to Australia, they'll give me a proper job. And you know what, I don't even care if they don't! Because this is exactly what I want—an opportunity, a ticket out of high school, out of Bready-Set-Go, out of Pippi Beach! I deserve this!"

"But . . . Wilson?"

"Just because you don't want him doesn't mean I can't have him!"

"But you don't want him either!"

"Yes I do!"

And Nicola said it with such conviction, and such hurt pride, that Lily had to stop arguing and believe her.

"Okay," Lily said. "I'm sorry."

"You should be."

"I said I'm sorry."

In the silence that followed, Lily felt their entire friendship collapse in on itself. This was Nicola, her best friend, whose volatile, impulsive heart had always been in the right place. Not anymore. Lily could understand why Nicola might want to take advantage of Wilson and vice versa, but she couldn't respect either of them for it.

"We're going out. I'm borrowing your green dress," sulked Nicola.

"Fine."

Lily sat on her bed with her eyes shut and her headphones on until she was sure Nicola had gone. Waves of emotion surged through her. As if she needed any more confirmation that the world revolved around money. At least this afternoon she had believed that Dorian's hateful, transactional view of relationships was something confined to his world, that it couldn't touch hers. And now here was her very best friend, with whom she had spent a good part of every day for the last five years, selling herself for social and financial gain. It was nauseating. She wanted to call Juliet but hesitated, unsure whether she could control herself in her current state of indignation. She'd be sure to blab what she'd found out about Casey and she couldn't bear for her cousin to know what he and Dorian thought of her. As this went through her mind, her phone dinged.

Are you busy?

It was Dorian. Ugh. Of all people, the one she least wanted to see. She was just about to text back "YES" when her phone dinged again. I'm out front. Do you have a minute?

Out front? What, he's dropping by unannounced now? She looked out the window. At the end of the driveway, beyond the tree canopy and past the gate, there was Dorian's car and Dorian himself. She was about to text some excuse but was overcome by a wave of rage. How dare he? How dare he be here and put her in the position of feeling like she had to lie to maintain her right to be undisturbed by an antisocial movie star? As it happened, she was not busy and she did have a minute—to give him a piece of her mind. She stomped down the stairs, out the door, and straight down the driveway to the gate.

"Yes?" she challenged him through the bars.

"May I come in?"

This momentarily confused her. But whatever confrontation they were going to have, it was probably better not to have it on the street.

She opened the gate, turned, and led the way back up the driveway to the guesthouse. But there was no way she was asking him to sit down.

"Are you okay?" he asked. "Franklin told me you seemed unwell."

"No."

"He said you just dashed off."

"I wanted to come home."

"Right. Here, home."

"Well, home home as well, actually," she admitted.

For the first time since she had arrived in the States, she felt homesick. The admission moved her and she no longer felt so very capable of telling Dorian what she really thought. She didn't even feel able to refuse permission when he asked to sit down.

"That's what I wanted to talk to you about. I understand you're leaving next week."

"Yes."

"I don't want you to go."

What? Was this some kind of nasty hidden camera show? That was what Wilson had said! Lily was too shocked to reply. Dorian continued.

"You must know that." He stood up again and paced. "I just keep thinking about you leaving and for some reason I can't bear it. I know it's ridiculous. I mean, I hardly know you, you're straight out of school, you don't know what you're doing with your life, you live in this bizarre beach commune, your mother's a cleaner." It seemed he could barely pronounce the word, it was so strange to him. "My life was perfectly fine before you came along; I certainly don't need the complications of a relationship. And yet—the thought of never seeing you again just makes me miserable." He stopped and looked deeply into Lily's incredulous eyes. "Don't go. Stay here."

Lily was dumbstruck. How could this be happening to her? Again and so soon? Was she exuding some kind of desperate sex appeal? Did she look like she needed a boyfriend?

"Or stay in a hotel somewhere, I don't mind, I'll pay for it," Dorian went on.

The mention of money jolted Lily back to herself. No. This was not her fault. A certain kind of person just assumed that a woman would fall at his feet the moment he looked at her. That she ought to be in a constant state of patient readiness that would swell to gratitude if chosen. It was despicable. She had done nothing to encourage Dorian, she had never wanted his attention, and she was under absolutely no obligation to protect his feelings. He'd clearly given no thought to hers.

"You can travel back to Australia with me in September," he went on.

"No," she said.

"No?" Dorian echoed. He seemed genuinely confused. "To the travel? Or the hotel?"

"No to all of it! No to you!"

Dorian took a step back, as if slapped. "Are you serious?"

"Are you?"

"Yes!" He slowed down, as though to explain something rather complicated. "I know it's bonkers, I know it can't possibly work. I've done everything I could to get you out of my mind, talk myself out of this. And yet here I am. Asking you to be with me."

He took a step closer and raised his hand to her cheek. She took hold of it and was somewhat surprised at its warmth and softness, but she was way too angry to care about that or how good he smelled up close. She snatched his hand away.

"You should have asked earlier and saved yourself some trouble. The answer is no," she said with cold fury.

He returned her anger with a fiery flash of his eyes. "May I ask why?"

"Because I don't like you, Dorian! And by the sounds of it, you don't like me much either!"

"Were you not listening to me?"

"Oh, I was listening. You said: ridiculous, bonkers"—she counted on her fingers as her outrage swelled—"this couldn't possibly work, you really don't want to be here, you don't want a relationship, and my mother's a cleaner. Like that's relevant."

"I'm only saying—"

"I know what you're saying. That I'm different. But you like me anyway. Is that supposed to make me feel special? Chosen? Because it doesn't; it makes me feel sick."

She expected Dorian to retort, try to convince her that it wasn't true, but he just looked surprised and then furious.

"I know I'm different," she went on. "I'm different because I don't want your approval and I don't care what you think! I have zero respect for you, Dorian Khan. You've shown time and again that all you care about is money, your career, and yourself, nothing and no one else."

"What?" he spat.

"Don't act so surprised," she went on, vaguely conscious that she was going further than she intended, but her rage was too hot to hold back now. "Alex told me everything."

"Alex? Alex King?"

"Yes. Remember him?"

"You want to talk about him now?"

"Just someone you trampled over on your way to the top."

"Alex King is a liar."

"He's my friend."

"Oh, he's great at making friends. Not so good at keeping them. He will cheat you and lie about it to your face and then ask you for money."

"You ruined his career!"

"Me? I did everything I could to save it!"

"No you didn't!"

"He was my best friend! I paid his rent, I did his laundry. When I booked Dan Danger, I felt bad for him, I really did, we were the final two. Could have gone either way. So after a few years, when I could, I got him a role. In a small indie, but a good role. And what does he do? Asks for more money, demands more scenes, then he turns up drunk, behaves like a total jerk on set, and

221

blames me. I nearly got fired myself. Then when I tried to reason with him, he dumped me and moved on to Stacy Black."

"That's preposterous," said Lily, a little unsure of herself but still too angry to care.

"He treated her like garbage, put her in the hospital, and between us we paid him a fortune to stay out of our lives forever. Which he did, until Pippi Beach. You don't know him."

"Yes I do, and I'd believe him over you or Stacy Black any day of the week. Because I know you too, I've seen you in action myself. You kept Casey away from Juliet, didn't you?"

His expression darkened. "What's that got to do with anything?"

"You broke her heart!"

"It was a summer fling! To keep it going would have been painful for everyone. You see how it is—what life is like for us. We're never in one place longer than a few months, we live with uncertainty—"

"That's not why you did it, though," flashed Lily. "And Casey would never have dumped Juliet like that. But you made sure he did by using Cecilia."

Dorian winced. "Yes I did."

Lily shook her head with disgust. To hear him admit

it brought back the look on Juliet's face as she hopefully texted Cecilia and waited days for a reply, any reply, and got nothing.

"That's so cruel. And childish. Casey can make up his own mind about who he likes."

"Casey is a child himself. He doesn't know what can happen."

"Sure, Franklin told me—stalkers, blackmailers, crazy fans. So that's what you think of Juliet? And me?"

"Not really." He actually looked sad. "I was worried about gossip and photos, leaks to the media, but not through you or Juliet."

"Who, then?"

"Your mother."

Lily turned scarlet. The truth of it stuck her like a knife. Her mother was very much capable of using any passing relationship with money and power to her own advantage. She had been doing it all her life—was still doing it to her sisters—and for Dorian to see this and judge her for it was unbearable.

"I don't mean to be harsh," he said. "But this business I'm in is brutal, it's dangerous. I've got to be careful. I've got contracts, responsibilities, whole productions that rely on me and the way I conduct myself in public. You want me to pretend none of that matters?"

"No, and don't you dare leave here thinking I'm just upset that you insulted my mother. I would have turned you down anyway; you've just saved me the trouble of feeling bad about it."

"Because I'm being honest."

"No, because you're being cruel! Not to mention arrogant, self-centered, entitled, smug, and offensive, exactly as you were the first time I saw you."

He seemed almost too angry to speak. That moment they first locked eyes at Pippi hovered in the air between them.

"This is what you think of me?"

She was about to reply but he stopped her with a stricken look.

"Don't answer that. It's obvious. I'm sorry I came. You won't see me again."

And with that, he was gone.

Lily stood there, unable to move. She heard his footsteps down the driveway, the creak of the gate, the slam of his car door, and the roar as he sped away and out of her life forever. Finally. She should be happy. Yet for some reason, all she could do was collapse on the couch and cry.

24

All her crying gave Lily a headache, so she didn't go out to dinner with Nicola and Wilson. They didn't really want her there anyway. Twenty-four hours ago, Nicola would have been the first person Lily told about her fight with Dorian, but now she couldn't tell her anything. Lily had never felt so alone. She called and texted Juliet but got no answer. She must have gone out. So Lily locked herself in the guesthouse and flopped down on her bed, feeling all jumbled inside.

Her anger cooled enough for her to approach the new information more clearly and logically. Might there be any truth to what Dorian had said? But even if there was, she reasoned with herself, why should she care? She was never going to see him again, and once she got home, she was going to kiss the whole of Hollywood goodbye. Except . . . she hated being wrong. And the only thing worse than being wrong was being willfully ignorant. At least if she found out he was telling the truth and she had completely misjudged everything, she could move on.

So Lily took out her notebook and wrote down in bullet-point form everything Dorian had said. On the opposite page, she wrote a second list: everything that Alex had said. His list was much shorter and had a lot more gaps in the timeline.

Lily wasn't exactly proficient in the way of cyber-stalking, but she'd picked up a few things from Nicola, who could find out anything about anyone from just a first name. Nicola's golden rules: be specific in your key words, click through to page two, and open links in separate tabs. And always use incognito mode.

She found the title of the movie Alex was fired from easily enough: *Standing Tall*, a feel-good drama about a group of private school boys. There wasn't much press coverage before it started filming, though Lily found a cast announcement listing "newcomer Alex King as Bobby, a member of Rupert's (Khan) friendship group." A three-star review of the film when it came out said that Alex King had been replaced due to "scheduling conflicts." But Lily had learned (unwillingly, in a very long and boring one-sided conversation with Wilson) that "scheduling conflicts" hardly ever actually meant what it said and was a catch-all term used for everything from quitting to firing. But none of the articles or reviews from the time seemed to know—or care—why Alex King had left the production. It was, of course, all about "rising star Dorian Khan."

But what else had Dorian said? Alex had put Stacy Black in the hospital? He'd said it so quickly and so brusquely that it had almost escaped her notice. But that was serious—and Alex hadn't mentioned anything about it. Lily typed: Dorian Khan Stacy Black Alex King hospital.

DORIAN KHAN, STAR OF THE DANIEL DANGER FRANCHISE, PHOTOGRAPHED EXITING ROYAL LONDON HOSPITAL

DANIEL DANGER 3 SUSPENDS FILMING IN LONDON FOR A DAY

FANS SAY DORIAN KHAN INJURED WHILE FILMING *DAN DANGER 3* AFTER BEING PHOTOGRAPHED OUTSIDE ROYAL LONDON HOSPITAL

DORIAN KHAN IS "NOT INJURED" SAYS PUBLICITY REPRESENTATIVE: "JUST VISITING"

But none of the articles mentioned Stacy or Alex. There was no proof it was Stacy Black in the hospital, and there was no proof Alex had been the one to put her there. But Stacy Black had enough power and enough money to keep that out of the press. And if Dorian was telling the truth . . . that was serious. What had Alex done? Dorian Khan Stacy Black Alex King assault

STAR OF DAN DANGER DONATES SALARY FROM FILM ABOUT SEXUAL ASSAULT TO CHARITY FOR SURVIVORS

DORIAN KHAN MAINTAINS DONATING HIS SALARY WAS "ALWAYS THE PLAN"

"I DIDN'T WANT TO MAKE A FILM ABOUT SEXUAL ASSAULT AND NOT ACCOMPANY IT WITH ACTION" SAYS DORIAN KHAN, STAR OF UPCOMING FILM *GONE NOW*

DORIAN KHAN DID "EXTENSIVE RESEARCH" FOR HIS ROLE IN *GONE NOW* AND "KEEPS IN TOUCH" WITH THE PEOPLE HE SPOKE TO

This had nothing to do with Alex King and Stacy Black either. But as Lily stared at the two lists in her notebook and the dozens of articles about Dorian donating his salary, Lily wondered if perhaps this was not about compiling lists or evidence or data or he-said-he-said. Perhaps it was about trust and sincerity and proof of character. When she thought about Dorian, she remembered his tact surrounding Juliet's injury. She thought of Franklin's generous praise. She thought of the courage it takes to tell someone the truth, even when it reflects poorly on the teller. Despite his casual cruelty and arrogance, Dorian had always been, as he himself said, honest. And what little he revealed about himself was always specific. Alex, on the other hand, had been all smooth talk and sweet words and was always rather vague on details. He hadn't shown up to New Year's when he said he would. He'd made grand plans and big claims and then forgotten about them a few days later. And he'd openly flirted with Rosie and her own mother, now that she thought about it. Dorian had been so rude and presumptuous, but at least he'd been forthright. Maybe Alex had only ever told her exactly what she wanted to hear. She didn't know whom to believe. And it wasn't like she could get advice or help from anyone around here. Casey, Franklin, Stacy, and Wilson were all under Dorian's thumb. Nicola didn't know anything. But . . . there was one person who might be able to help her find out the truth, even though Lily had never heard her speak more than two words. She was close enough to all the key players to know what had really happened—and closest of all to Stacy Black. It was her daughter, Inez.

But how could Lily possibly get in touch with her, let alone engineer a casual conversation about Alex King? Then she remembered the movie screening at the end of the week. Wilson had invited her as well as Nicola; it was a work event at the production office. Stacy Black would be there. Maybe Inez would come too. Dorian, she was pretty sure, would stay well away. This would be her only chance to find out more.

Wilson and Nicola were only too happy to discover that Lily wanted to attend the screening after all. "Of course we want you to come and enjoy yourself," they urged with tilted heads and smiles. Once there, they both proceeded to ignore her completely. It was perfect. As everyone jostled to squeeze into the most important conversations in the lobby and the best seats in the small theater, Lily found it very easy to get close to Inez. She didn't pay much attention to the movie, even though it was an all-star-cast heist movie she would usually enjoy. She kept sifting through her encounters with Dorian, her memories of Alex, all the headlines she had read and the articles that accompanied them, and the one image she couldn't escape: Dorian's angry and hurt face as he walked out the door.

As the credits rolled and Wilson and Nicola gushed to Stacy about the film, Lily had the perfect opportunity to start a conversation with Inez. But how could she broach the subject? Especially when it was, according to Dorian, such a delicate one. Hey, Inez, what do you think of Alex King? Did he somehow hospitalize your mother? But Inez, surprisingly, spoke to Lily first.

"So, you're, like, going home tomorrow, right?" she said to her phone as she chewed gum.

"Yeah."

"And the flight's superlong, right?"

"Fifteen hours."

"I would die."

"I'm looking forward to getting home."

"I hate my home," she remarked with no hint of irony. "My mom's the worst."

"Mmm," replied Lily, to somehow suggest agreement without being directly insulting to Stacy Black. "I miss my friends a lot. The people at Pippi, they're all really great. Actually, I think you know someone there. Alex King?"

Not her smoothest transition, but Inez didn't seem to notice. Whatever feelings that name triggered in Inez, they were not positive. Her face turned sour.

"Alex King? That cockroach?"

"You're not friends?"

"He has no friends. He has targets."

"Are we talking about the same guy?"

"Tall, handsome, so English it makes you want to vomit."

"I guess."

"My mom, she's a nightmare, right? I know it, you know it, whatever. He went after her like she was Marilyn freaking Monroe. And she believed him. Suddenly she's in love, he's in her movie, he's moving in, he's spending all her money, he's kissing up to her, creeping onto everyone in a skirt behind her back, and she thinks he's just the best."

"I don't think—"

"Until she's a couple hundred thousand down, he ruins the movie, totals her car, and the maid turns up in his bed. She confronts him. They fight, he shoves her down the stairs, breaks her arm."

Inez spoke like she was listing shopping, but to Lily, the revelation was a blow that left her winded.

"Really?"

"Yeah, really. Whaddya think I am, a liar?"

"No, it's just . . . there's nothing out there—"

"Of course not, my mom's not stupid."

"Oh."

"She was in love. Got over that pretty quick."

"So no one knows about this?"

"She doesn't like to talk about it." Inez snapped her gum. "I love talking about it."

"But how—"

"She fixed him. Dorian fixed him, actually. Paid him off, took some of the heat himself. Mom would have just made everything worse. You know, most movie heroes are dogs in real life. Dorian's not. He's actually cool. You're lucky he likes you."

"Right," Lily said finally because that was all she could think to say.

But Inez had already gone back to texting on her phone.

That night as Lily packed her suitcases, Inez's words roiled around in her head. How could they possibly be true? She tried desperately to discount them by checking against her own experience and found nothing but more confirmation. She remembered the very first day she'd spoken to Alex at the party, all he'd told her about Dorian, and the way he had dismissed Stacy Black. At the time, she'd thought it brave—his clear disregard for fame, money, and power. But now she realized it had been a self-pitying, self-aggrandizing anecdote designed to make him look good and another person, someone she barely knew at the time, look bad. He'd kept a low profile while Dorian was at Pippi, even stayed away from New Year's Eve. Then as soon as anyone who might challenge him had gone, his story became public knowledge. She remembered that Cecilia and Aunt Kitty had both warned her, and Dorian himself had done so too, on Stacy's behalf. She had ignored them all. Lily suddenly felt sick at the thought that she had defended him. She had to face a truth so painful it made her cry: at least part of the reason it had taken her so long to realize the truth about Alex was that she didn't want to admit he had duped her. She'd been wrong.

Lily's phone rang just as she closed the zipper on her last suitcase. It was Juliet on video call. She was back home after her trip to Melbourne and she gave the appearance of happiness, but Lily couldn't miss the hope in Juliet's voice when she asked if Lily had seen or heard from Dorian recently—or Casey.

"I saw Dorian briefly," Lily said truthfully. She wanted to tell her everything there and then, but Juliet's sad, hopeful eyes stopped her. How much could she reveal without also telling her the truth about what Dorian did to stop her and Casey getting together? Should she tell Juliet? But what good would it do? Wouldn't it just upset Juliet even more to know she'd been deliberately kept away from Casey—and the reason why? It was still all so raw and jumbled in her head that she decided it could wait. She'd be home soon enough and could tell the story in person.

"Casey's still in Australia," Lily acknowledged. Juliet looked disappointed but tried to hide it by turning the conversation back to Lily.

"Are you all right? You seem low."

"Just tired."

"Sad to be leaving?"

"Ha! I cannot wait to get home."

After hanging up with Juliet, Lily knew she should be a good daughter and call her mum and sister. They answered bundled up in thick cardigans. It appeared to be a cold wintry morning at Pippi and Lily could imagine the steel gray color of the water. Though LA's eternal summer had been great, it was beginning to look more and more plastic under the bright sun and she looked forward to getting back to Pippi. Even when gray and stormy, it was always real.

"Can't you stay any longer?" said Lydia. "Don't come back here, it's cloudier than chicken soup and just as wet."

"Please come back, Lily," Rosie whined, "but only so you can pick me up and take me back to LA with you. School is so boring I'm actually losing brain cells."

"There is nothing going on here, nothing. Nicola's got the right idea, getting herself a job! Why didn't you get yourself a job?" asked Lydia.

"Lily, did you get me that eye shadow? You have to, I can't get it here and I want to make everyone jealous," said Rosie.

"Have you got that Stacy Black woman's number? Call her. Do it now. If anyone should have that job, it's you," said Lydia.

"Also, can you puh-lease put something interesting on social media? None of my friends believe you're actually hanging around movie stars and Hollywood producers," said Rosie.

"Nicola makes a mess of everything and she dresses like a tart. Tell Stacy Black. Tell them all!" said Lydia.

"Oh, and can you pretty pretty please tell Inez Black to follow me back? She's got, like, twenty million followers," said Rosie.

Lily felt like bursting into tears after she hung up. She had been so angry at Dorian for how he'd interfered with Juliet and Casey, and how he'd been so rude about her mother in the process, but now she saw her family through Dorian's eyes: her mother grasping, her sister naive. She hadn't considered Lydia as part of the equation when it came to Juliet and Casey, but there she was—a bright red X inserting herself into any situation she thought she could benefit from. Anything Dorian had done to keep Casey from Juliet, however cruel it may have seemed, was done only in response to the threat Lydia had posed to them. The strikes against Juliet were not her fault; instead the blame fell on Lily's avaricious family. She was embarrassed by them, and she felt so ashamed for it.

25

Lily felt lighter as she put her shoes back on at the airport on the other side of security. No longer on the fringes of luxury or the movie business, she was back to being herself. But so much had changed!

Now she was by herself. She felt a fresh pang of sadness when she thought of how much fun it had been when she arrived at this very airport with Nicola. Her best friend at the time. Not anymore. They weren't exactly enemies, but they both knew that trust and intimacy were gone, replaced with an air of aggrieved suspicion on both sides. The Nicola of Pippi Beach no longer even existed. She had become Wilson's girlfriend.

Lily felt that she too was a different person now. The whole business with Dorian kept playing over and over in her head like a bad song. For the first time in her life, she was living with the knowledge that she had misjudged, misunderstood, and been in the wrong. Before, she had never given too much weight to what others thought of her. Now she felt the burden of Dorian's contempt. She was used to moving on from altercations, but the words she had used against him still caused her cheeks to flame. "Cruel," "arrogant," "self-centered," "entitled," "smug," and "offensive." She had flung those words in his face and nothing could ever take them back.

As she lined up for boarding, Lily wondered about those traveling up front. Business class, first class. For a lot of the people she had met in LA, that was the norm, and for the rest, it was what they wanted. Special treatment and privilege. Lily could see why, she mused, as she entered the plane and threw a casual glance over her shoulder toward the luxurious reclining pods in business class, where the lucky few were already being served champagne and offered hot towels. She edged into her narrow seat in the middle section, between two strangers, one of whom was already unpacking their snacks. The other was listening to music that escaped through their enormous headphones and their hood, which was almost completely closed over their face with a little drawstring bow. It would be a long fifteen hours wedged in between the crackling chip packets and the techno, but Lily reminded herself she was lucky to be traveling at all and settled in. The experience of living in a mansion in Beverly Hills was not one she would ever forget, but it had not tempted her to demand, desire, or expect luxury. She had seen the downsides too.

The flight was one long, dark night and Lily was surprised at how soundly she slept. How wonderful it was to shuffle off the plane, through the maze of passport control and baggage collection and then customs, to finally emerge on the other side, home again, and put the world's biggest ocean between herself and Dorian and everything associated with him. She bounded out into the arrivals hall and the first thing she saw was Juliet's lovely face. In her embrace, she felt truly whole again.

"Honey!" Juliet exclaimed. "You're crying!"

"I'm just so, so inexpressibly happy to be home!" Lily gushed through her tears.

How could a happy person cry so much? Juliet would just have to take her at her word.

"So. Tell me everything," she insisted once they were on the road. "Are you okay? Is Nicola okay?"

"I think I am and she thinks she is." Lily had to laugh.

"Does she know what she's doing? With Wilson, I mean?"

"Absolutely. I know it seems incomprehensible from

here, but over there—where things like cars and clothes and jobs and connections really matter—I don't know. Wilson was worth it. To her. It all felt like a big game."

"Is that really what it's like?"

"It's like . . . living in a theme park." Lily tried to explain. "Everything is exciting, beautiful, and fun and brightly colored and kind of magnificent."

"But?"

"But nothing. That's what it's like. And Nicola likes it."

"But did you get deeper? What's it like beyond the surface?"

Lily laughed. "It's all surface! Not to say it's superficial. I mean, that facade, it goes deep. You're just not supposed to sit with anything too much or for too long. Everything we saw was for show, everything was about the look."

"But you saw more?"

Lily smiled, shook her head, and didn't trust herself to answer.

Juliet drove north, destination Pippi. Now that Lily was back, Juliet would spend more time with her at the beach. Both of them gave a little squeal of delight when they glimpsed the sparkling water.

As they pulled in at the ferry wharf parking lot, a

massive bang on the passenger window made them both jump.

"SURPRISE!" shouted Rosie.

"What are you doing here? It's a Wednesday!"

Rosie tossed her head and shrugged her shoulders. Her school uniform was so short, tied up and accessorized with dangly things, that it looked like a costume for a music video.

"I wanted to welcome my big sister home! And I'm only missing math," she said with a pout. "And while you're here with the car, Juliet, can we pop down to the mall just quickly? Pleeeze? It won't take long and we can show Lily the new pub on the way."

Juliet was too kindhearted and Lily was too tired to resist Rosie's pleas. So they detoured to the mall and let Rosie prattle on about the backpackers, who was dating whom, and how much Lily had missed. After the high-profile and highly secretive gossip of LA, hearing about Pippi's lawn-mowing dramas and Rosie's high school parties was comforting and familiar.

"I got new earrings—see? Florence made them. Theo wears them too, all the boys do, and I'm getting my thirds done with Ludo next week."

"I got the makeup you asked for."

"Which one? Oh God, no. Florence has it and it's awful. Maybe I'll find someone at school who won't mind it—me and Florence are totally into this new Australian brand that's really big in Paris. It's ethical. You'll have to come to the pub with us tomorrow and meet everybody."

"Since when can you go to the pub?"

"Oh God, Lily, don't be such a grandma. With makeup on, I look older than you. And if you want to make any impression at all, you'd better step up—I thought you said they bought you some new clothes? BUT, oh yes, I'm dying to tell you, your darling Alex King is totally unavailable."

Lily drew in a breath at the mention of the name, but no one seemed to notice and she had time to compose herself as Rosie babbled on.

"He's hooked up with the daughter of the lady who owns the backpackers' hostel, and you should have seen her face when she found out."

"Are you serious?"

"Deadly. He'd been staying in the daughter's room; took the lady owner, like, weeks to finally realize he'd been hanging around the common areas and not paying for a bed. It was so funny—she turned red."

"Did you know about this?" Lily asked Juliet.

"No."

"Oh, it's no big deal," Rosie continued. "He's staying over at Pippi now, in one of the empty places, mowing lawns, I think. Anyway, it won't last long; they're all going to Queensland during the holidays, so who cares."

I do, thought Lily, but she was careful not to give that impression as Rosie would most definitely misinterpret the reason why. Lily's interest in Alex now was nothing but forensic.

"What's the daughter like?" she asked.

"I don't know. She's got a big nose."

They finally caught the midafternoon ferry to Pippi, and Rosie talked the whole way. Then Lydia was in a terrible mood because she'd been working all day on a cleaning job she'd only accepted because she thought Lily could do it and was personally affronted that Lily had arrived home a day later than Lydia had thought, even though it was the day written on the wall calendar all along.

Lily had to laugh. And when her bare feet touched the sand, she knew she was home and nothing else mattered. Pippi was about as far as Lily could get from Los Angeles and she was glad of it. She wanted to distance herself from that world as much as possible. Lily hadn't told anyone what had happened between her and Dorian, and the secret was burning a hole in her stomach that hurt a little bit more any time she was reminded of him. Which, unfortunately, was a lot. Dorian's face still glowered at her from the covers of magazines, her news feed, and posters plastered on bus stops everywhere.

As soon as the opportunity arose, she took Juliet for a long, quiet walk up to the north end of the beach and revealed the whole story: their time at the observatory, his invitation to stay with him ("No way!" said Juliet), her accusations, and his explanation. The only thing she omitted was any reference to Casey. In that regard, what was done was done and it wouldn't do Juliet any good to know. The real issue she needed help with was what to do about Alex King. He was staying at Pippi and was very much a part of their circle; Lily would have to encounter him sooner or later. They were supposed to be friends.

"The problem is someone is lying!" Juliet said. "Alex definitely got fired from that movie—but why? Who is the villain?"

"Has to be one of them."

"Or neither?"

"Or both?"

It was a conundrum.

"Who do you believe?" asked Juliet. "Alex or Dorian?"

"Inez," admitted Lily with a laugh. "You know how much it pains me to say this, but I think I was wrong about Alex. I think he might be the snake."

"But everyone really likes him!"

"He makes himself likeable."

"So if he's the snake . . ." wondered Juliet.

"Should we tell people?" finished Lily.

"Wow." Juliet frowned and rubbed her eyes as if this was all too much for her to take in.

"Rosie's hanging around him all the time. We could at least warn her that he has a past?"

But even as she said it, Lily knew it was impossible. She'd been warned too, hadn't she? By Cecilia and Dorian and even her own aunt Kitty. Lily had only ever seen the side of Alex she wanted to see. Warnings would do nothing to keep Rosie away from a hot guy, especially if the warnings came from Lily.

"She'll never listen," they said simultaneously.

Lily gave a rueful laugh.

"Anyway," said Juliet, "we don't know what really happened. Not for sure. And even if we did, it's not our business."

"You're right," agreed Lily. "And it's not like Rosie's marrying the guy. He's with someone else."

"Wait." Juliet frowned. "Rosie's not going to Queensland with him, is she? With the whole gang?"

"She wants to but she can't. She doesn't have the money and there's no way Mum will let her go."

"Whew."

Lily threw her head back and let out a long sigh. Relieved of (most of) her secrets and finally back home, she could forget about Dorian Khan.

"I just hope Alex stays away from me, goes to Queensland, and never comes back. I need some quiet time to think about what I'm going to do with the rest of my life," said Lily.

26

The rest of Lily's life started with solitary walks on the beach and taking over most of what little work there was over the winter from her mother.

"Guess you need the money. This is why I never go on holiday," tutted Birdie-Round-the-Back. "It's just not worth it."

Lily wanted to get back to normal, but somehow, after the trip to the US, she had completely lost her sense of what normal was. Nicola's friendship, which had been part of her daily life for years, was gone, as was Nicola herself. The school routine they had shared was over, and the void it left yawned deeper and wider than ever. It still rankled her that both Dorian and Wilson had seen her lack of concrete plans as evidence that she was looking for love, as though having a boyfriend would give her the purpose she obviously lacked. It was infuriating that neither of them would ever be judged that way. She had been so confident in the way she saw the world, and now Dorian, stupid Dorian with his stupid face, had thrown her into doubt. She now saw Dorian and Alex and everything they had said and done in a completely different light—and looked back on her own snap judgments with dismay. To make matters even worse, Dorian was all over the media as he had arrived back in Australia to make his movie. And Alex himself was there at Pippi, walking around, smiling cheerfully, and waving at everyone, as handsome and charming as ever. Whenever Lily encountered him, which she did as little as possible, he insisted they must catch up properly soon, but luckily something always got in the way.

Lily's sister and mother's chorus of shrill complaints was loud enough to keep her from dwelling quietly on anything for long. As the spring holidays approached, Rosie's campaign to follow Florence, Theo, Ludo, Alex, and the gang to Queensland became more and more fevered.

"I'm in Year Ten! I haven't been anywhere in months! Lily went overseas! All my friends are going skiing, no one will be here! I won't need money, I can stay with Florence and Ludo! I can borrow money! Pleeeeezze! You're such a cow, you're ruining my life! Lily, make her let me go!"

But Lily had no intention of letting Rosie go. Rosie was too young, too silly, and way too reckless to be allowed pretty much anywhere other than school, and certainly she should not be allowed on holiday with a shady character like Alex King. So Lily put some effort into explaining to Lydia (without mentioning Alex specifically) why Rosie most definitely shouldn't go anywhere, which only made Rosie complain louder.

"Oh God, shut up with the whingeing!" shrieked Lydia. "The pair of you! You're like some terrible comedy act. I wish I could go to Queensland and leave you two here to moan about it." Which led to Lydia spending the rest of the evening looking at websites of airlines, train and bus timetables, and campgrounds. The next day she announced that she had the perfect solution and her word was final, so suck it. She would take Rosie to Queensland herself.

Silence.

Both girls looked at her with confusion and a little fear.

"Everyone else is booked into a youth hostel," said Rosie eventually.

"I'm youthful," trilled Lydia. "And I love unisex bathrooms."

Oh dear.

"Mum, do you really think that's a good idea?" ventured Lily.

"Yes. Yes, I bloody well do, Miss Hollywood USA," she barked. "I never get to go anywhere."

"What about the business?"

"It's winter, there's nothing going on anyway."

"There are lots of places let over the spring holidays."

"Then you do them."

"Aunt Kitty invited me to Melbourne."

"Then I'll do them when I get back. Or Birdie-Round-the-Back can do them; God knows she needs the exercise."

"Mum, I don't think—"

But Lydia didn't hear her; she was busy looking up a discount coupon for a wax. "And find the keys to the back pavilion, Rosie. We're getting out the designer bikinis!"

Lily could barely contain herself, but she knew there was nothing she could do now that Lydia had made up her mind. She would just have to trust that Lydia's instincts as a parent were strong enough to keep Rosie or herself from getting into serious trouble. And after all, this was better than Rosie going alone, right? Right? She tried desperately to believe it. Lily vented to Juliet when she next came to visit and Juliet comforted her with her usual optimism and faith.

"With both of them going they probably won't have much to do with the others," she assured Lily. "Lydia's a lot older than them and Rosie really is too young. And Alex is with some other girl anyway."

Lily grimly reflected that neither Lydia nor Rosie ever seemed to display much sensitivity to what was age appropriate or who was off-limits.

"And I don't think either of them is interested in him," Juliet added.

"If it's not him, it'll be someone else."

"Why shouldn't they have some fun?"

"Rosie's idea of fun is practically criminal," railed Lily. "And so is Mum's! Not to mention expensive. She can't afford to go, she's supposed to be saving for a new car. The old one probably won't even make it back."

"She still needs a holiday."

"She's always on holiday."

"You went away and it was good for you. Maybe all they need is a bit of time out."

At that moment, who should saunter past but Alex King on his way to the jetty with a fishing rod and a beer. He waved to them both and flashed one of those smiles that made the world seem a better place.

"They're biting," he said. "Care to join?" The girls smiled and declined, but later, when Lily took the rubbish out after sundown, Alex was still there in the chill of the early evening.

"Good to see you home," he said cheerfully.

"Looks like home to you too now," Lily commented.

He smiled and shook his head.

"It's divine here and I wish I could stay. I feel it's become a part of me. Like you said—it's not just the people or the beauty, it's the place, isn't it? But the people I'm house-sitting for come back next week so I'm moving on out. Following the sun. And the work. There's not much around here for me anymore."

"No bed at the backpackers'?"

"Can't afford it," he answered with no hint of embarrassment.

Lily wondered at him. Either he was a brilliant actor or he really thought she didn't know about the fling with the owner's daughter. But how could he?

"I'm quite destitute. Lucky I know how to fish."

Lily smiled. "People are always happy to help out someone who is resourceful."

"Your family is good to me. They've kept me from starvation while you were away. It was your mother who found the place for me here, actually, while you were being fancy in LA. How did you like it?"

"It was . . . beautiful. And weird."

"So the high-flying Hollywood life isn't for you?"

"I was very glad to get the chance to see it up close—and very glad to come home again."

"Well, when home is this—"

He gestured to the expanse of dark water in front of them, the distant glitter of lights on the opposite shore and the stars. Silence.

She felt his closeness—the easy warmth of him right next to her—and reflected on how this romantic setting with Alex King would have thrilled her last summer. She could still see how handsome he was, but now his friendliness, ease, and charm seemed to have an undercurrent. A smugness, a self-interest. She couldn't resist a little jab to see if that confidence could be touched.

"I saw a bit of Dorian Khan."

"Really? He widened his circle to admit mortals?"

"I know. It was extraordinary."

"So you got the five-star treatment, then?"

"Some of it."

"Not all."

"No, not all."

"Good. High flying is fun. Even Dorian Khan gets that and he never has fun. It's the crashing and burning afterward that hurts." He smiled ruefully. "I'm glad to be out of it now, to be honest. But what can you expect from people who make money off pretense? I'm just happy you have the sense to see them for what they really are."

"Yes. I've been lucky, really. The more time I spent with Dorian, the clearer everything became. I found I got a very good sense of what was fake and what was real."

Alex kept his eyes on the water and slowly started to reel in his line.

"Was that something? No . . ." He turned again to Lily with his most dazzling smile and she could tell that something in him had shifted.

"So. A master class in acting, then, from one of the best," he said. "Lucky you. Do you mind, I'm starving—do you think I could take your mum up on that offer of a meal?"

And they walked back to the house in silence.

27

After their little talk, Alex steered clear of Lily, and this gave her confidence that he would leave her mother and sister alone. Perhaps the trip to Queensland wouldn't be such a disaster after all, and the anticipation of it had already improved Rosie's and Lydia's moods. Meanwhile, Lily threw herself into work. It was out of necessity, of course, and a good distraction. As she cleaned, Lily listened to podcasts, caught up on reading via audio books, scrubbed away any residual unpleasant memories from the LA trip, and reset her mind for her visit to Melbourne. It would be so good to spend time with Aunt Kitty and Hanna. Maybe they could give her some clarity about what kind of adult life she wanted to pursue.

For the first time in a long time, the beachfront house lay empty. Lydia and Rosie drove north, while Lily caught a bus south. She had been to Melbourne only a few times—sometimes by train, or if she and Lydia had saved up, they flew—and she really liked the city. What it lacked in beautiful beaches and harbor views, it made up for in café culture, art galleries, and shopping. Whether polished and proper or gritty and grungy, everything and everyone in the city seemed to have style.

Kitty and Hanna lived in an uber-cool yet slightly falling-down two-bedroom terrace house in a trendy part of the inner-city fringe. Their black, drapey clothes and colorful jewelry fit right in with their eclectic midcentury modern décor. This time, Lily was the one who looked out of place in her linen pants and hoodie. She was a beach girl, but with Aunt Kitty she always felt at home.

"You poor darling, in two years you've barely had a moment to breathe," soothed Kitty as she poured a homemade oat milk latte into a handmade ceramic mug. "School, exams, jet-setting, working. While you're here, I just want you to relax. Okay? Make it all about you."

"I'll try!"

"And stop worrying about your future. All we have is now. When you find what it is that you want to do, you'll know."

"Thanks, Aunt Kitty."

"You're only eighteen! When I was your age, I had no idea. I was a disaster. And your mum was worse."

"You know she's—"

"Gone to Queensland with a bunch of kids half her age, I know. I guess she hasn't changed."

Lily had to laugh. "That's what I'm afraid of."

"Oh my darling, please don't worry about her. Lydia will do whatever Lydia wants to do. All anyone can do is stand by to pick up the pieces."

"So I should save my panic for later?"

"Absolutely. And meanwhile, just relax. Sometimes even the biggest disasters turn out all right in the end."

Lily's first few days in Melbourne were wonderful, despite the dreary weather. Kitty and Hanna took her to the exhibition Juliet had loved and they went to the theater to see a dark, incomprehensible play with lots of nudity (it was about the evils of social media). Lily caught up with a friend from school who'd moved to Melbourne a few years ago and it was nice to talk about old times with someone who knew nothing of the movie stars at Pippi. But Hollywood's influence reached everywhere and Lily's respite from all things Dorian Khan didn't last very long.

"You'll never guess what," said Hanna with a secret

smile on her face as they sat down to dinner (homemade vegan dumpling soup). "A friend from uni days just texted me and she is working on Dorian Khan's new movie! They're filming just outside Melbourne and she says we can visit the set!"

Lily's stomach plummeted. How was it even possible that their paths should get so close again so soon? Australia was supposed to be big. Hanna looked eager and Lily tried to twist her face into a smile, but it wasn't convincing.

"I thought you'd be excited?" Hanna said.

"I know he was a bit standoffish at Pippi," said Kitty. "But didn't you see him again in LA?"

"Dorian and I . . . we're not friends. He's a celebrity, it's hard for him to . . . have normal friends. It's a different world . . ."

Lily knew this wasn't much of an explanation.

"We don't have to go if you don't want to," Kitty said. Hanna looked a bit disappointed, and Lily was disappointed in herself too.

She felt cowardly. She should have poured out the whole story to them—of course they would be supportive, they would understand—but Lily just couldn't bear going through it all. And the thought of facing Dorian himself just made her feel sick. He'd been such a presumptuous turkey—and she'd called him on it—and then she found out that he most likely wasn't a turkey at all. She was the turkey. It was too complicated.

"It would be great to visit a movie set," said Lily. "But I really don't want to see him again."

Kitty sensed there was more to the story that Lily didn't want to share and so she let it lie. But Hanna didn't.

"You don't have to go when he's there," Hanna said. "I'll ask." She was already pulling out her phone and tapping away.

Kitty looked at Lily with concern in her eyes, but Lily just shook her head.

"Good news!" said Hanna. "He's not on tomorrow at all. Bronte says they're doing a stunt with his double—wouldn't that be so cool, to see a stunt?"

"Yeah, I guess . . ."

"You don't have to go if you don't want to," assured Kitty again.

"I'll think about it," said Lily.

Later, alone in her room, Lily searched "Dor" and @doriankhan came up straightaway. She tapped on his profile and sifted through the collection of publicity shots, magazine shoots, and travel photos. His latest post was a picture of him with a horse in a paddock,

259

film camera equipment behind him, just outside of Melbourne. Posted three days ago. Lily then tapped on Dorian's most recent video post: a ragged, rocky beach at sunset. Aha. He's gone there for the weekend! Could it be safe to visit his set after all?

Ding. Lily tapped on the notification at the top of her screen. It was Rosie, pictured on a beach in Queensland, smoldering at the camera while her mother adjusted her sarong in the background.

Having fun in the sun. Sucks to be you in dreary Melbourne.

Whether Lily went to the set or not, she definitely wouldn't tell Rosie or Lydia.

Just then, Kitty knocked on Lily's door and let herself in. Lily hastily locked her phone.

"You all right?" Kitty asked, sitting down next to her on the bed.

"Yep."

"Now, you don't have to tell me anything," Kitty began. "I'm a cool aunt and it's your business . . ."

Lily gave a little laugh.

"But . . . did anything . . . happen between you and Dorian in LA?"

"Are you asking if I'm pregnant?"

"No! Unless you are?"

"Of course not!" laughed Lily. "Honestly, there was

nothing between us. Just lots of talk—and a bit of bad feeling. I don't really like him much."

"I see."

"And he most definitely doesn't like me."

"I find that very difficult to believe, but I take you at your word. In any case, he definitely won't be there. Hanna and I are going and we'd love for you to come, but absolutely no pressure. Happy either way."

"Where is it?"

"Somewhere up north."

Lily paused. The nearest beaches were a couple of hours south and Dorian was at a beach. And when it came down to it, this was a chance she didn't want to miss. To be on a real live film set!

"Okay," she said. "Let's do it!"

"Yay!" said Kitty.

"As long as he won't be there," affirmed Lily.

"Of course," agreed Kitty.

28

On the way to the film set, Lily thoroughly stalked social media once more to make absolutely certain Dorian wouldn't be there. The risk of a chance encounter— even from a distance—made her stomach turn. But an early-morning sighting of Dorian by a fan at a beach, documented on social media with much pride, put her mind at rest, and once she banished the sick feeling in her stomach, she felt free to look forward to the visit. In LA she had only seen the machinations on the production side of the movie business. Here she would see creativity at work, and that was exciting.

Their car looped off the freeway, curved through some picturesque farmland, and emerged on the edge of a tiny one-main-street town. There was one old grand pub, now empty upstairs; a delightfully decorative Mechanics' Institute Hall, now a dance studio; a handful of utilitarian businesses, cheerful homes, and gardens;

and dilapidated farmhouses and sheds, built or adapted over the years to the town's fluctuating fortunes. All seemed peaceful until they reached the traffic barrier and security guards blocking off the main street. Beyond them, a line of tents flapped as production crew popped in and out. In the distance, there was the hum of generators and the sound of building. A nearby paddock looked like a crowded trailer park, and the side streets were lined with enormous white trucks, all open at the back, revealing piles of mysterious metal equipment, guarded by crew members with tool belts.

"Wow," breathed Lily.

"I didn't realize it was such a big operation," gasped Kitty.

She spoke to the security guard and soon Hanna's friend Bronte appeared, sporting a remarkable jangling array of lanyards around her neck and a walkie-talkie on her hip.

"Yay!" she bubbled. "This way—park in here, anywhere you can. So glad you're here!"

She chased the car to the paddock and greeted everyone with a hug and a lanyard marked VISITOR.

"Sorry, protocol. This production is next level. It's so good to be working on something that's got big money behind it."

The lines of trailers and trucks sprawled right to the edge of town and into the fields beyond. Everywhere they looked there were crew members hauling equipment or talking into headsets or mobile phones. Cast members dressed in nineteenth-century farm gear clustered in the shade, sipping water from bottles marked with the film title logo. Curious locals could be seen looking on from their own front yards or curtained kitchens.

"Isn't this supposed to be just a small Australian film?" asked Kitty.

"Well, it's smallish, but once the big DK signed on, he brought overseas interest and then here you are—mind your step—with a team of—copy that—ROLLING!"

Bronte put her finger to her lips and motioned for them to stop where they were—in the field of cars and trucks, with spaghetti of electrical cords at their feet. All around them everyone stopped walking or talking or carrying things. Then a few seconds later—"CUT!" And everyone started moving again. Bronte continued as though nothing had happened.

"And you'd be amazed the difference it makes. I mean, of course we were all worried he'd be a huge snob and demand blue candies in his trailer or whatever."

"We've heard that's what stars do," Kitty put in with a wink at Lily.

"Well, he is next-level nice," gushed Bronte. "See those trailers?"

Lily looked at the line of square white boxes with doors at each end.

"Dorian Khan could have had a whiz-bang thing three times the size of those all to himself. Actually, the producers assumed that's what he wanted, but he intervened and asked to get the same as everyone else. Said it would save money and time and he's right, of course—those huge bedroom-ensuite trailers are a pain to set up."

"Do you have much to do with him?" Kitty asked.

Bronte answered her with a raised hand.

"Copy that. ROLLING!"

They tiptoed around a corner of a tent. Before them a cluster of people sat on camp chairs under an umbrella, watching monitors. In the street in front of them was an athletic figure who looked just like Dorian Khan! Lily's heart skipped a beat, then she realized all at once it wasn't him, it was his double. Someone yelled "ACTION!" and he took off down the street like a rocket, with an older guy hot on his heels. They pelted past a general store and a horse and cart, then as Not-Dorian flew over the verge, the older guy caught him and tackled him to the ground.

"CUT!"

It was only when it was over that Lily even spotted the camera beyond the monitors and tent, strapped to a man with what looked like some kind of spinal brace.

The two stunt performers helped each other up and the atmosphere immediately flipped back to the everyday as people started moving around again, distant power tools revved up, and the cluster of people around the monitor huddled closer with their headphones on to watch the replay. The stuntmen lumbered over and had a good look too, pointed things out, and discussed what had happened or not happened. Lily was fascinated. This was filmmaking. Not the Sunset Room, fancy pool parties and yachts and social media. This was a moment of real drama, happening right here and now, that would be strung with hundreds of other real moments like beads on a string to make a story that moved people.

After some downtime in which nothing much seemed to happen or be decided, the call went up.

"Going again! Resetting! We're going again! Back to one!"

The calls echoed around the set, yelled by various people at various distances. The stuntpeople and crew ambled back into position, there were more calls of "ROLLING!" someone leaped out of nowhere with

266

a genuine electronic clapper board, some incomprehensible phrase was shouted out, the clapper clapped, someone yelled "ACTION!" and the chase began again, exactly as before. But this time, when the chase was halfway down the street, Lily's and everyone else's attention was drawn to the highly incongruous approach of a bearded man riding a pink cruiser bicycle.

The entire group around the monitor groaned. One of them called "CUT!" as a couple of the crew converged on the man on the bicycle, who despite being a fair distance away, was speaking loudly enough to make it pretty clear to all concerned that he was not happy.

"But youse are still here!" he shouted. "Youse were here yesterday! And all I want to do is ride me own bike down me own bloody street and youse are still here!"

Reactions around the set ranged from amusement to annoyance to disbelief or a mix of all three. Lily looked on, eyes wide. The conciliatory efforts of the crew members seemed to stall as the rider was now declaring, "I don't care about your movie, mate!" and telling people to get their hands off his bike. Finally, one small person near the monitor stood up and wandered over with an air of patient authority.

"That's the director!" whispered Bronte.

To Lily, the director looked just like a PE teacher

crossing the playground to break up a fight. Lily couldn't hear what she said, but whatever it was, it satisfied the bike rider to the extent that he rode off, back the way he came, rather than straight through the performing area and tents. And just at the point where everyone seemed about to relax into giggles and headshaking, he shouted back at them, "But youse better be gone tomorrow!"

"So sorry," said Bronte to her guests. "That does not happen every day!"

While Kitty and Hanna burst into questions about how often such things happened, why, and what would happen next, Lily kept an eye on the director, who slid back into her seat and replaced her headphones with a quick word to another important-looking producer type. They nodded. Clearly, there was a plan in place to deal with recalcitrant locals and it had failed and there would have to be further measures. The crew buzzed across the set, all talking and laughing a little at the intrusion, and it made Lily think more about how the production had taken over the town and what that meant for the people who belonged there. Lily wondered whether anyone had asked the man on the bike how he felt about his everyday life being upended.

"LUNCH!"

The call rebounded around the set. There was much

dropping of tools, removing of headsets, and securing of equipment, then everyone gathered in a huge tent in another paddock.

"It's the best part of the day," gushed Bronte. "The catering on this set is unbelievable."

She led the way and they lined up with cast and crew for a magnificent buffet, then found a seat at a trestle table with her colleagues.

"Everyone tends to sit with their kind. High school's never over," she laughed. She pointed at the table of people in colorful shirts and wide-brimmed hats. "Hair and makeup and costume." She nodded toward a big table of burly folk in button-down flannels. "Gaffers. Lighting," she explained. The table of athletic-looking muscly types in a mix of costume and sports gear. "Stuntpeople. I'll take you to say hi later if you like; they're super friendly. So are the actors." She gestured to another table of people in costume.

"Anyone we know?" asked Kitty.

"I think they're all background performers today."

"The stars wouldn't eat here anyway," put in Hanna. "With everyone else. Would they?"

"They do on this set," assured Bronte. "Because this set is gold. No status games, no sucking up, no special treatment. Every other thing I've worked on, the stars eat in their trailer. But with this mob . . ." She gestured toward the director and producers. "And Dorian Khan being so awesome, this is no kidding the nicest set I've ever worked on. I don't even care if it turns out to be a terrible movie. Seconds?"

Lily couldn't resist another serving of the delicious paella and headed back to the buffet table, where the line had now slowed to a trickle. She accepted another generous bowl, turned around, found herself in someone's way, was about to say excuse me and duck past . . . when she saw who it was.

"Lily!"

"Dorian!"

Lily stood there, her mouth open, clutching her paella with a rising sense of panic.

"What are you doing here?" he finally said, at which Lily could only manage a confused mumbling.

"Nothing. Just. Kitty—visit. Omigod. I'm so sorry."

She shoved her bowl back at the server and sprinted back to her table.

"We have to go. Now!" she yelled, tugging furiously at her lanyard.

Before Kitty and Bronte could establish what was wrong, Dorian appeared with two bowls of the unlucky paella.

"Lily—please, it's fine. Hi, you're Bronte, aren't you? Do you mind if I join you?"

Having stood up in confusion, everyone now sat back down again. Lily shriveled, too horrified to even look up as Dorian politely shook hands with Kitty and Hanna, asked what they had seen so far, what they thought of it, and how they knew Bronte. It was a perfectly normal, easy, amicable conversation, during which Lily stewed in a pool of hot embarrassment, unable to say anything at all. How it must look! Like she was a starstruck stalker following him around the country—around the world even! Exactly the deplorable behavior that he had suspected of her and her family, and she'd denied. And nothing she could say would change the fact of it. She could die when she thought of how easy it would be for Dorian to triumph in her misery with one look. She dreaded the moment she would have to meet his eyes.

But as the conversation continued, it became clear to Lily that Dorian was doing his absolute best to be polite. No, not just polite—actually friendly and engaged. There was none of the distance and haughtiness he'd shown at Pippi or in LA. He was smiling, even joking, not just with Bronte, whom he worked with, but also with Kitty and Hanna. She had never seen him so comfortable. Surely this couldn't be the real

271

Dorian? Maybe he was waiting for a chance to drop the facade and turn on her in fury. Or maybe this was the only place Dorian could relax. He was still a movie star on set, but he was just another part of the team, like everyone else.

"Copy that!" said Bronte into her headset. "I'll be right back," and she slipped away, leaving a gap at the table and a gap in the conversation just as Lily began to hope that the situation would soon be over and forgotten. She was just about to make a carefully framed comment to make it crystal clear that she wasn't expecting to see Dorian, and indeed would never have come if she'd known he was here, when they were interrupted.

"There you are!" A young woman put her hand on Dorian's shoulder and slid into the seat next to him with all the familiarity of a very close friend. Extremely close, thought Lily.

"I thought you got lost. Hi. I'm Sigrid." She offered her hand and beamed an impossibly beautiful smile.

Lily couldn't help thinking, with a little bit of resentment, that perhaps relationships weren't so difficult for Dorian to manage after all.

"Sorry," Dorian apologized to the young woman, then turned back to the others. "This is my sister."

Ah! Lily felt a stab of relief, quickly followed by a

rushing sense of her own foolishness. She had no interest in Dorian or his relationships, she reminded herself, as she observed (with quite a bit of interest) that Sigrid's dark skin, posh accent, and handsome bone structure were very much like her brother's. But her manner had none of his reserve, and within minutes Lily found herself chatting with her easily, as though they were old friends. Sigrid turned out to be visiting from the UK, where she was studying psychology.

"Pippi Beach!" she exclaimed. "Of course, Dorian told me all about it. And the photos! My gosh. Paradise. I was in the Lake District at the time with some friends, up to my ears in mud, positively kicking myself that I wasn't there with you. But now here I am—desperate to spend time with my little brother—and he's very selfishly making a movie."

"I did warn you," Dorian put in.

"So I'm spending most of my time on set and the rest of it strolling around museums and gardens all on my own."

Lily laughed. "I'll be doing the same next week, when they go back to work." She indicated her aunts. "Maybe we should join forces."

"Yes, let's!" Sigrid pounced. They proceeded to make such absorbing plans to visit exhibitions, libraries, and parks that Lily became completely unselfconscious about Dorian and indeed almost forgot he was even there.

"WE'RE BACK ON!"

The call went around the tent and the entire set and the party was swept up in some confusion about where they were all going next. Bronte urged them in one direction to watch more of the stunt, while Dorian and Sigrid were needed somewhere else. There was a lot of hugging and leave-taking, then somehow Lily found herself shaking hands with Dorian, feeling rather red in the face, apologizing again for bursting in on him at work.

"Don't worry about it, really," he assured her as he continued to hold her hand. He pulled her closer. "I'm very glad you came."

And he said it into her eyes with such deep sincerity that it really did seem like a line from a Hollywood movie—a good one—and the others all stopped talking and stared a little.

Then he and Sigrid were both gone and Lily was faced with some very pointed looks. She was obliged to spend some time explaining that no, she really didn't know Dorian Khan that well, and yes, she was as surprised as they were.

29

Lily spent a delightful day in Melbourne with Sigrid, ambling from museum to café to library. At first, Lily had worried about what Sigrid thought. What had Dorian told her? Was she protective of her brother or suspicious of Lily's motives? But within minutes of meeting again, her nerves were forgotten. Sigrid had a ready laugh and a blithe sense of humor. She was full of easy banter and provocative insights into art, literature, food, architecture, and comedians, and Lily soon gave up being careful. She found herself enjoying Sigrid's company so much that she opened up to her completely. If Sigrid hadn't steered well clear of any talk about her brother, Lily probably would have told her the whole story. At twilight, bundled up at a rooftop bar beneath a gas heater, sipping on mulled wine, talk inevitably turned to the future.

"I just don't know what I should do," mused Lily.

"You don't have to decide now," reassured Sigrid.

"I have to eventually."

"Why? I mean, really, the whole idea that we're in control of our lives is such a lie. Don't you think? So much of it is just chance."

"But you decided to do psychology."

"Barely. I fell into it. I wanted to be an actor. More than Dorian did. He didn't choose his path; he just got lucky."

"You think so?"

"I loathe this pretense that he did it all himself, you know, that any of us ends up anywhere through choice and hard work. So much of our lives is determined by circumstance, opportunity."

"Not to mention fate. And maybe more importantly, the algorithms," Lily added, smiling. She looked at the drinks menu. "Maybe this is the only real choice we've got?"

"What to drink. And who with," laughed Sigrid.

"It doesn't seem like a lot, but this is a really long list."

"And no one says you have to like what you get."

"You can always politely send it back."

"Or impolitely." Sigrid's mouth twisted. "Although last time I tried that I just sounded exactly like my mother."

"There's no escaping family," Lily had to admit.

"Come on, let's go back to the apartment. No one else will be there and it's super close. We can get some food delivered. Unless you've got plans?"

Lily had to admit that she had none, so Sigrid led the way to the penthouse apartment of a flashy high-rise.

"Production got it for him," she explained as they emerged straight from the elevator into a well-lit, minimally decorated space with floor-to-ceiling views of the gardens and city. Sigrid led Lily into a cavernous living area, then suddenly stopped short as a figure rose from the couch.

"Casey!" she exclaimed.

"Sigrid! So great to see you!" he gushed as they embraced.

"You're supposed to be coming tomorrow!"

"Didn't Dorian text you? Oh my gosh, it's you!" He whooped with excitement as he took Lily into a big bear hug that lifted her off her feet. "What are you doing here? It's been too long! You gotta tell me everything!"

But before Lily could answer, another figure drifted up from the couch, and Lily found herself face-to-face with . . . oh dear. Cecilia.

"Oh my God. It's that girl. Lizzie," she said with a dazzling smile.

"Lily."

"Of course. I've missed you so much!"

Cecilia wafted closer in what passed for a delicate hug.

"What are you even doing here?" said Cecilia.

"Just visiting."

"You seem to do that a lot."

"Not as much as you, Cecilia, surely," breezed Sigrid. "I've never known you to stay in one place longer than a month."

"Hi. You got my text, then?" It was Dorian himself, emerging from the butler's pantry in the lavish open-plan kitchen, holding a tea towel.

"What text?"

"The change-of-plan text."

"You know, changes of plan usually warrant an actual phone call," Sigrid laughed.

"It's okay, I can head on home," Lily said, but Sigrid wouldn't hear of it and the others assured her very loudly (Cecilia with a little less enthusiasm) that she should indeed stay.

"It's not my fault my brother doesn't know how to communicate. Anyway, now it's a party."

And soon Lily found herself in sociable conversation with Sigrid at her side, drink in hand, view of Melbourne at her feet, feeling more comfortable in this company than she ever had before. Indeed, she felt like herself, and somehow this situation of being in a penthouse with movie stars who had just flown in for a movie premiere the following day didn't even seem weird.

"Melbourne is so cool," gushed Casey. Lily and Sigrid had to agree, which sparked a pleasant conversation about the personalities of cities.

"I need another drink," announced Cecilia. "No, not that, something good. Dorian? Where's the good stuff?"

She wandered off to the kitchen, where Dorian was making a salad, and left Lily, Sigrid, and Casey to discuss the differences between Sydney, Melbourne, and London. Sigrid knew all the cities well, although she hadn't lived in Australia since she was a child.

"We moved back to England with Mum after she and Dad divorced," Sigrid explained to Lily. "They came out here together just after they married. Dad loved it, Mum not so much."

Lily could feel Dorian's eyes on them but didn't dare to look. Was he worried Sigrid was revealing too much? Did he think Lily would make his private business the new hot gossip at Pippi? Lily didn't want to seem nosy, but Sigrid was as open as Dorian was closed.

"I come back and visit Dad whenever I'm on break,

and Dorian whenever I can pin him down," Sigrid went on. "How perfect that they're both in the same place at the same time!"

"This is not the same place as Geelong," corrected Dorian from the kitchen. "Tell her how much you love Geelong."

Lily flicked her eyes to him. Far from disapproving, he seemed to be listening with approval, even encouragement.

Sigrid made a face.

"I wish Dad would move to Melbourne, but he's so stubborn," Sigrid continued. "He loves Geelong. Have you been there? It's a nineteenth-century industrial relic with beautiful water views and chain stores and drive-through fast food."

"Does it still feel like home?" Lily ventured.

Sigrid laughed. "Not really. How about you, D? Does your soul belong to an old colonial outpost? Or London? Or Hollywood?"

"My soul belongs with those I love. Wherever they may be," said Dorian with a smile.

"Oh, same!" declared Cecilia.

Over a delicious dinner, conversation flowed amicably and Lily was quietly delighted. Any residual social fears evaporated. Sigrid was so welcoming and relaxed and

Dorian remained surprisingly pleasant. Cecilia's ongoing performance of overfamiliarity was so roundly ignored by Sigrid that it wasn't even annoying.

After they'd eaten, Lily helped clean up and found herself working companionably alongside Dorian in the kitchen.

"How did you enjoy your day on set?" he asked.

"It was really interesting." Lily smiled. "And I'm glad I went but—" She dropped her voice. "I'd never have gone if . . ."

"You weren't there to see me," Dorian said. "I gathered."

His face darkened and Lily felt his old, cold manner emerge then clear as swiftly as a passing cloud.

"It was a good day to be there," he said. "Better to see the stunt guy than me, really."

"I also loved the cameo by the guy on the bike."

"Who?"

"The guy on the pink cruiser."

"Oh no. Again? Honestly, we've tried everything—"

"It was fine," laughed Lily. "It's his town, after all."

"So it would seem."

"Why shouldn't he ride his bike down his own street?"

"Because we paid him not to."

"I guess there are still some things money can't buy."

"What? What can't money buy?" demanded Cecilia from the other side of the room. "Have you ever noticed that people who say that just can't afford what they want?"

An awkward lull.

"No offense," she added. "So what's everyone wearing to the premiere?" "Everyone" clearly did not include Lily. "The weather's so weird, I can't decide between a dress or a suit."

"I think something subtle would suit you," suggested Sigrid, and Lily had to suppress the urge to laugh.

Dorian turned to Lily. "Sorry, I meant to ask you earlier. Would you like to join us at the premiere?"

Lily and Cecilia looked at him, both dumbfounded. Sigrid seemed less surprised.

"Please come," Sigrid urged. "It sounds grand, but really it's just a movie and drinks."

"If you're not in the industry," Cecilia muttered into her drink.

"Our dad's coming," added Sigrid.

Lily avoided Dorian's expectant look as she tried to figure out what to say. Was he asking her out? Even after she'd rejected him? Of course not. This couldn't be a date; Sigrid had seemed in on it. It was a casual invitation. But why? When he already had his sister and his father and his best friend and Cecilia, who had clearly been to premieres before and looked stunning on a red carpet?

"No pressure, of course," Dorian said as Lily paused. "If you're busy, I understand. Or if it's just not your thing. Big crowds, you know."

"No, I'd love to come, thank you."

She wasn't quite sure what had made her say it. Maybe it was to gratify Sigrid, who seemed keen, or to irritate Cecilia, who was obviously against it. Maybe she wanted to see more of Dorian, who was so clearly working to repair the rift between them. However she had felt about him previously, this was a chance to start over. He was being nice, she was enjoying his company, maybe there was potential for friendship that had previously been thwarted by her misconceptions and his former arrogance. Whatever it was, she abandoned her resolve to avoid Dorian for the rest of her life and decided instead to pursue the strange force that kept throwing them together.

30

"What in the name of holy hell are you going to wear?" exploded Aunt Kitty.

Lily shrugged. The premiere was that night and she had not considered red-carpet wear when she packed, nor did she have money to buy something new. Hanna and Kitty were happy to lend Lily anything she wanted from their supercool wardrobes, but Hanna was much taller and Kitty was two sizes bigger and neither of them had a taste for glamour.

"Seriously, it doesn't matter," Lily insisted. "No one will be looking at me anyway."

Nevertheless, the three of them took some time to put together a simple look of Lily's plain black dress and one of Kitty's vintage coats that sat all right even though it was loose. With good boots, a sparkly evening bag, and nice earrings, they felt they'd hit the mark. Lily didn't do much makeup, but she made the effort to blow-dry her hair so it didn't frizz. She felt pretty and elegant, yet still like herself.

"I'm so glad you're here!" said Sigrid when Lily arrived. "It's getting awkward," she whispered in her ear as they hugged. She ushered Lily into the living room, where Cecilia was lounging on the sofa in a silk jumpsuit that plunged to her navel.

"Oh, hi! You look so cute," Cecilia drawled with zero enthusiasm.

Behind Cecilia, hovering in a no-man's land between the sofa and the window, was a middle-aged man in chinos and an unironed shirt and tie, with his hands thrust deep into his pockets and a look on his face that suggested he would much rather be somewhere else.

"Dad, this is Lily. Lily, this is my dad, Ehsun."

"Pleased to meet you," he said gruffly, shaking Lily's hand.

"Boys won't be long," reassured Sigrid as she filled a glass of bubbly for Lily and topped up her own and Cecilia's. "They're still doing their hair."

"Can't rush perfection," joked Lily.

"Mine took thirty seconds," Ehsun said without a trace of humor.

"Not everyone can be as efficient as you, Dad."

"Never took your mother this long."

Lily and Sigrid shared a glance in which they silently apologized to each other for not knowing what to say. Cecilia, who hadn't been listening, inadvertently came to the rescue.

"This champagne just isn't it," she complained. "I always get jittery before red carpets, I don't know why. It's not like it's my first." She threw a glance at Lily, then unfolded herself from the couch and wandered toward the kitchen. "Can we do shots?"

Sigrid winced as Ehsun's disapproval visibly deepened and Cecilia began opening and closing cupboards in search of something stronger.

"My dad doesn't drink."

"Oh, me neither," said Cecilia as she took a last swig of champagne before tipping the rest of it down the sink. "I mean, it's so bad for you, all that sugar. If it's not, like, pure vodka, it just makes me feel sick."

Luckily, Casey strode in at that moment, wearing a fab cream suit and a huge smile.

"Lily! You look so great!" He enveloped her in a bear hug. "Sigrid, you are an absolute vision. Sir, it's a pleasure to meet you," said Casey as he shook Ehsun's hand. Within moments, he had drawn Ehsun into a conversation about his manufacturing business and successfully steered Cecilia away from her hunt for alcohol.

"Thank God," whispered Sigrid to Lily. "Now, if we can just get out the door without any more drama—"

"Dad!" exclaimed Dorian as he strode in, red-carpet-ready in black, looking so devastatingly handsome that Lily had to momentarily look away and pretend to be interested in the view. "It's a formal event, Dad. I said formal."

"I am wearing a tie."

"You look like you're going to work."

"I've been at work all day."

"I tried to tell him," Sigrid said with a sigh.

"This isn't a staff meeting, though, is it?" said Dorian in a tone Lily had never heard him use before. Was the great Dorian Khan actually being a little petulant?

"You said to wear a tie," returned Ehsun. "I am wearing a tie, I look professional."

"But it's not your work. It's mine. My profession."

"I think you'll find that acting is more of a trade."

Sigrid's eyes went heavenward as Ehsun folded his arms and Dorian looked thunderous.

"Look, we've got twenty minutes before the car gets here," Sigrid began. "Do you have something else he could wear?" she asked her brother.

"I have no desire to wear something else," announced Ehsun.

"I think you look great," put in Casey.

"It doesn't really matter; no one will know who he is," slurred Cecilia. "No offense."

This sparked a fresh round of discussion about the appropriateness (or not) of Ehsun's outfit, whether he could change, whether he should, and whether he wanted to. Which he most certainly did not. Lily couldn't help thinking that the whole scenario was one that had played out dozens of times on her front deck, with her own mother. She understood Sigrid and Dorian's frustration. There was nothing worse than trying to get your parent to act according to social nuances that they had already decided to ignore. But she also shared Ehsun's reluctance to yield to theatrics. This was just a performance after all, and like Ehsun, Lily only wanted to participate on her own terms.

Finally, with the help of a stylist who magically appeared from another room, Ehsun allowed his shirt to be steamed on the understanding that it wasn't really necessary. He followed the stylist into a bedroom.

"Parents," said Sigrid with a shrug.

"If only we didn't owe them our lives," laughed Lily.

"Yes," Dorian agreed without smiling, and in that

admission Lily heard a vulnerability that was almost like an apology. She could see him regretting how he had judged her family, and she herself regretted that she had judged him for doing it.

"So tell me," she said, turning back to Sigrid, "I've never been to one of these things before. What's going to happen? Do we have to curtsy?"

"Oh my God, are you serious? No!" burst out Cecilia, whose hearing was particularly selective today. She launched into a description of what it would be like, with plenty of caveats targeted at the unsophistication of the Australian film and media industry. She rambled on with dos, don'ts, and anecdotes of previous occasions in which other people had made fools of themselves while she had emerged unscathed and largely triumphant. The rest of the party were relieved that they didn't have to find other conversation, particularly after Ehsun reappeared in a crisp new suit and nobody commented on it. Cecilia rambled on right through proceedings as a PR manager sporting spiky, black designer heels and a tense expression took them in the elevator down to the lobby and out to a waiting limousine.

Miraculously, the same PR manager met them ten minutes later in the driveway of a luxury hotel and escorted them to a function room for the private preshow event. They plunged into an atmosphere thick with power talk, perfume, bare shoulders, impeccable suits, and champagne flutes. Dorian and Casey were instantly surrounded, the ever-present PR manager at their elbows piloting them around while keeping one eye on her phone. Cecilia tried to cling to Dorian's side but was soon edged out. She took refuge with Sigrid and Lily, to whom she complained about the PR manager's unprofessionalism and the tackiness of the décor. Ehsun surprised all three of them by recognizing a well-dressed couple and engaging them instantly in confident, comfortable conversation. His success inspired Lily. She felt safe in the glow of Sigrid's friendship and started to enjoy herself. She watched Dorian shake hands, smile, and chat with an endless stream of eager strangers, with the precise intensity of a surgeon. She could see that he was not comfortable, but it wasn't obvious to anyone who didn't know him. She had new appreciation for the energy it required for him to be sociable, and the pressure of such intense scrutiny.

As she was watching Dorian, a familiar figure loomed out of the crowd beyond him. Stacy Black. The PR manager drove off anyone within striking distance. "Hey ho, ladies, are we ready for this?" Stacy Black inquired of Casey and Dorian as she air-kissed them. She scanned

Dorian up and down with much approval, then Casey with a little less. Cecilia took advantage of the space around Stacy to breathe her way into the inner circle. Stacy noticed the cool move.

"You're Casey's sister, aren't you?"

Cecilia gave her most languorous smile but Stacy's gaze had already gone past her to Sigrid. "Oh, hello there!" And then she spotted Lily. "And you're here too." An expression of mild disappointment crossed her face. "Well, yes, I suppose you're Australian, that makes sense. Okay, so let's get out there and do this thing. After I have a drink. Skinny martini," she demanded of a frightened-looking waiter who subsequently shrank and disappeared. "God, Australia would be so much better if the service was good."

"I know, right?" gushed Cecilia. "And it's so far away."

"I swear I was on that plane for a week. But then you still run into people you know." Stacy flicked a glance at Lily.

"Isn't it weird?" gushed Cecilia. "Everyone I know is on the Gold Coast. Like, half of LA."

"Well, it's an American movie," said Casey.

"But not just people working on the movie! We see people we know everywhere," Cecilia protested.

"No we don't," laughed Casey.

"Yes we do! Dorian! You know. What about that guy at the beach—what was his name?"

"Who?" asked Casey.

Lily knew exactly who and so did Dorian. Stacy's attention was wandering but Cecilia persisted.

"You know, that guy who used to be Dorian's friend. Andrew? Alex? Alex."

"Alex who?" said Stacy, her voice like metal.

"I think we might be moving—" said Dorian with some desperation. He looked to the PR person for help.

"No, we've got time," she said, and smiled.

Her colleagues, likewise black-suited and clutching clipboards and mobile phones, were ushering out the lesser-caliber guests.

"Alex King!" shouted Cecilia.

Stacy's face turned to ice.

"You saw him? Here?"

"Not here," assured Dorian.

"I'm so sorry," Lily interrupted brightly. "Should I stay here or go now with everyone else? I have no idea how these things run."

Stacy turned her pale eyes on Lily, flicked them back to Cecilia with suspicion, but decided that patronizing Lily was a better use of her time than chasing her own misery.

Lily smiled. Her ruse worked. "I must look a bit ridiculous."

"Well, the boots don't help, honey," Stacy Black drawled.

Dorian inserted himself between Cecilia and Stacy and shot Lily a look of gratitude.

Within minutes the bulk of the guests had been funneled out, taking the party atmosphere with them. In the lull they left behind, Lily felt the mood shift to one of tense anticipation. It was like being in the wings of a huge stage, waiting for the show to start. Dorian fell silent, Casey became more ebullient. Cecilia adjusted the tendrils of her hairstyle and lifted her chin even higher. All around them publicity and event professionals ramped up whatever it was they were doing (Lily couldn't precisely tell what that was). Soon, the party was being ushered out of the function room, through the lobby, and out into the street, surrounded at all times by security guards who were so discreet that Lily wasn't even aware of them until Sigrid pointed them out. Then somehow they emerged miraculously onto a red carpet in front of a cinema, on the celebrity side of a velvet rope, and Dorian was ushered toward the photographers' backdrop screen amid a pop of camera flashes. Photographers and fans alike shouted his name. In the chaos, the PR person orchestrated photos of Dorian on his own, then with cast members, the producers, the director, through all of which Dorian somehow managed to remain devastatingly cool. He was then piloted toward a waiting barrage of reporters with cameras and microphones, where he was obliged to smile politely and answer every question that was bellowed at him.

Lily hung to the side, trying to get away from all the cameras and flashes. The noise was deafening and the magical aura around the stars drew light, eyes, microphones, and all conversation. They moved in a halo created by everyone else's attention. Every single person there, even Stacy Black, was self-consciously playing a supporting part. The PR person swept Cecilia and Sigrid along in Dorian's wake, while Lily resisted and found a quiet ally in Ehsun. The two of them stood back and watched the parade. It was liberating to reflect that she, Lily, was not being judged.

Yet at that moment, as she hung back with Ehsun, smiling, enjoying the bursts of laughter and light, the gloss and sparkle on gowns, the fixed smiles, the furtive looks and checks between those who knew each other, Dorian was actually looking at her. Their eyes met across the confusion in a smile that everyone saw but few understood.

Cecilia followed his gaze and smirked. "So nice of you to show her all this," she murmured, making him bend to hear her. "Poor thing, though, she looks very out of place."

Dorian turned on her. "She is." And he drifted back toward the cameras, leaving Cecilia with the obviously nonsensical impression that he thought being out of place in this crowd was a good thing.

It was the first Dorian Khan movie Lily had watched since she met him. The experience of seeing him on the big screen, while he himself was right in front of her in the cinema, was somewhat odd. Sometimes she didn't recognize him—his eyes were too bright, his face was half in shadow, or he wore an expression she'd never seen. In those moments she saw only the character. But most of the time, she just saw Dorian. Now that she knew the nuances of his smile, and the way he moved his hands when he spoke, she couldn't see anyone but him. Watching his face up close for so long seemed so intimate that afterward she felt strangely shy when he asked her what she thought.

"I loved it," she confessed.

"I'm glad. I'm way too close to have an opinion. It's always great to see a movie come together as a finished product, but I don't like watching myself."

"I don't think anyone does, really."

A flash went off nearby as Cecilia took a selfie, looked at it with a critical air, then took another.

"Or very few people," Lily corrected herself with a smile. "No one I know well."

They didn't stay at the after-party long and instead went back to Dorian's apartment to continue the celebration away from photographers and fans. Everyone was in good spirits, even Ehsun. Lily felt very warm with friendship and champagne. She realized she should head home before she offended Cecilia or got into an argument with Stacy Black.

"My driver can take you," said Dorian.

"I don't need a driver," Lily laughed.

"Really. He's waiting to take Stacy anyway and she'll be here for hours."

Lily protested, but Dorian wouldn't hear of her taking a taxi. He texted his driver and Lily accepted the offer with thanks. She said farewell to Sigrid, Casey, and Ehsun (warmly), and Stacy and Cecilia (not so warmly), and Dorian accompanied her down to the parking garage. After the buzzing atmosphere of the party, the elevator was so quiet she thought she could hear Dorian breathing. Was the elevator this small before? He seemed very close.

"Thank you for coming tonight," he said, and Lily was surprised to hear such warmth in his tone.

He was being sincere and vulnerable and it made her feel all fuzzy inside—or maybe that was just the champagne.

"Thank you for inviting me," she said. "It was . . . interesting to see that side of moviemaking."

God, why had she said that? With such cool judgment? But to her relief, Dorian just laughed softly.

"Interesting is a nice way of putting it," he said. "You made it better."

Lily blushed and blinked. He was gazing at her with big brown eyes, just like the ones she had seen onscreen, except now they were gazing at her. But to her disappointment (though she didn't know why), Dorian seemed to catch himself and looked at the floor. He shook his head slightly as if to clear his thoughts.

Ding. Parking garage. The doors slid open and directly in front of them was the shiny black limousine.

"Would you like to come to the theater with me?" he asked in a rush. "I've got two tickets to opening night, it's—"

"Yes," Lily said, interrupting him, then she laughed at her own indelicacy. "Sorry. Go on."

"You don't want to know what it is?"

"Too late, I said yes," she joked. "Surprise me."

But she knew she didn't care what play it was or when. She just wanted to hang out with him again.

Dorian gave her the biggest smile she'd ever seen him give anyone. She couldn't help but mirror it.

"Okay, great," he said. "I'll text you."

They stood there smiling at each other for what seemed like a very long time until the driver got out and opened the back door of the limousine, and Lily felt she had no choice but to get in.

She looked out the window for as long as she could see Dorian's silhouette. Then she slumped back in the seat, confused and elated at the same time. Had she imagined it or had he been about to kiss her and then thought better of it? Or were they interrupted? Everything seemed significant and stretched out when she was tipsy; it was probably nothing. After everything, his declaration, their shouting match, her firmly rejecting him . . . he couldn't still like her. And she . . . well, she had never liked him. In that way. Ever. But he had invited her to the theater. Just the two of them. And she had said yes.

31

"Lily!"

"Can I call you back later, Rosie? I'm going to the theater—I'm getting picked up any minute."

"No, Lily, it's serious!"

Lily paused, an earring halfway to her ear. Rosie sniffled through the phone's tinny speaker and Lily recognized her all-or-nothing sobs. She discarded the earring and sat down on her bed.

"What happened?"

"Mum left me!" Rosie howled.

"What?" Lily said sharply. "What do you mean?"

She hoped this was a case of Rosie exaggerating for dramatic effect as she was prone to do, but though Lily didn't believe in gut feelings, she heard alarm bells sound in her head telling her this was not a drill.

"She's gone off with Alex! I knew something was going on, but—"

"Wait—Alex King?"

"Yes, Alex King, what other Alex do we know?" Rosie swallowed a sob, then continued. "He wanted to go to some island and I didn't want to go so I went to the beach with Florence, and Mum tried to call me but I didn't pick up and then when I got back they were both gone!" Rosie broke down into more tears and sobs. "And now she won't answer her phone and I hate her!"

Lily was so shocked she couldn't see for a moment. Her breathing was shallow, her heart pounded, and she felt a strong desire to just hang up. But she couldn't hang up. She'd have to handle this. Just like every other disaster that happened in the family, she'd have to be the grown-up and sort it out. Deep breath.

"Okay, Rosie, do you know where they went exactly?"

"Some stupid island."

"Have you tried calling her?"

"No, Lily, I've been shouting across the ocean—of course I called her! I told you, she hasn't picked up!" And Rosie let out another mournful sob.

"Did you call him?"

"He dropped his phone in the toilet."

"Is anyone with you right now? Where's Florence?"

"God, I don't need a babysitter, Lily. I'm not five years old!"

"I'm only trying to help!"

"You can help by getting Mum back!"

"Rosie, just—" Lily stopped herself and took a deep breath.

The doorbell rang. Oh dear. Lily heard Kitty open the door and Dorian's voice as he greeted her.

"Hold on, Rosie. I'm going to give you to Aunt Kitty. I'll only be a minute, I promise. Don't go anywhere."

"I can't go anywhere; I've got no money."

"What, none?"

"She took her card and mine's maxed out."

Lily winced as she worked to keep the panic out of her own voice.

"Don't worry. I'll be right back."

"Okay, Lily! Just . . ." Lily heard the real vulnerability in her little sister's voice. "Don't be long, okay?"

"One minute," Lily reassured her.

Lily caught a glimpse of herself in the mirror as she left her room. She looked terrible. Pale face, shaking hands, sweat on her upper lip, only one earring in. It was a horror show. She took a deep breath and went out to face Dorian.

"I'm sorry, I have to cancel the theater."

"Is everything okay?"

"Yes, just—a family situation," Lily responded.

"Anything I can do?" asked Dorian.

"What happened?" demanded Kitty, who had hovered nearby when she saw Lily's tragic face.

There was no time to be coy.

"My mother and Alex—Alex King—have left Cairns and gone to some island together. Rosie's by herself. We need to get her home."

Lily tried desperately not to cry.

"Lydia," said Kitty through gritted teeth as she took the phone. "Rosie? Rosie, hey, it's me. Don't worry, sweetie, it's going to be okay."

Kitty wandered down the hall talking soothingly.

"I'm sorry, Dorian," Lily said. "We've got to sort this out."

It was an invitation for him to leave but he didn't take it. He glanced past her down the hall to make sure Kitty couldn't hear.

"Let me," he said in a low voice. "I'll get her a flight right now; she can be here tonight."

"What?"

"Where is she? I'll get her a car, a private plane." He whipped out his phone and looked at her expectantly. "What's the address?"

Lily gaped at him and had a confused thought that she was not being offered what she wanted most.

"It's okay," he was saying, clearly misinterpreting her hesitation. "No one has to find out."

Lily felt her face flush red. "Find out what?"

"About this," he said, frowning at her. "The money," he tried again. "Please. I can afford it and—"

"As long as no one knows."

"I don't want to cause any unpleasantness," he said, coldness creeping into his voice, "through a public connection."

"For me or for you?"

"I'm trying to help," he said defensively.

"With money."

"Yes, with money for the moment and then—"

"Well, we don't need it," Lily snapped. Dorian's face reddened, then iced over. "Thank you. We're not completely helpless or friendless—or broke," she added, thinking of her aunts Jane and Elizabeth. Better to be in financial and emotional debt to them than to Dorian. Better, even, to go it alone and risk everything than remain so dependent on others.

"I didn't mean to offend," he said coldly.

"No. You meant to control."

He looked like he was about to contradict her but thought better of it. Dorian, Lily had learned, was not a liar.

"I feel at least partly responsible."

"You're not responsible for Alex King and you're definitely not responsible for my family," Lily said, her anger giving way to a desperate need to make him understand when she barely understood herself. "I know it's normal for you, but I've never felt in control of my life. I have to be able to look the truth in the face and deal with it, no matter how bad it is. I don't want you to save me." I want you to support me, she added in her mind, but she knew it was too late for that.

There was silence as they both recognized the uncrossable gulf between them. Naively, she'd thought it was possible to bridge it. But it was glaringly obvious: Dorian lived in a different world and as long as she felt powerless within it, they would never be able to meet on equal terms.

"I see. Good luck, then," he said, and turned on his heel.

Lily couldn't do anything but nod as she shut the door behind him. She stood a moment, listening to his footsteps and the sound of the car door opening and closing. The engine started up, surged, then receded as he drove off to join the hum of the rest of the city. How odd that they had ever been thrown together. She knew it would never happen again.

She turned back to face the reality of her reckless, selfish, and utterly suburban family, involved in a fresh disaster that wasn't even much of a surprise. Thank goodness she was with Aunt Kitty.

Together, Kitty and Lily transferred Rosie some money, booked her a flight back to Sydney, and arranged for her to spend the rest of the holidays with Juliet. Rosie accepted the arrangement without complaint. It seemed that a week of cruising the backpackers' hostels and bars of Cairns had not been as liberating as she'd hoped.

"Florence is being a cow," she sniveled.

Lily thanked Kitty and promised to pay her back somehow.

"Don't worry about it," Kitty assured her. "It's not the first time I've had to bail your mum out. Mostly to keep Lizzie and Jane from knowing the worst. But God, Lily, how are we going to keep this under wraps? How old is this Alex King anyway?"

"Twenty-two," Lily confessed miserably. "And that's not the worst of it. He's done this before."

"What?"

"Hooked up with women for—I don't know. Money."

"Well, Lydia hasn't got any."

"She probably told him she owns the house."

"What was she thinking?"

They didn't have to wait long to find out. Lily's phone rang. It was Lydia.

"Guess where I am," she crowed. "I don't even know, ha! But it's paradise. You know the beach at Pippi; well, this is a million times better, the sand is so soft and white it squeaks."

"Mum."

"And the trees are so—I don't know. Everything's green. Moist."

"I've spoken to Rosie, Mum."

"It's not messy like Pippi."

"Mum? Rosie? Remember your fifteen-year-old?"

"Oh God, yes, stop nagging. I know, that's why I'm calling. Honestly, it's the last time I ever go anywhere with her; she was absolutely miserable from beginning to end."

"You left her in a hostel in Cairns with no money, Mum."

"That's what she wanted, that's hardly my fault!"

"She didn't want to be stranded."

"Well, I didn't want to stay there. I know it might not mean much to her or you or my bloody judgmental sisters. I know you're listening, Kitty, hi, by the way, go ahead and tell Lizzie and Jane, I don't even care. And you know why? Because I've found love. For the first time in my life. And that is the most important thing and I deserve it too!"

"With Alex King? Are you serious?"

"Now, I don't want to hurt your feelings, honey, I know you liked him, but there are some things about men and women that you're too young to understand."

"MUM! He's twenty years younger than you!"

"See? There you go. Exactly what I knew you'd say, there's no point in talking to you about this—"

"And he's done this before. He's using you."

"Oh right, you know everything, do you? As per usual. Well, let me tell you, Miss Hang-Around-Movie-Stars, I have plenty to offer and Alex is giving me exactly what I need right now. I am the center of his world and he is everything to me and after all I've done for you and Rosie and everyone else, with no help, single parenting, dealing with mental health issues and an emotionally abusive ex—yes he is—I deserve some time in the sun. Yes I do. So you sort yourselves out and call me when you're ready to be supportive because I don't have to take this from you. I've got a wedding to think of. You heard. We're getting married. Suck on that."

Slam.

If it was possible to slam a mobile phone down, Lydia did. Lily stared at Kitty's horrified face.

"Did she say . . . married?"

"She said married."

The two of them sat for a minute and contemplated all the ramifications of that word. Tears sprang to Lily's eyes.

"It's okay, sweetie," Kitty soothed. "You know what your mum's like. She won't do it. You know she loves you, right? You and your sister? You're everything to her."

Lily believed this was true. But Lydia didn't always act like it. And right now she was acting as though the only worthwhile person in her life was Alex King. How frustrating that Lydia could fall for someone like that! But then Lily had fallen for him too. She remembered with some shame how safe and special she had felt in the glow of his smile. She'd dressed for him on New Year's Eve, scanned the crowd for him, and drooped when she realized he wasn't there. How could she have let such a lizard have any effect on her at all?

But she couldn't blame herself for too long. Her own sense of shame soon gave way to indignation and anger. Alex King had played her, just as he was playing her mother right now. It was low stakes for him. But for Lydia and so many other people Lily knew, a life without romantic attention was no life at all. Somehow the world was always working to convince women that men were their only ticket to happiness. Lily thought of her own father, whom she had met exactly twice since he bailed on them when Rosie was born. Handsome, energetic, fun to be with. Alcoholic, unreliable, then completely absent. Why, why, why would Lydia risk going through all that again? But deep down she knew why. Because Lydia, like everyone else, just desperately wanted to be adored.

32

Lily: Flying home to Sydney today. Sorry everything turned into a mess. Good luck with the rest of your shoot.

Dorian: I'm sorry we couldn't say goodbye properly. Let me know if there's anything I can do.

Lily left it at that. Her farewell text exchange with Sigrid was similarly regretful, brief, and somewhat cool. She was so deeply embarrassed. For the first time since she met Dorian, they'd finally been on good terms. She liked being around him and she thought he liked being around her too. But Lily hadn't been allowed to feel that way for long. Just as she finally started to understand him and his world, Lydia had yet again demonstrated that Lily didn't belong in it. What made it ten times worse was that Dorian had seen it months ago. Lily couldn't blame him for wanting to steer clear of her family. They were constantly being pulled into Lydia's riptide and fighting to drag her out unscathed. As Lily said goodbye to Kitty and Hanna, she wondered if this was part of the reason they had moved to Melbourne: to be farther away from Lydia's mess.

When she arrived in Sydney, Lily went straight to Juliet's house. Rosie had arrived just hours before on a morning flight from Queensland, having spent the night in a fancy airport hotel courtesy of Aunt Lizzie's loyalty points. Aunt Lizzie and Uncle Fitz were happy for Rosie to stay there with them, but school was starting on Monday and Lily was determined to get Rosie back home to Pippi Beach in one piece, with or without her mother.

Lizzie opened the door, and at the sight of her beautiful, reassuring face, Lily let go of all the tears she'd been holding in on the journey home. Aunt Lizzie pulled her into a comforting hug on the doorstep. No words, just a warm embrace, and that was exactly what Lily needed.

Lizzie took her into the beautifully furnished living room, where Rosie was slumped on a midcentury couch. She sprang up at the sight of her sister and gave her a tight hug. With all Rosie's tough talk and makeup and bravado, Lily often forgot how young she was.

"What took you so long?" Rosie said, her voice muffled by tears and Lily's sleeve.

"I'm so sorry," Lily said. "I should have been there."

They broke apart and sat back down as Aunt Jane, who lived nearby and would never miss a family crisis, delivered cups of tea.

"You would have hated it," said Rosie. "It sucked."

"Well, you're safe now," soothed Aunt Jane.

"I wish I'd never gone."

"You'll feel better when we get home," assured Lily.

"About that," began Aunt Lizzie from one of the armchairs opposite them. Jane sat down in the other.

Uh-oh, thought Lily. This is starting to look like an intervention.

"Given that we don't know when Lydia will be home," said Lizzie, her voice tight with exasperation, "we—your aunt Jane and aunt Kitty and I—think it would be best for you girls to stay with Aunt Jane for the time being. We don't want you living at Pippi by yourselves."

Lily's heart sank. She should have expected this. But after everything that had happened, Pippi was the only place in the world she wanted to be—the only place that could possibly make her feel okay again.

"Are you serious?" said Rosie, going all pink in the face.

Lily thought for a minute that Rosie would start screaming at Jane and Lizzie, and they looked prepared for that too. But to everyone's surprise, Rosie just leaned back on the couch and closed her eyes, defeated.

"I'm eighteen," said Lily, with an urge to fight Rosie's battle for her. "Legally, I'm an adult. I can take care of Rosie at Pippi until Mum comes home. We can do without the car. And I can work."

Lizzie and Jane shared a glance. Though Jane was the eldest, Lizzie had always been the leader and she always had the final word.

"I don't doubt your ability to be responsible and take care of Rosie and the house in the short term," she said gently. "And I know that Pippi is your home. But we don't know how long your mum will be away or what she might do next."

Lily remembered Lydia's voice on the phone. "We're getting married," she'd said. "Suck on that," she'd said. Maybe she would never come home at all. Tears sprang to Lily's eyes as she thought of all the times Lydia had ranted about the girls' father—her ex-husband—and the freedom he had to do whatever he wanted. Maybe she was walking out on them just as he'd done. Lily knew this was what her aunts were thinking too.

"We want you close by so we can take responsibility for you."

Lily didn't push it any further. She knew they were right.

"Lily," began Lizzie, pausing as if still undecided

about saying whatever it was she was thinking. But she took a breath and continued with resolve. "Jane and I have been bailing Lydia out of scrapes since she was fifteen. And it's just not sustainable anymore—for us or her. This is Lydia's choice. She has to deal with the repercussions and bear her responsibilities. It's not for us—or you—to fix."

Lily nodded, a lump forming in her throat again. How many times was she going to cry today? She didn't know what to feel anymore. All her embarrassment, shame, fury, disappointment, pity, it all mixed together into an underwhelming numbness. All she wanted to do now was sleep.

On Sunday, Juliet drove Lily and Rosie up to the ferry to Pippi to retrieve as many of their belongings as they could fit in the car. Aunt Jane had enrolled Rosie at the private school her own daughter, Kat, attended, "for some routine and stability," she said. Which seemed a little terrifying to Rosie, but at least her cousin would be there. Lily felt a new wave of shame at the thought of how much a last-minute enrollment would cost. Yet another sum to add to the pile of debt they owed their aunts.

During winter and spring, Pippi was a much quieter place. Few people came to visit and the locals kept to themselves. Without the constant stream of visitors and outdoor activity, it seemed a little lonely. Rosie and Lily packed slowly and sadly. Life as they knew it really did seem to be at an end. The only person they saw was one they had absolutely no desire to see: Birdie-Round-the-Back. She popped in while walking her dog when she saw the blinds up.

"So moving out, are you? Just as well, really, without your mum. I mean, I told her I'll take over your clients, no skin off my nose, and if she wants to go start a new life in Queensland, good luck to her, I say. And people are always on the lookout for cleaners, half of them don't care where they're from or if they're reliable or anything, so it won't even matter that she can't get references. And she's got a new man anyway—one of the young backpackers, I hear! What a cougar! Ha ha. So is she definitely not coming back at all? Just that the clients have been asking and I do like to offer some certainty. I know some people don't go for that these days, call me old-fashioned, but I've always found people respond best if you do what you say you're going to do."

"Thank you so much for stopping by," interrupted Juliet. "Do you mind very much helping me? I've got to take these to the bins."

Juliet very kindly and gently ushered Birdie-Round-the-Back away from Rosie and Lily before either of them got violent or burst into tears.

At sunset the girls stood at the end of the wharf with their bags at their feet and the wind in their faces. The ferry appeared around the headland and Lily had never been sadder to see it, knowing that it was to take them away from the longest, best, and most secure chapter of their lives. She could still remember other big shifts and escapes from the era before Lydia brought them to Pippi to stay. Those were times of late-notice flights from rental houses and road trips across the country. They always left without saying goodbye and arrived unannounced at strange addresses, either in pursuit of a man or getting away from one. Lily had been too young then to know what was really going on. Now she felt all the pain of an insecure existence and the pressure of an uncertain future.

"I don't want to go," whispered Rosie.

"Me neither," said Lily, "but that's what we're doing and it will be okay." She wished fervently she were old enough to make her own decisions, and protect Rosie and herself from the consequences of their mother's.

33

Aunt Jane, Aunt Lizzie, Juliet, and the other cousins did all they could to help Rosie and Lily carve out a new place for themselves in Sydney. Jane's house was large and messy, so the girls didn't feel in the way and the cousins Kat and Martin were happy to have them around. Yet they were still intruders in a life that didn't belong to them. Waking up every morning in Aunt Jane's guest room with very little to fill the day ahead left Lily feeling anxious and depressed. She worried about things. She couldn't even think of her mother up on some tropical island resort with Alex King without imagining a fresh humiliation, danger, or disaster. The thought of Alex King as her stepparent filled her with dread. The very real possibility of a new half brother or sister was even worse. And Rosie seemed to have left her personality behind in Queensland. She was pale, quiet, and sad. When Lily finally got her to talk, she burst into tears and wanted to know why everyone kept abandoning her. It was grim.

Thinking about the past offered no relief. Lily saw nothing but the mistakes she had made, all of which seemed to have led to her current state of limbo. She should have done something, anything, to keep Alex King away from her family. The fact that she hadn't, or couldn't, was just more evidence of her helplessness. Here she was with no prospects, a recent history of misfired nonstarter relationships, her best friend Nicola not talking to her, and her mother uncontactable. Thinking about the future was even worse. She flicked through university websites and career advice pages with a growing sense of certainty that there was nowhere she would fit. She didn't want to do just anything. She wanted meaning and purpose. Right now, nothing seemed achievable.

She felt the need to stay positive and impress upon her sister, cousins, and aunts that she was everything her mother Lydia was not. Reliable, dependable, driven, with the intelligence and staying power to see anything through. That had been the impression she had always wanted to make, and everyone around her still seemed to be falling for it. While Rosie was showered with concern, the only attention Lily seemed to attract was occasional mild praise for handling everything so well. She got up each day, helped around the house, attended to any little tasks that Aunt Jane had for her, and spent time with her sister and cousins. But as the situation dragged on, playing the role of the capable one seemed like a big lie. And when Aunt Lizzie visited to drop off some books she thought Lily might like, Lily thanked her and promptly burst into tears.

"Hey! What's wrong, darling?"

"I don't know. I just—I don't—I don't know what to do," Lily sobbed.

"They're for reading."

Lily laughed through her tears.

"And if this is about your mother—there's nothing you can do. She's a grown-up, you're not responsible for her. She'll change if she wants to and when she's ready."

"I know. It's not that. It's me. It seems so selfish and stupid, with everything that's going on, but I don't know what I'm doing with my life."

"I see."

"I know I'll be fine, thanks to you and Aunt Jane, and really I could do anything and it wouldn't even matter, but I want to make what I do count. You know?"

Lizzie enveloped her in a warm, scented hug that solved nothing and everything all at once.

"I know."

"It's got to be worth it. Otherwise—oh wow, I know, I just sound arrogant."

"You've got so much to offer, Lily. It's natural for you to search for meaning, to want to dedicate yourself to something worthy of your attention."

"But I don't know what that is."

Lizzie paused.

"When I was younger, I had very little control over what happened to me and in some ways I think that made it easier to carve a meaningful path. You've got so much choice, you can afford to take your time. And in the meantime, just do whatever is in front of you."

"Read these books?" Lily smiled a watery smile.

"Maybe start with something that needs to be done."

Lily's mind cast about. What needed to be done?

The next day, she took the bus up to Pippi Beach.

She wasn't living there anymore, but she still considered it her home. And as long as Lydia was away ignoring her responsibilities, including all the maintenance and administration associated with the beachfront house, Lily was best placed to fulfill them. Aunt Jane, whose house it really was, agreed that it was a splendid idea and would save her having to go up there herself to pick up the mail or check on things. Lily sat at the back of the bus, opened a window to enjoy the breeze on her face, and felt better than she had in weeks. At the Point post office, the sight of their mailbox jam-packed with letters and bills filled her with a sense of purpose. Here was work to be done. She continued on to the wharf to catch the ferry over to Pippi, and the smell of the salt air made her feel happy.

Salt water has cleansing, healing properties. That was one of the first things Lily learned when she moved to Pippi. When she was younger, Lily had often cut herself on the oyster shells that lined the underside of the jetty's steps. She used to run back to the house with bloody knees or feet and bite back tears as Lydia doused her cuts in antiseptic and dug out the broken shards of shell with tweezers. Then she became friends with Nicola, who taught her that the best thing to do was just keep swimming. The seawater would wash away any leftover bits of shell, sanitize the wound, and even numb the pain. Now, as she plunged into the cold water, Lily wondered for the first time if salt water had emotional healing powers too. The water seemed to do more than just chill her skin and clear her lungs. It drowned her negative thoughts: her lingering anger at her mother, at

Alex King, her self-reproach and shame. She ran back to the house to snuggle into a towel and felt all her wounds start to heal.

Not even a visit from Birdie-Round-the-Back, who happened to be passing, could dampen the quiet spark. Indeed, she rather welcomed the opportunity of getting all the gossip over all at once. The county council was replacing the signage, clearing old vegetation or planting new vegetation, upgrading the path or eliminating it altogether. Whatever they were doing, it was certain to be a disaster because nobody had asked her, Birdie. Real estate agents were all sharks who were cheating everyone at Pippi, except the clever ones like herself who refused to deal with them and would rather receive an envelope of cash, thank you very much, even if it was half the commercial holiday rental rates, because Birdie, who owned two cottages around the back, wasn't going to have her business made public on the internet. Unless, of course, she was advertising. Lily took most of what Birdie said with a smile and noncommittal agreement, but when Birdie began talking about a particular visit from some Americans, Lily's interest was piqued.

"Spent thousands already, they have, looking for a place to make their movie. Been up and down the coast, but it's Pippi they want. Going to buy the whole thing, buy everyone out for months, then they're going to turn it into some sort of studio just to make a single stupid movie."

"Really? A movie at Pippi?" Lily could barely believe it. After all she had heard and seen about moviemaking, surely Pippi Beach would be hugely inconvenient as a location. "But there are no roads in."

"That's exactly why they want it," declared Birdie triumphantly. "Privacy. And of course, for its pristine natural beauty. But I'll tell you something for free: they won't get their hands on my property without a fight."

Lily found county council letters buried deep within the pile of mail, notices up in the jetty shed, and other locals who confirmed what Birdie said. There was indeed a very elaborate and advanced plan for Pippi to be used as a filming location early the following year. Exclusive access to all public property, including the beach, for three whole months! The weekend residents were very concerned about what it would mean for the environment and the wildlife, not to mention their own access. The permanent residents were justifiably alarmed. As much as the Pippi community had enjoyed flirting with Hollywood last summer, no one wanted anything more. They had little idea what could be done beyond complaining vigorously to each other that they weren't going to stand for it. The council hadn't officially approved it yet, but there was a general feeling that the decision was all but made and the council never listened to what residents had to say anyway.

"It'll be a bloody circus," Bob-with-One-Dog confirmed to Lily when she found him at the jetty unloading his boat that afternoon. "All the works and lights and what-not. This is what happens when you let celebrities in."

"Really? You think Casey Brandon—or Dorian Khan—is behind this?"

Bob-with-One-Dog grunted and shrugged. "You'd know better than me."

Lily felt she did know. They couldn't possibly have anything to do with it. Surely they would have said something?

"Is the Pippi Committee doing anything about it?"

"Everyone wants something done, but no one's got the time, as per usual. I got on the horn to the council, was on hold for an hour."

"Maybe there's something I could do?" Lily wondered.

"Knock yourself out. Want a lift? Come on, Grom."

Lily followed Grommet-the-One-Dog into Bob's boat and was back on the other side in time to get an earlier bus. The entire way back to the city she thought of nothing but the filming. She knew what it meant for the whole of Pippi to become a film set. It would be overrun more than it had ever been, even on the busiest of summer days. Filming equipment, lights, and tents for months at a tiny settlement with no escape. The residents would leave and the natural landscape would be transformed, possibly forever. No one at Pippi wanted that.

As soon as she got home, she researched the film and the film production company behind it to see if it had anything to do with the people she knew. No. Extensive internet trawling revealed no connection to Casey, Dorian, or Stacy Black, who were making something different. Good. That would make her task much easier. She would take up the fight to preserve Pippi Beach without the added complication of having to deal with people she wanted to avoid.

Over the next few weeks, Lily threw herself into the task of defending Pippi. She researched. She spoke to everyone she could, transcribed what they said, selected important quotes, and collated results. She found articles on the local ecosystems, recent changes to the shoreline, and what was needed to maintain the populations of endangered species that lived on Pippi. She spoke to council representatives and environmental campaigners and finally, after weeks of work, delivered a comprehensive document that had the best possible chance of convincing the council to prevent filming at Pippi Beach and maybe even take up some of her environmental recommendations instead. The work had given her a sense of purpose, restored her interest in the world around her, and reminded her that her efforts were worth something. Whether her submission influenced the council decision or not, she had awakened her motivation to strive for positive change. Now she knew what she wanted to do for the rest of her life.

34

One school day afternoon, exactly four weeks after running off, Lydia turned up at Jane's house unannounced with her luggage, a new haircut, and an apology in her eyes. Lily, who had answered the door, just stood there.

"Who is it?" Aunt Jane called out—and then she saw. "Lydia!"

Jane stood motionless, long enough for doors upstairs to open and voices to call down asking who that was and if they'd heard right.

"Well, can I come in, then?" Lydia asked somewhat snappishly as Rosie and the cousins thundered down the stairs.

"Of course. Of course. Martin, get your aunty Lydia's bags."

Jane ushered her in and Lydia, Lily, and Rosie stood silently in the hallway and stared at one another while

Aunt Jane and the cousins fussed around them with doors and bags.

"Well," said Lydia finally. "This hallway's obscenely big, isn't it? Jane, your hallway's like a ballroom."

"What are you doing here, Mum?" Lily asked.

"I'm on my way home," Lydia said. "Wherever that is. I mean, I think it's Pippi. I hope it's Pippi."

She looked hopefully at Jane, who was attempting a tasteful retreat while waving at her children to take bags away and making signs at Lydia to talk to her daughters now. Lydia took the hint and faced her children.

"Anyway. Pippi's not home without you." And she hugged her girls tight and cried a little. Shortly after, they all settled into a very large meal, during which she complained about how cold it was in Sydney and how bad the food was in Queensland.

"They put egg in the risotto! Can you believe it?"

No one mentioned Alex. Lily didn't ask any questions. She was still too angry with her mother and resentful that she should again be put in the position of having to take the lead. This time, she wouldn't.

She remembered what Aunt Lizzie had said. Lydia would do what she wanted to do and Lily couldn't force her to admit to anything, or to apologize for anything, or to change. Lily felt she had finally accepted that. But that didn't mean she wasn't upset.

A few days later, after many long and serious behind-closed-doors discussions among the aunts from which Lily was excluded, Lydia and her girls returned to Pippi on the condition that Lydia start paying proper rent. Other details were kept secret and Lily knew nothing about what had really gone on. Her mother's return instantly undermined Lily's newly won feelings of power and independence. Once again, she felt shielded and infantilized.

Lydia patched up her feud with Birdie-Round-the-Back and returned to work with minimal public complaint—although plenty in private—and Rosie, overjoyed, returned to her beloved local high school, bubbling with gossip about her truly terrible experience at a private girls' school in the city. Lily marveled at their ability to slip straight back into their previous lives and willfully ignore its recent disruption. For Lily, it wasn't that simple. On the surface the routines were the same, but unasked, unanswered questions hovered in every room. The name Alex King hadn't been uttered once. Then one weekend Lydia's phone rang in the kitchen.

"Who is it?" Lydia yelled from the next room.

"Alex King," Lily said after a beat.

Lydia appeared in the kitchen in a flash, her face pale. She fixed her gaze on the caller ID and pressed reject. Lily and Lydia stood there a moment and stared at the phone. As Lily wondered if now was the time to ask for the full story, the phone rang again. Alex. Lydia pressed reject again. Almost immediately, the phone rang for a third time.

"Slow learner," Lydia muttered, and turned away.

But Lily didn't want to let him off that lightly. She picked up the phone.

"Yes?"

"Lydia?"

His voice on the line was urgent.

"No, it's Lily."

"Oh, hey!" He affected some of his old charm. "How was Melbourne?"

"What do you want, Alex?"

"Wow. Okay. Um—can you put your mum on?"

"No."

He changed gear again.

"Look, Lily . . . I know you must think I'm such a loser. And I'm glad you answered, actually, because I've been meaning to call you."

"Why?"

"I've been thinking of you. I wanted you to know how much I care about you."

Lily's skin crawled.

"And your mum," he continued. "She's an amazing woman—"

"Why are you calling?"

"I just told you! Because I care."

She could hear the lie in his voice and a flicker of anger at being challenged.

"To tell you the truth, I'm in a bit of a situation here in Queensland. I did something stupid . . . like I always seem to do."

He attempted a self-deprecating half laugh, but Lily stayed as silent as a statue.

"Anyway, I've been let off with a fine. A huge fine, actually. And Lily . . . I've got no one to turn to and nowhere to go. I'm swimming in debt, I can't afford a place to live, my parents have cut me off—"

"Alex—"

"And to be honest, none of it would have happened if—"

"Alex!"

He stopped talking at Lily's firm tone.

"We're not doing anything to help you."

Lily glanced at her mother. Lydia bit her lip and clenched her fists as if to stop herself from grabbing the phone and saying she would do anything, anything! Tell her what he needed and she'd make it happen! But Lily stood firm and shook her head.

There was a short silence on the other end of the line and Lily knew Alex had finally realized none of his tricks would work.

"Unbelievable," he scoffed quietly. "After everything. I can't believe you're being like this."

Lily felt rage slice through her.

"After everything? Everything? Alex, you took my mother away from my fifteen-year-old sister—"

"She left her! How is that my fault?"

Lily caught her mother's eye and saw the shame in her face. In that moment, they were both done with Alex King.

"She chased me, for the record. She seduced me."

"Don't you—"

"Go on, ask her! I did her a favor!"

"Ever—"

"You know what she's like! She owes me!"

"I know her and I know you too, Alex King. You called to ask for money. You're not getting it. I'm blocking your number and if you call me or her or anyone I know again, I'll report you to the police."

And she hung up.

Lydia stared at Lily, mouth agape.

"Did I do the right thing?" Lily asked. She was shaking.

Lydia flew to her daughter and enveloped her in the tightest hug.

"You are perfect," Lydia said. "And I'm going to make it my life's mission from now on to be worthy of you."

35

Lily still worried about her mother. The irony was agonizing because Lydia was doing everything Lily had always wished she would do or nagged her to do, and all without complaint. She prepared meals in advance, remembered Rosie's school timetable, hugged her girls, appreciated them, asked questions of them, and took genuine (if slightly distracted and fleeting) interest in their answers. She listened to the story about the film-making at Pippi and finally seemed to understand the threat it posed. She praised Lily for doing something about it and even showed interest in the council decision, which was still some weeks away. But mostly she floated around the house like a much politer zombie version of her former self. She spent time on the deck bundled up in a blanket against the cool air, and when Lily brought her cups of tea, she accepted them with wan smiles, sometimes through tears. She watched her girls laughing and bickering as they did chores or walked along the beach together.

"Are you okay, Mum?"

"Of course. I'm here with my two favorite people in the whole world!"

One morning, without explanation, Lydia dressed in her city clothes, hugged the girls tightly, and caught the first ferry.

"I'll be back tonight. I'll call ahead so you can make me a cocktail."

Lily spent the day wondering what she should do. Her mother had always been such an open book; all this secrecy was confounding. What could possibly take her into the city on her own like that?

Lydia returned on the last ferry, which in the cooler months made its final circuit around the bays and headlands in the dark. She was pale, unsmiling, and looked older and more tired than Lily had ever seen her. She made it through dinner with an effort at brightness that failed dismally and the meal ended with Rosie bursting into hysterical tears.

"You've got cancer, haven't you!" she blurted out in a sea of sobs. "Or some other terrible disease, you're going to die or leave us and I'll have to go back to St. Clair's and—" She descended into unintelligible ranting as Lily and Lydia tried to soothe her.

"Cancer!" laughed Lydia. "My God, Rosie, I don't look that bad!"

Lily cleaned the kitchen while Lydia put Rosie to bed. Half an hour later, Lydia retreated to the deck with a blanket. Lily joined her with two cups of tea and a blanket for herself.

"Is Rosie okay?"

"Yes. She's all good. I just—you know—apologized. Again. I've done lots of filthy things in my life but leaving her with the backpackers was the worst."

Lily couldn't think of what to say. To agree would be harsh, to reassure her would be a lie, so she said nothing.

"In my defense, she was being really obnoxious and said she never wanted to see me again."

"She didn't mean that."

"I know. No excuse. My fault." Lydia stared moodily out at the lights on the water. "Always my fault."

"What happened today, Mum?"

"I went to the police."

"What? Why?"

"It's all right. I'm not going to jail. I just had to make a statement, that's all, get the ball rolling on something."

"Are you okay?"

"Yes. Yes, I am, actually. I think today, even though the whole thing was rubbish and I feel like a wet mop, honestly, just embarrassed and hurt and ashamed and all of that stuff—now that it's done, I also feel proud."

"What happened?"

"How old are you again?"

"I'm eighteen, Mum."

"And have you—yet—oh God, never mind. I don't know; there's no manual for parenting."

"There's literally hundreds of books on parenting."

"I never thought I'd need one! How was I to know there'd be moments of crisis?"

Lily was growing increasingly alarmed, the breath rising in her chest.

"Just tell me what happened."

"The thing is, honey—men are ratbags. I mean, not all men, of course, hashtag whatever, but you know, a lot of them, most of them, are on a sort of sliding scale of ratbaggery. Even Lizzie's most fabulous husband, your uncle Fitz, who is so incredibly wonderful and the best husband and father in the whole wide world, can be so rude. He was very disdainful of Lizzie taking up needlepoint. And he's no fun at all at stand-up comedy nights, he'll ruin it for everyone 'cause he's got no sense of humor."

"Mum—"

"I know. He's actually great, it's just an example. You've got to keep your standards high, front and center, and not let these ratbags get away with treating us like we don't matter, because that's their default position, you know? That's what they'll do if they can."

"Are you talking about Dad?"

"Oh, your dad, bless him, he's probably as good as he's capable of being. Such a loser. No. It's Alex King I'm talking about. He, well—there's no good way of putting it, really—he abused me, honey. Threatened me. I pushed back—that shut him up for a bit. Then next time he got mad . . . he hit me."

Lily gasped. For the first time, she saw her mother unmasked and vulnerable.

"Not hard. I'm okay. He apologized, cried like a baby, promised it would never happen again, blah blah, but then . . . There was some other stuff I don't want to talk about. And I thought, well, I kind of deserve it, you know? Who am I? I'm nothing. Just some over-the-hill hot mess he's picked up somewhere who is quite literally a servant, and when he smiled at me and when he touched me, it was like Christmas."

Lydia's eyes welled up through a wry smile. "That is how pathetically starved I am. And so was he. Underneath

338

it all, he just wanted someone to love him, love all of him, this angry, damaged soul. And I did. We both thought if we got married, that'd somehow prove that we were worth something. That things would get better. Then I caught him with a barmaid. Ha. What a cliché. Anyway. She reminded me of Rosie, that young woman. You know, sparky like her, not much of a thinker, feels all the joy of life. And I thought, I don't care what he does to me, I can handle it. But he's going to hurt her too. And he won't stop hurting people until someone makes him stop. So I dumped him. I talked to her. And between us we have enough evidence of what he did to both of us to actually prosecute."

Tears sprang to Lily's eyes. It had been some years since she recognized her mother as a survivor, but she never thought Lydia would ever see herself that way, let alone actually use the word "abuse" in relation to herself.

"And I made that decision on my own, Lily. Because that's what women need to do—stand up for ourselves and support one another."

"I'm really proud of you, Mum."

Lydia grimaced. "Yep, well, enjoy the feeling. It's only taken me your whole life to get there, probably won't last," she muttered. She adjusted her blanket. "Did you know he knows Dorian Khan? What a pair. A couple of prancing chihuahuas, only tall. Did you know they were friends?"

"Does it matter?"

"Not really. Just more evidence of widespread male ratbaggery. Who cares?"

"I don't."

"Me neither."

They lapsed into silence. Lydia was calmer, unburdened, while Lily's mind was a whirl. She was very conscious of how massively her opinions of Dorian and Alex had changed since the summer. She couldn't dwell on her history with either of them without flaming cheeks, an intense desire to do better next time, and the sad realization that there never would be a next time with Dorian Khan.

Lydia broke the silence. "Just remember. Please. You are important and you are powerful. Just as you are, in yourself, standing alone. Don't let anyone, and especially no man, treat you as anything less."

"I won't."

"It's taken me a really long time to know that. I know I'm just a ridiculous, vain little flirt who would do anything for a smile from a hot guy. Just—do as I say, not as I do, okay?"

"I'll try."

36

The warmer sunshine washed away the drama of the past months and lured visitors back from the city. Council workers in high-vis came on the barge, real estate agents in suits jumped off each ferry, and hired yachts brought lunch parties of fifty-somethings in button-down shirts, blow-dried hair, and shoulder-slung cardigans. Lily observed the parade of newcomers largely unseen. As a barefoot local swimming or lounging on the deck, she was just part of the landscape; as a worker hauling mops, buckets, and a vacuum cleaner, she was invisible. But she felt no resentment or bitterness. She had a new sense of vitality and purpose that could not be touched by social circumstances. Her activism at Pippi had inspired her to enroll in an environmental science degree, starting next year. She felt she was growing up. Finally.

So was Lydia. She had started dating Fire-Chief-Steve by publicly announcing, somewhat embarrassingly for

Lily and Rosie, that she was not going all the way with him until they had been on ten dates or he confirmed their relationship on social media, whichever came first. At least she was setting some kind of standard. And Fire-Chief-Steve could hardly believe his luck. He'd taken to haunting the house with his tool kit, fixing everything within reach, and had bought paint to reseal the deck in the autumn.

Community concern about filming at Pippi was also resolved. After weeks of no news, Lily called the council to find out what was happening and discovered that they had read her submission and viewed it very favorably, but before they had voted on it, the production company had withdrawn the application. Lily was so relieved that she didn't even care that her submission had nothing to do with it. She and her family could continue to live and work at Pippi and next year she would start studying. She was ready for her new life in which her mother was an ally and Dorian Khan and everything connected with him was in the past. If only she could stop thinking about him so much.

Now that the Pippi community had demonstrated how little it cared for the moviemaking business, its connection to Dorian and Casey seemed even more special and there was much speculation about whether they would return this summer. Any fancy yacht scudding toward Pippi or new helicopter scouting low could indeed be theirs. So when a helicopter actually landed on the flat of green close to the beach, all shiny and loud and as completely out of place as an alien ship, the noise brought everyone out of their houses and onto their front lawns or decks. At first, everyone wondered aloud who'd had a heart attack, snakebite or broken limb, and why had they not been told or appealed to for help? But as the rotors thudded to a stop, a security guard stepped out, followed by a stately figure in a floppy hat and sunglasses. This was not a medical emergency. Everyone knew at once: this was Hollywood.

"Is that . . . ?" Rosie whispered as they watched the figure make her way up the path, straight toward their deck.

"Stacy Black," Lily replied. "It's fine," she called to concerned locals. "I know her. Thanks, Steve, we don't need the defib."

"Who? The fancy-pants producer? What's she doing here?" Lydia shrieked, and Lily caught a grimace on Stacy's face. She kept walking, however, right up to their front deck. Her black leather loafers clomped on the wooden planks.

"Stacy. This is a surprise," Lily said as casually as she could.

"Lily," Stacy replied, as though she landed helicopters in people's backyards all the time. Which she quite possibly did.

"Um . . . this is my mum, Lydia, my sister, Rosie, and my cousin Juliet."

Stacy smiled coldly but didn't greet them or shake anyone's hand. For once, Lydia and Rosie were too shocked for words.

"A word with you," Stacy announced.

Her tone reminded Lily of her scary French teacher, but Lily was no longer at school and she refused to be intimidated on her own front deck. But she was baffled. What could Stacy Black possibly have to say to her?

"Of course," Lily said politely, careful not to express any surprise. "Would you like to come inside?"

"No, no. Let's walk."

Stacy turned swiftly on her heel and Lily had no choice but to follow. She glanced back at her terrified-looking family and shrugged. Stacy caught the gesture and bristled.

"You know why I'm here," Stacy snapped.

"I . . . no, I don't." Lily's head whirred, searching for explanations, each one wilder than the next. A job offer? Something about Nicola? Alex King? Dorian? No. Please don't be here to talk about Dorian.

Stacy stopped abruptly on the green overlooking the south end of the beach, at precisely the spot Lily had first locked eyes with Dorian when he called her "suburban." The coincidence was almost comical. Stacy's mouth was pressed into a haughty line but her sunglasses were so dark it was impossible to discern what she was thinking. Lily waited.

"I run a very successful business, Lily," she began. "I've been making movies for over twenty-five years, and I know how to make a really good one too. And that's because I don't tolerate applesauce. From anyone."

Lily felt her heart rate increase as Stacy paused. This sounded threatening—but what did she have to fear? She'd done nothing to Stacy or her business—that she knew of. What was she supposed to do? Apologize for something she didn't know she'd done?

Stacy let out a short sigh at Lily's silence.

"Nothing to say for yourself?"

Lily just stared at her, bewildered. "I don't know what you're talking about."

"Don't play dumb with me. We both know you're a terrible actress."

Still, Lily said nothing.

"A month ago," said Stacy, "we had everything locked in to film here. We had put deposits down on construction, equipment, travel, the potatoes at the local council were all on board. But then in swoops your knight in shining armor and says to me we can't possibly film here! He says it'll 'ruin the landscape and wildlife'—take a guess which one you are, Lily."

Lily's eyes widened. "Dorian said that?"

"Yes, Dorian, who else?"

So it had been Stacy Black who was going to take over Pippi.

"But the name of the film, the production company—"

"My film. My company."

"The names were all different!"

"Of course they were; we use pseudonyms, don't you know anything?" she barked. "Let me put this in a way you can understand. This is my business and Dorian is my actor. My lead actor," Stacy repeated. "He says he won't do the movie here."

"I had no idea," said Lily indignantly. "I didn't—I never asked him to do that."

"Do you think I care?" snapped Stacy. "Whether you did or didn't, he's jeopardizing this production because of you. So you're going to be the reason he changes his mind."

"What are you talking about?"

"You're not stupid. Tell. Him. To do. The film. At Pippi."

346

Lily was speechless for a moment. All she could say was: "But I don't want the film here."

"So?"

So, indeed. Pippi Beach was just a small corner of the world, with a tiny local council and a handful of residents. And hundreds upon thousands of lizards, snakes, wallabies, jellyfish, stingrays, native plants, pristine sand . . . and it was her home. This was Pippi and Lily was prepared to fight for it.

"I'm not going to do that," she said.

Even though Stacy was still wearing her sunglasses, Lily could tell she was rolling her eyes.

"How much do you want?"

"Excuse me?"

"How much do you want? Give me a number, I'll give it to you, whatever."

"I don't want money."

"Of course you do."

"No I don't."

It was all so ridiculous that Lily had to laugh.

"Bet your mother does. I'll up the money—every resident gets a goddamn hotel room and a car. How about that?"

"I'm not for sale and neither is my family!"

Stacy drew herself up, took her glasses off, and stepped

right up in Lily's face so her floppy hat scratched her forehead and Lily got a mouthful of expensive perfume, hair product, and freshly applied lipstick.

"You think you're a hero with your whole noble stand act. Well, you're not. You're a nobody from nowhere. And you are poison to Dorian's career."

"I don't care."

"Yes you do!" Stacy spat. "Because you're in love with him!"

Lily stopped smiling.

"Aren't you?"

And it came to her all at once that Stacy was right. That was this feeling, a feeling that went all the way back to the day she had met him on set. She had thought of him every day since. She loved him!

"That's none of your business!" Lily snapped back.

"Dorian is very much my business."

"But I'm not! You don't own me and you don't own Dorian either."

"I think you'll find that I do."

"Then what are you talking to me for?"

Stacy shook with fury. Her intimidation, though impressive, hadn't worked. And she wasn't used to it.

"Are you and Dorian together?" she asked.

"Are you serious?"

"Just tell me. I'm not leaving until you do."

Lily shot an exasperated look out at the water. "No. No, we're not."

Stacy stepped back and eased off her threat with a faint smile. "Okay. So just tell him you're fine with filming going ahead."

"I wrote a twenty-page submission to the council arguing against it."

Stacy looked at her with distaste. "Tell him you've changed your mind."

"No!"

"Yes!"

"How can you even expect that? You can't just land a helicopter and tell people what to do! You're not in charge of me."

Stacy turned red and was about to retaliate, but Lily couldn't be stopped.

"You can't make me go against what I believe, and if you go ahead and fight for this, then you'll be walking over me and Dorian and everyone else here. And we matter, Stacy. Pippi matters."

She turned and stalked back to the house, legs shaking. She expected Stacy to shout after her, but she heard nothing and Lily didn't turn around, not even when she heard the blades chop the air and Stacy Black fly away.

Everyone had watched the interaction and her family pestered her with questions when she got back. She didn't know what to say, so she brushed the whole episode off as a misunderstanding, which was true, and slipped away to her bedroom. She was shocked, disturbed, upset, proud. She couldn't believe Dorian had saved Pippi, but had he really done it for her? Or just to stay away from her? Either way, he was out of her life and, for the first time, Lily was forced to acknowledge to herself how much she cared.

37

Luckily, people were too busy with Christmas preparations to spend more than three days discussing Stacy Black's helicopter visit. Lily managed to fend off questions with evasion and distraction. Some surmised that Stacy was in the market for another beach house, and this explanation satisfied most. However, Bob-with-One-Dog correctly identified Stacy Black as a player behind the failed film location offer and became quite vocal about how he had single-handedly saved Pippi from becoming an international filming destination. Much worse, Wilson, who was now working in preproduction on that very film, either knew or guessed the real reason behind Stacy's visit to Pippi. Unhappily for Lily, he came to lunch especially to tell everyone else.

"Omigod, it's so great to be back, you guys! You have not changed," he gushed while running his hand through his new haircut and flexing his newly pumped, tanned, and tattooed biceps. (Wilson had found solace in the gym after he and Nicola had broken up a couple of months ago when she moved on to another production company in London.) Lily attempted to keep the conversation light and well away from Dorian Khan and Stacy Black, but of course it was impossible.

"I'm so sorry," Wilson went on unapologetically. "You must have wondered where I've been all year—there was so much to do in the LA office and then when I got here last month I wanted to visit, but Stacy was so down on even the mention of Pippi Beach and you know how it is with her. Then when she asked me to book the chopper I was like, wow, this is triple-shot-Frappuccino serious. I don't know what you did to Dorian, Lily, but you have to stop. Seriously."

"What?" snapped Lydia.

"It's nothing, Mum."

"Is that why she came?"

"No," said Juliet.

"Yes," said Wilson.

"Does it matter?" begged Lily.

"You know what we always say: the only thing that matters is what matters to Stacy."

"I do not matter to her."

"Well, duh, but Dorian does and that helicopter cost

two grand. All jokes aside, Lily, you have to stay out of Dorian's grille."

"Wait, wait, wait," crowed Lydia. "That woman paid two thousand dollars to tell Lily to stay away from Dorian Khan?" She burst into laughter. "Tell her I'd do it for half! And Lily would do it for free!"

Lily squirmed.

"It's nothing to laugh at," Wilson claimed, a little miffed that everyone seemed to think it was so funny.

"Lily hates Dorian," Rosie explained.

"Always has," Lydia guffawed. "That's so hilarious. Like paying a shark to swim! Ha ha!"

"Remember that time?" Juliet smiled, turning to Lily. "You said you wouldn't even walk to the end of the jetty with him."

Lily nodded, not trusting herself to speak.

"But then you did. I saw you," Rosie added. "You should have pushed him in."

"I wanted to at the time," Lily had to admit.

As soon as she could, she made her excuses and escaped for a solitary walk at the north end of the beach. How humiliating to have her own words and feelings flung back at her like that, now that everything had changed.

Time sped up as the weeks rushed toward the end of

the year. Juliet started spending most of her time up at Pippi, and preparations were underway for a big family Christmas.

"It's going to be a good one," Lily asserted firmly to Juliet. "The whole family all together, like when we were little. And your parents will be here for a whole week!" Aunt Lizzie and Uncle Fitz were notoriously difficult to pin down. "No backpackers, no movie stars."

Juliet smiled. "What movie stars? I don't know any movie stars," she joked, and Lily regretted even mentioning them.

Lily and her mother opened up the back pavilion and cleaned it together, excited about the prospect of another summer.

"You'll never guess what I heard," said Lydia.

"What?"

"Guess which two boys are coming back to the cliff house!"

"No."

"Yes."

"Definitely?"

"Ever so."

Lily turned away and stuck her head in a cupboard to hide her flushed face.

"Wow. Wouldn't have thought that," she said loudly to a pile of beach towels.

"Maybe somebody likes somebody after all."

Lily pulled her head out of the cupboard in alarm.

"Who told you that?"

Lydia stopped dusting, surprised at Lily's tone.

"You did."

"I did not."

"Yes you did. You say it all the time. You think Casey loves Juliet and Juliet loves Casey. What's your problem?"

"Oh. Oh, of course."

"Who did you think I was talking about?"

"Nobody."

"Dorian Khan?"

Lydia put on a surprisingly accurate fake English accent.

"Darling, I would love you, but my heart is a very tiny little piece of stone, shaped like a luxury yacht. Also, if I kissed you, it might ruin my hair."

Lily laughed tightly, pinched with regret at having ever shared such an opinion. Lydia found herself funny enough not to notice.

That afternoon on the deck, Lily carefully packaged the news for Juliet, who took it with surprising equanimity.

"Casey's coming back! Wow. Great!" She smiled. "It'll be so nice to see him again. I mean, he might not want to see us at all, which is totally fine. If they come here with that yacht thing, he won't even need to pass by our house."

At that very moment the ferry tooted as it backed away from the jetty, leaving two tall men with backpacks.

"Surely not!"

"Oh my God!"

Each of them felt a pang of panic—I am so NOT READY. And then each mentally cursed herself for feeling self-conscious about an encounter that would at most be a casual wave from afar to a boy she really didn't know that well anymore and hadn't seen in months, who most likely didn't care about her. For Lily, the feeling was most uncomfortable because it was so unfamiliar. But she knew exactly what it was, as though she were finally following a part written for her years ago. This is what they've been talking about and acting out in novels and movies and TV my whole life, she thought. This is what it is to have a crush on someone! It was just like being out of control in the surf. She was riding a surge of need that she had seen so often in her mother's face. She cringed as Lydia hurtled out of the house and dangled over the deck railings as though the two young men were not

356

just walking by on the only possible path but had come to see her especially. Oh God, why had they come here at all? For Juliet. Of course, for Juliet. Lily shot a look at her cousin, whose face was frozen in a kind of half-expectant smile of surprise. How conspicuous or weird would it be if she just slipped inside now? Too late.

"Ahoy!" Lydia called out.

"Ahoy!" Casey shouted back.

"So you couldn't keep away!"

Casey practically jogged up to the deck and smothered all three of them with hugs while Dorian hung back.

"It's so great to see you all! So great!" he repeated, looking only at Juliet. "So glad you're here. I was worried . . . I dunno . . . I thought maybe you wouldn't be."

Pause. Casey and Juliet looked into each other's smiling faces and eleven and a half months disappeared for them, along with Lydia, Lily, and Dorian, who were stranded outside their bubble.

"You want dinner?" Lydia asked eventually. "It's almost six—you can't have any food in those bags." She flung a look over her shoulder at Dorian. "I guess you can stay too." She turned to Lily and winked. "If you're allowed."

Lily crumpled a little inside. Luckily Dorian didn't seem to have heard that last remark. He and Casey readily accepted the invitation and took seats at the table, surrounded on all sides by the aunts, uncles, and cousins. Casey was delighted by everyone and everything; Dorian was quiet but not grave. Over glasses of wine, big bowls of pasta, and Casey's exuberant monologue about the entire year's activities, everyone relaxed and Dorian escaped much notice. But not Lily's. She was painfully aware of every glance, every expression, every gesture. What was he thinking? Why was he here? Would she ever get to talk to him alone? When would her mother say something ridiculous? Luckily, Lydia was too charmed by Casey to be very embarrassing. Everyone could see his open delight at being there again. Juliet blossomed in his presence. When darkness fell and Dorian retreated to the cliff house alone, Juliet and Casey walked on the beach in the moonlight, where the hope and promise of New Year's Eve was finally sealed with murmured declarations and a kiss.

"Can you believe it?" Juliet said to Lily later. "The messages I sent to Casey through Cecilia never got through! Things got all mixed up. She's got too many social media accounts. He thought I had his number all along and I was the one deliberately avoiding him! Isn't that weird?"

Weird—or a deliberate plan, Lily thought ruefully.

But at least whatever roadblocks Dorian and Cecilia had built were now gone. The way ahead for the cutest couple ever was clear.

"And guess what? He's actually asked me to join him on the Gold Coast next year! For, like, six months!" Juliet gushed.

"Are you going to go?"

"No, I have uni," said Juliet indignantly. "I'm not going to sit around and just be a girlfriend."

"That is not a thing people do anymore," Lily agreed.

"Not full-time."

"Weekends only."

"Absolutely."

They turned out the light and Juliet whispered to Lily that she had never ever been so happy to be alive. No matter what happened in the future, and whatever had happened in the past, she would always have this day—when she embraced and was embraced by a person who made the rest of the world fall away.

38

The next morning, Lily wandered out to the deck in her pajamas and smiled to see Juliet already out at the end of the jetty, swimming and laughing with Casey. How much had changed! This time last year Casey had been a stranger and Juliet was so reserved around him. Now he was part of the family and Juliet was bubbling with happiness.

But. What was Lily to do? For all this change, she felt she had very little to show except for her university enrollment and a squirming kind of agony that the person she most wanted to talk to about it was Dorian Khan. She squinted up at the cliff house and wondered what would happen when she finally got to speak to him on his own. And when would that be? This morning? Now? Ever? She scurried back to her room in search of some equilibrium, but within minutes found herself agonizing over what to wear and had to sit down and give herself a stern talking-to. What she wore or how she did her hair was irrelevant to anyone's happiness but her own. She slipped into the swimsuit on top of the pile, glad that it happened to be her favorite and also happened to be flattering. And anyway, she might not even get to spend any time with Dorian today at all. But she hoped she would. How much, she hardly realized herself until she arrived on the deck and saw Dorian striding toward her. She felt physically sick with anticipation. Why was it that she used to be so capable of saying anything that came into her mind and yet now she felt like a big wet frog with an empty brain and bulging, desperate eyes? Oh dear.

"Would you like to go for a walk?" Dorian asked, with something of his past abruptness.

"Yes," Lily declared a little too loudly, and steeled herself.

They strolled up to the north end together in silence. Lily made sure to keep her distance so their hands wouldn't accidentally brush. But with the sound of the water boosting her spirits and no pressure to look at each other as they walked side by side, after some minutes Lily felt safe enough to say what was on her mind.

"I've decided to study environmental science next year," she began, her eyes on the sand.

"Good for you."

"I want to advocate for places like Pippi. Protect natural spaces from overdevelopment."

Dorian stayed silent beside her.

"I know what you did for Pippi," she continued. "I'm really grateful—everyone's really grateful."

"They know?"

"Well, they don't know it was you. Bob-with-One-Dog is taking all the credit for single-handedly fending off Stacy Black and her helicopter. But I'm the one who wrote to the council."

"Lily, I'm so sorry," Dorian said suddenly.

Lily glanced at his troubled face. She recognized his expression immediately—the same one she'd so often mistaken for anger or disdain. He was embarrassed.

"I told her from the start Pippi was out of the question. She just got it in her head that . . . maybe . . . if you—"

"It's okay," Lily said, and Dorian let out a small sigh of relief. "It was quite funny, actually."

"I wish I could see the humor in it," he said grimly. "I can't believe she ambushed you like that, put it all on you—the whole weight of my 'career'—as if filming at Pippi is going to make or break this film or my career or anything! It won't."

Lily heard anger creep into his voice and she was

362

surprised. A year ago, Dorian had seemed much more passionate about his work than anything else.

"She only fought so hard for it because she hates being told no," he said.

The memory of the times Lily had said no to Dorian hung in the air between them.

"It's rare for her to come up against someone who can't be bought out. She's come to expect that everyone has a price," he added.

"Then I feel sorry for her."

"So do I—when she's not flying around in helicopters harassing people. She's been treated really badly so many times. What happened with Alex King isn't even the worst of it."

Lily felt her stomach sink, as it did every time she thought about Alex. How he had used her mother was unforgivable, and he had done it before and worse.

"I'm sorry, Lily, I hope this isn't overstepping a boundary, but I know what happened with your mother after she ran off with Alex."

Lily's face burned with embarrassment, and fury at being embarrassed when Alex was the one in the wrong.

"Alex called me, told me he was in trouble with the law, blamed your mother. And asked me for money," Dorian explained.

"We were on his list too."

"I didn't help him. Not this time. But I'm sorry for all the times that I did. I knew what kind of person he was when he showed up at Pippi and I should have told you, or someone, or at least gotten him to leave, then none of it would have happened. I understand if you blame me; I blame myself too. Stacy doesn't want anyone to know what happened, but I could have said something and kept her out of it. Truth is, I was ashamed of the connection myself."

"It's okay," Lily interrupted. "It's over now."

She didn't blame him any more than she blamed herself. She wished she'd warned Lydia about Alex too, but knowing her mother, at the time it probably wouldn't have done any good. But things were different now.

"My mum's helping with the prosecution," Lily said, "along with another woman she met at the resort."

Dorian nodded.

"I'm glad. Let me know if I can help in any way."

"She can handle it."

"Yes. Of course."

A comfortable silence grew between them as they made their way to the top of the north end. Without looking at each other, they perched side by side on a large rock. They sat in the quiet relief of apologies offered and forgiveness granted and took in the view spread out before them of sand, water, bushland, and sky.

"So peaceful," whispered Lily. "The way it should be."

"Pippi Beach is lucky it has you to fight for it."

Lily's stomach tightened.

"I'm sorry, I have to know," he said. "If you feel the same as you did in LA, then I'll leave Pippi and never bother you again. I promise."

Lily turned to look at his soft, vulnerable face. A face that she had misunderstood so many times was finally open to her with just a simple question.

"Please tell me the truth," he said.

And Lily kissed him. It was a gentle, delicate kiss. They both felt surprise at such a tender moment shared between them so soon, but Lily knew it was right.

"I was so wrong to judge you," she began, but Dorian cut her off.

"No you weren't! I was awful."

"I was worse!"

Dorian smiled at her and it was like the sun melting the last barriers between them. There was no stiffness or awkwardness and nothing left to hide. It was the most intense relief she'd ever felt. The ocean looked bluer, the cicadas screamed louder, she could taste the salt in the air, and she could see her own reflection in Dorian's dark eyes.

"Can I ask . . ." He hesitated.

Lily reached out and squeezed his hand.

"What changed?"

She contemplated the question for a moment. Had it really been that sudden? To an outsider, maybe. But she had felt something brewing for a while now. She'd just refused to acknowledge it.

"Maybe I never really disliked you at all."

"But you were right when you said—"

"Please don't remember what I said!"

"Arrogant, self-centered, entitled, smug, offensive—"

"No!"

"And then controlling."

"I'm so sorry!"

"I thought of nothing else for days, weeks afterward. Both times."

"I was upset."

"It was the truth. And I needed to hear it. So when Stacy told me . . ."

"What? That I'm poison to your career?"

"She said that too."

"And what else?"

He smiled and drew her closer.

"She gave me hope."

They kissed again and walked back down the beach talking of other, more familiar things. For the first time together, they each felt seen and understood, and a whole new world opened up before them.

39

"What's up with you?" Juliet asked.

"Nothing," squeaked Lily.

"Yes there is, you're all smiley and dreamy. What's going on?"

Big breath.

"Well. It's like this. Um. Okay, Dorian and I . . ."

"No!"

"Are . . ."

"You are not!"

"Actually, kind of, yes we are!"

Juliet squealed, Lily squealed, and they hugged and stared at each other in amazement that such a thing could possibly be true.

"But how? When? Why? This is outrageous—I thought he was the worst!"

"So did I! This is the thing—I was wrong!"

"You're never wrong."

"Well, okay, I made some assumptions from which I drew some incorrect conclusions and on top of that, I was just stupid!"

The words rushed out in a torrent as Lily explained in how many ways Dorian was actually not the stand-offish, stuck-up, avaricious, arrogant monster she had previously thought.

"I can hardly believe it!" said Juliet.

"Please, you have to," laughed Lily. "If you don't believe me, no one else will. Everyone thinks he's so terrible—completely unjustly, I have to add—that I'm going to need your help to convince them otherwise."

"But how did it happen exactly? You really didn't like him. When did you realize that you did?"

"I don't know. It seemed to happen gradually, but I think it might have been the moment I turned down his offer of a private plane!"

Juliet was always ready to see the best in people. She stood by Lily that evening on the deck in front of absolutely everyone—Aunt Lizzie, Uncle Fitz, Aunt Jane, Uncle Charles, Lydia, Rosie, and all the cousins— as they announced they were both going up to the cliff house for dinner.

"Ugh. Why?" groaned Lydia. "I mean, of course I

369

know why for you," she added, looking at Juliet, "but you'll just be in the way," she said to Lily.

"Dorian," Lily announced a little too loudly, "has invited me."

Lydia made a face.

"So? Who cares what he wants! Bloody movie star."

"Lydia," warned Lizzie.

"Well, he is," Lydia mumbled. "Thinks he can have whatever he wants. Lily, if I've taught you anything this past year, and I hope I have, it's that you don't have to let guys like that boss you around."

"I want to be with him."

"No you don't."

"Yes I do!"

Rosie and Kat squealed and started peppering her with questions. Juliet jumped up and down and clapped her hands, and Uncle Charles said, "Wait, who are we talking about here?" All the while, Lydia ranted at full volume that no daughter of hers was going to sell out for fame and money, and anyway if it was official, why wasn't it on the socials? He must just be using her for his own convenience and she was having none of it. But her ranting was lost in a fresh round of squeals as the lightning-fingered Rosie found Dorian's latest post—two pippi shells on the smooth sand at the north end, bathed in golden afternoon sun. And if you looked hard enough, the two shells made the shape of a lopsided heart.

"So," bellowed Lydia. "That doesn't mean anything."

"But he's following her!" squealed Rosie.

"I follow lots of people."

"Dorian Khan doesn't follow anybody."

As the younger ones tried to explain to the older ones the significance and intricacies of who followed whom and how this sign most definitely meant nothing but love, Lily snatched Juliet's hand. They escaped up to the cliff house together and didn't come back home until the moon was very high.

40

"Put the telescope down, Lydia," said Aunt Jane as the two sisters lounged on the deck on Christmas Eve.

"I'm just—"

"Down!"

"You never let me have any fun."

Lydia pouted as she placed the telescope in her lap but kept her hand on it, ready to pick it up again as soon as Jane left the deck.

"There's a beautiful yacht out there," she complained.

"You can look at the yachts."

Lydia didn't want to look at the yachts. She wanted to look at Dorian and Lily on the north end of the beach, sitting in the shade of a rock, talking quietly, in their own bubble of present attention and future hopes.

Juliet and Casey were in the kitchen making dinner for everyone. Fire-Chief-Steve, now Steve-Lydia's-

Boyfriend, was on the jetty talking boats with Charles. Lizzie and Fitz were out on the water kayaking strongly through a vigorous discussion. Lizzie's laughter drifted over the water to the deck like a ringing bell, echoed by an occasional ripple of giggles or squeals from the younger ones up on the back lawn.

Jane sighed and leaned back in her deck chair.

"I love it when we're all together like this," she murmured. "Remember when all the children were little, how loud it always was? How quickly the time goes. I wish we could bottle it. Put moments in a bottle. That would be good."

They lapsed into silence and surveyed the glittering bay before them. Dorian and Lily had disappeared among the rocks. Lizzie and Fitz paddled beyond them and around the headland. Steve and Charles came to some sort of satisfactory conclusion regarding the boats and loped back to their seats on the deck.

Lydia reached for Fire-Chief-Steve's hand. He took it, smiled at her, and then returned his eyes to the water.

"Better be heading home," he said.

"I thought you were staying!" said Jane, surprised.

"Nah, my daughter's here."

"You go," urged Lydia. "Go on, see you tomorrow."

They kissed briefly, softly, then he was gone.

"He's nice," Jane mused, and wondered if this one would last.

"It doesn't matter," said Lydia, as if answering Jane's unspoken question.

"What?"

"Whether it, you know, lasts. I don't need a man to make me happy. Whether it starts, finishes, goes on forever—we're all just bumbling about in the dark, aren't we? I mean, they're so happy now."

She threw out a gesture to the headland that took in Dorian and Lily and also Lizzie and Fitz. "And now is forever in a way, isn't it?"

"Who said that?"

"I don't know. I did."

As the sun went down, Lily and Dorian strolled along the beach, hand in hand, and marveled at this moment that couldn't be bottled. There was no certainty where it would lead. They might not be together in two years, or five, or ten, but they were together now and there was comfort in yielding to the certainty of constant change and knowing that this feeling of complete devotion would always be part of them. Whether their future was together or apart, their stories would be forever intertwined.

Acknowledgments

Thank you to the teams at Walker Books and Zeitgeist Writers for believing in us and our book. Thank you to the teams at CPM and WME, who have given me incredible opportunities to do what I love. Thank you to Jane Austen and our real-life Pippi Beach. Thank you to my family for making summer holidays loud and fun and full of board games. Thank you, Daddy, for being a better father than all those in this book, and Kalliope, for being all the best parts of all the Bennet sisters. And thank you, Mummy. We have shared so many wonderful experiences, but writing this book was one of the best. —*Angourie*

Thank you to the family, friends, collaborators, colleagues, teachers, acquaintances, and institutions that have supported me in my life as a writer. Thank you, Angourie, for coming with me on this ride. Thank you, Jeremy and Kalliope, for believing we could do it. Thank you, Jane Austen, for showing the way. —*Kate*

About the Authors

Angourie Rice is an actor with international feature film and television credits, including *Mean Girls*, *Mare of Easttown*, *Spider-Man: No Way Home*, *Black Mirror*, and *Ladies in Black*. She also writes, produces, and hosts a literary podcast, *The Community Library*. When she's not acting or writing, she's knitting, baking, reading, painting, or doing half a crossword before giving up.

Kate Rice is an award-winning Australian playwright with a PhD in ethical creative process. She is also a parent, partner, chorister, knitter, dancer, and dog-lover. She has written theater for young people and several plays based on real events. She tries to spend at least ten minutes of every day in a rational manner.